LIGHT FREIGHTS

W. W. Jacobs (1879–1943) was one of the leading popular writers of the 1890s, the golden age of the short story, when readers of weekly magazines seemed to have an insatiable appetite for such tales. His speciality was the humorous sketch, at which no less a critic than F. R. Leavis considered him a greater master than P. G. Wodehouse. The settings for his stories, unlike Wodehouse fantasies, are strictly realist, among the sailors and riverside inhabitants of the Thames.

"Every moment [in *Light Freights*], from the nonchalant opening to the gentle click of the closing door, is deliberately planned and faultlessly controlled. . . . His economy of language, his perpetual understatement, his refusal himself to be the joker but the suggestion in a rapid exchange of conversation by his characters of the ludicrous catastrophes which have overtaken them or are about to overtake them—these are qualities in a writer granted only to a master of his craft." Michael Sadleir in *Dictionary of National Biography*.

LIGHT FREIGHTS

W. W. Jacobs

THE BOYDELL PRESS

First published 1900

Reprinted in the BOOKMARKS series 1982
by The Boydell Press
an imprint of Boydell & Brewer Ltd
PO Box 9, Woodbridge, Suffolk IP12 3DF

British Library Cataloguing in Publication Data
Jacobs, W. W.
Light Freights
I. Title
823′.8[F]   PR4821.J2
ISBN 0-85115-202-3

Photoset in Great Britain by
Rowland Phototypesetting Limited, Bury St Edmunds, Suffolk
and printed by Nene Litho, Wellingborough, Northants

Contents

LIGHT FREIGHTS

AN ODD FREAK

"Speaking o'money," said the night-watchman, thoughtfully, as he selected an empty soap-box on the wharf for a seat, "the whole world would be different if we all 'ad more of it. It would be a brighter and a 'appier place for everybody."

He broke off to open a small brass tobacco-box and place a little quid of tobacco tenderly into a pouch in his left cheek, critically observing at the same time the efforts of a somewhat large steamer to get alongside the next wharf without blocking up more than three-parts of the river. He watched it as though the entire operation depended upon his attention, and, the steamer fast, he turned his eyes back again and resumed his theme.

"Of course it's the being short that sharpens people," he admitted, thoughtfully; "the sharpest man I ever knew never 'ad a ha'penny in 'is pocket, and the ways 'e had o' getting other chaps to pay for 'is beer would ha' made 'is fortin at the law if 'e'd only 'ad the eddication. Playful little chap 'e was. I've seen men wot didn't know 'im stand 'im a pot o' beer and then foller 'im up the road to see 'im knock down a policeman as 'e'd promised. They'd foller 'im to the fust policeman 'e met, an' then 'e'd point them out and say they were goin' to half kill 'im, an' the policeman 'ud just stroll up an' ask em wot they were 'anging about for, but I never 'eard of a chap telling 'im. They used to go away struck all of a 'eap. He died in the accident ward of the London Horsepittle, poor chap."

He shook his head thoughtfully, and ignoring the statement of the watchman at the next wharf that it was a fine evening, shifted his quid and laughed rumblingly.

"The funniest way o' raising the wind I ever 'eard of," he said, in explanation, "was one that 'appened about fifteen years ago. I'd just taken my discharge as A.B. from the *North Star*, trading between here and the Australian ports, and the men wot the thing 'appened to was shipmates o' mine, although on'y firemen.

7

"I know it's a true story, becos I was in it a little bit myself, and the other part I 'ad from all of 'em, and besides, they didn't see anything funny in it at all, or anything out of the way. It seemed to them quite a easy way o' making money, and I dessay if it 'ad come off all right I should have thought so too.

"In about a week arter we was paid off at the Albert Docks these chaps was all cleaned out, and they was all in despair, with a thirst wot wasn't half quenched and a spree wot was on'y in a manner o' speaking just begun, and at the end of that time they came round to a room wot I 'ad, to see wot could be done. There was four of 'em in all: old Sam Small, Ginger Dick, Peter Russet, and a orphan nevy of Sam's whose father and mother was dead. The mother 'ad been 'alf nigger an' 'alf Malay when she was living, and Sam was always pertickler careful to point out that his nevy took arter 'er. It was enough to make the pore woman turn in 'er grave to say so, but Sam used to say that 'e owed it to 'is brother to explain.

"'Wot's to be done?' ses Peter Russet, arter they'd all said wot miserable chaps they was, an' 'ow badly sailor-men was paid. 'We're all going to sign on in the *Land's End*, but she doesn't sail for a fortnight; wot's to be done in the meantime for to live?'

"'There's your watch, Peter,' ses old Sam, dreamy-like, 'and there's Ginger's ring. It's a good job you kep' that ring, Ginger. We're all in the same boat, mates, an' I on'y wish as I'd got something for the general good. It's 'aving an orphan nevy wot's kep' me pore.'

"'Stow it,' ses the nevy, short-like.

"'Everything's agin us,' ses old Sam. 'There's them four green parrots I brought from Brazil, all dead.'

"'So are my two monkeys,' ses Peter Russet, shaking 'is 'ead; 'they used to sleep with me, too.'

"They all shook their 'eads then, and Russet took Sam up very sharp for saying that p'r'aps if he 'adn't slep' with the monkeys they wouldn't ha' died. He said if Sam knew more about monkeys than wot 'e did, why didn't 'e put 'is money in them instead o' green parrots wot pulled their feathers out and died of cold.

"'Talking about monkeys,' ses Ginger Dick, interrupting old Sam suddenly, 'wot about young Beauty here?'

"'Well, wot about him?' ses the nevy, in a nasty sorty o' way.

"'W'y, 'e's worth forty monkeys an' millions o' green parrots,' ses Ginger, starting up; 'an' here 'e is a-wasting of 'is opportunities, going about dressed like a Christian. Open your mouth, Beauty, and stick your tongue out and roll your eyes a bit.'

"'W'y not leave well alone, Ginger?' ses Russet; and I thought so too. Young Beauty was quite enough for me without that.

"'Ter 'blige me,' ses Ginger, anxiously, 'just make yourself as ugly as wot you can, Beauty.'

"'Leave 'im alone,' ses old Sam, as his nevy snarled at 'em. 'You ain't everybody's money yourself, Ginger.'

"'I tell you, mates,' ses Ginger, speaking very slow and solemn, 'there's a fortin in 'im. I was lookin' at 'im just now, trying to think who 'e reminded me of. At fust I thought it was that big stuffed monkey we saw at Melbourne, then I suddenly remembered it was a wild man of Borneo I see when I was a kid up in Sunderland. When I say 'e was a 'andsome, good-'arted looking gentleman alongside o' you, Beauty, do you begin to get my meaning?'

"'Wot's the idea, Ginger?' ses Sam, getting up to lend me and Russet a 'and with 'is nevy.

"'My idea is this,' ses Ginger: 'Take 'is cloes off 'im and dress 'im up in that there winder-blind, or something o' the kind; tie 'im up with a bit o' line, and take 'im round to Ted Reddish in the 'Ighway and sell 'im for a 'undered quid as a wild man of Borneo.'

"'*Wot?*' screams Beauty, in an awful voice. 'Let go, Peter; let go, d'ye hear?'

"''Old your noise, Beauty, while your elders is speaking,' ses 'is uncle, and I could see 'e was struck with the idea.

"'You just try dressing me up in a winder-blind,' ses his nevy, half-crying with rage.

"'Listen to reason, Beauty,' ses Ginger; 'you'll 'ave your share of the tin; it'll only be for a day or two, and then when we've cleared out you can make your escape, and there'll be twenty-five pounds for each of us.'

"''Ow do you make that out, Ginger?' ses Sam, in a cold voice.

"'Fours into a 'undered,' ses Ginger.

"'Ho,' ses Sam. 'Ho, indeed. I wasn't aweer that 'e was your nevy, Ginger.'

"'Share and share alike,' ses Russet. 'It's a very good plan o' yours, Ginger.'

"Ginger holds 'is 'ead up and looks at 'im 'ard.

"'I thought o' the plan,' 'e ses, speaking very slow and deliberate. 'Sam's 'is uncle, and 'e's the wild man. Threes into a 'undered go——'

"'You needn't bother your fat 'ead adding up sums, Ginger,' ses Russet, very polite. 'I'm going to 'ave my share; else I'll split to Red Reddish.'

"None of 'em said a word about me: two of 'em was sitting on my bed; Ginger was using a 'ankerchief o' mine wot 'e found in the fireplace, and Peter Russet 'ad 'ad a drink out o' the jug on my washstand, and yet they never even mentioned me. That's firemen all over, and that's 'ow it is they get themselves so disliked.

"It took 'em best part of an 'our to talk round young Beauty, an' the langwidge they see fit to use made me thankful to think that the parrots didn't live to larn it.

"You never saw anything like Beauty when they 'ad finished with 'im. If 'e was bad in 'is cloes, 'e was a perfeck horror without 'em. Ginger Dick faked 'im up beautiful, but there was no pleasing 'im. Fust he found fault with the winder-blind, which 'e said didn't fit; then 'e grumbled about going bare-foot, then 'e wanted somethink to 'ide 'is legs, which was natural considering the shape of 'em. Ginger Dick nearly lost 'is temper with 'im, and it was all old Sam could do to stop himself from casting 'im off for ever. He was finished at last, and arter Peter Russet 'ad slipped downstairs and found a bit o' broken clothes-prop in the yard, and 'e'd been shown 'ow to lean on it and make a noise, Ginger said as 'ow if Ted Reddish got 'im for a 'undered pounds 'e'd get 'im a bargain.

"'We must 'ave a cab,' ses old Sam.

"'Cab?' ses Ginger. 'What for?'

"'We should 'ave half Wapping following us,' ses Sam. 'Go out and put your ring up, Ginger, and fetch a cab.'

"Ginger started grumbling, but he went, and presently came back with the cab and the money, and they all went downstairs leading the wild man by a bit o' line. They only met one party coming up, and 'e seemed to remember somethink 'e'd forgotten wot ought to be fetched at once.

"Ginger went out fust and opened the cab-door, and then stood there waiting becos at the last moment the wild man said the winder-blind was slipping down. They got 'im out at last, but before 'e could get in the cab was going up the road at ten miles an hour, with Ginger 'anging on to the door calling to it to stop.

"It came back at about a mile an' a 'alf an hour, an' the remarks of the cabman was eggstrordinary. Even when he got back 'e wouldn't start till 'e'd got double fare paid in advance; but they got in at last and drove off.

"There was a fine scene at Ted Reddish's door. Ginger said that if there was a bit of a struggle it would be a good advertisement for Ted Reddish, and they might p'r'aps get more than a 'undered, and all the three of 'em could do, they couldn't get the wild man out o' that cab, and the cabman was hopping about 'arf crazy. Every now and then they'd get the wild man 'arf out, and then he'd get in agin and snarl. 'E didn't seem to know when to leave off, and Ginger and the others got almost as sick of it as the cabman. It must ha' taken two years' wear out o' that cab, but they got 'im out at last, and Reddish's door being open to see what the row was about, they went straight in.

"'Wot's all this?' ses Reddish, who was a tall, thin man, with a dark moustache.

"'It's a wild man o' Borneo,' ses Ginger, panting; 'we caught 'im in a forest in Brazil, an' we've come 'ere to give you the fust offer.'

"Ted Reddish was so surprised 'e couldn't speak at fust. The wild man seemed to take 'is breath away, and 'e looked in a 'elpless kind o' way at 'is wife, who'd just come down. She was a nice-lookin' woman, fat, with a lot o' yaller hair, and she smiled at 'em as though she'd known 'em all their lives.

"'Come into the parlour,' she ses, kindly, just as Ted was beginning to get 'is breath.

"They followed 'em in, and the wild man was just going to make hisself comfortable in a easy-chair, when Ginger give 'im a look, an' 'e curled up on the 'earthrug instead.

"''E ain't a very fine specimen,' ses Ted Reddish, at last.

"'It's the red side-whiskers I don't like,' ses his wife. 'Besides, who ever 'eard of a wild man in a collar an' necktie?'

"'You've got hold o' the wrong one,' ses Ted Reddish, afore Ginger Dick could speak up for hisself.

"'Oh, I beg your pardin,' ses Mrs. Reddish to Ginger, very polite. 'I thought it was funny a wild man should be wearing a collar. It's my mistake. That's the wild man, I s'pose, on the 'earthrug?'

"'That's 'im, mum,' ses old Sam, very short.

"'He don't look wild enough,' ses Reddish.

"'No; 'e's much too tame,' ses 'is wife, shaking her yaller curls.

"The chaps all looked at each other then, and the wild man began to think it was time he did somethink; and the nearest thing 'andy being Ginger's leg, 'e put 'is teeth into it. *Anybody* might ha' thought Ginger was the wild man then, the way 'e went on, and Mrs. Reddish said that even if he so far forgot hisself as to use sich langwidge afore 'er, 'e oughtn't to before a poor 'eathen animal.

"'How much do you want for 'im?' ses Ted Reddish, arter Ginger 'ad got 'is leg away, and taken it to the winder to look at it.

"'One 'undered pounds,' ses old Sam.

"Ted Reddish looked at 'is wife, and they both larfed as though they'd never leave orf.

"'Why, the market price o' the best wild men is only thirty shillings,' ses Reddish, wiping 'is eyes. 'I'll give you a pound for 'im.'

"Old Sam looked at Russet, and Russet looked at Ginger, and then *they* all larfed.

"'Well, there's no getting over you, I can see that,' ses Reddish, at last. 'Is he strong?'

"'Strong? Strong ain't the word for it,' ses Sam.

"'Bring 'im to the back and let 'im 'ave a wrestle with one o' the brown bears, Ted,' ses 'is wife.

"''E'd kill it,' ses old Sam, hastily.

"'Never mind,' ses Reddish, getting up; 'brown bears is cheap enough.'

"They all got up then, none of 'em knowing wot to do, except the wild man, that is, and *he* got 'is arms tight round the leg o' the table.

"'Well,' ses Ginger, 'we'll be pleased for 'im to wrestle with the bear, but we must 'ave the 'undered quid fust, in case 'e injures 'isself a little.'

"Ted Reddish looked 'ard at 'im, and then he looked at 'is wife agin.

"'I'll just go outside and talk it over with the missus,' he ses, at last, and they both got up and went out.

"'It's all right,' ses old Sam, winking at Ginger.

"'Fair cop,' ses Ginger, who was still rubbing his leg. 'I told you it would be, but there's no need for Beauty to overdo it. He nearly 'ad a bit out o' my leg.'

"'A'right,' ses the wild man, shifting along the 'earthrug to where Peter was sitting; 'but it don't do for me to be too tame. You 'eard wot she said.'

"'How are you feeling, old man?' ses Peter, in a kind voice, as 'e tucked 'is legs away under 'is chair.

"'Gurr,' ses the wild man, going on all fours to the back of the chair, 'gur—wug—wug——'

"'Don't play the fool, Beauty,' ses Peter, with a uneasy smile, as he twisted 'is 'ead round. 'Call 'im off, Sam.'

"'Gurr,' ses the wild man, sniffing at 'is legs; 'gurr.'

"'Easy on, Beauty, it's no good biting 'im till they come back,' ses old Sam.

"'I won't be bit at all,' ses Russet, very sharp, 'mind that, Sam. It's my belief Beauty's gone mad.'

"'Hush,' ses Ginger, and they 'eard Ted Reddish and 'is wife coming back. They came in and sat down agin, and after Ted 'ad 'ad another good look at the wild man and prodded 'im all over an' looked at 'is teeth, he spoke up and said they'd decided to give a 'undered pun for 'im at the end o' three days if 'e suited.

"'I s'pose,' ses Sam, looking at the others, 'that we could 'ave a bit of it now to go on with?'

"'It's agin our way of doing business,' ses Ted Reddish. 'If it 'ud been a lion or a tiger we could, but wild men we never do.'

"'The thing is,' ses Mrs. Reddish, as the wild man started on Russet's leg and was pulled off by Sam and Ginger, 'where to put 'im.'

"'Why not put 'im in with the black leopard?' ses her 'usband.

"'There's plenty o' room in his cage,' says 'is wife, thoughtfully, 'and it 'ud be company for 'im too.'

"'I don't think the wild man 'ud like that,' ses Ginger.

"'I'm sartain sure 'e wouldn't,' says old Sam, shaking 'is 'ead.

"'Well, we must put 'im in a cage by hisself, I s'pose,' ses Reddish, 'but we can't be put to much expense. I'm sure the money we spent in cat's meat for the last wild man we 'ad was awful.'

"'Don't you spend too much money on cat's meat for '*im*,' ses Sam, ''e'd very likely leave it. Bringing 'im 'ome, we used to give 'im the same as we 'ad ourselves, and he got on all right.'

"'It's a wonder you didn't kill 'im,' ses Reddish, severely. 'He'll be fed very different 'ere, I can tell you. You won't know 'im at the end o' three days.'

"'Don't change 'im too sudden,' ses Ginger, keeping 'is 'ead turned away from the wild man, wot wos trying to catch 'is eye. 'Cook 'is food at fust, 'cos 'e's been used to it.'

"'I know wot to give 'im,' ses Reddish, off-handedly. 'I ain't been in the line twenty-seven years for nothink. Bring 'im out to the back, an' I'll put 'im in 'is new 'ome.'

"They all got up and, taking no notice of the wild man's whispers, follered Ted Reddish and 'is wife out to the back, where all the wild beasts in the world seemed to 'ave collected to roar out to each other what a beastly place it was.

"'I'm going to put 'im in "'Appy Cottage" for a time,' says Reddish; 'lend a hand 'ere, William,' he says, beckoning to one of 'is men.

"'Is *that* "'Appy Cottage"?' ses old Sam, sniffing, as they got up to a nasty, empty cage with a chain and staple in the wall.

"Ted Reddish said it was.

"'Wot makes you call it that?' ses Sam.

"Reddish didn't seem to 'ear 'im, and it took all Ginger's coaxing to get Beauty to go in.

"'It's on'y for a day or two,' he whispers.

"'But 'ow am I to escape when you've got the brass?' ses the wild man.

"'We'll look arter that,' ses Ginger, who 'adn't got the least idea.

"The wild man 'ad a little show for the last time, jist to impress Ted Reddish, an' it was pretty to see the way William 'andled 'im. The look on the wild man's face showed as 'ow it was a revelashun to *'im*. Then 'is three mates took a last look at 'im and went off.

"For the fust day Sam felt uneasy about 'im, and used to tell us tales about 'is dead brother which made us think Beauty was lucky to take arter 'is mother; but it wore off, and the next night, in the 'Admiral Cochrane,' 'e put 'is 'ead on Ginger's shoulder, and wep' for 'appiness as 'e spoke of 'is nevy's home at ''Appy Cottage.'

"On the third day Sam was for going round in the morning for the money, but Ginger said it wasn't advisable to show any 'aste; so they left it to the evening, and Peter Russet wrote Sam a letter signed 'Barnum,' offering 'im two 'undered for the wild man, in case Ted Reddish should want to beat 'em down. They all 'ad a drink before they went in, and was smiling with good temper to sich an extent that they 'ad to wait a minute to get their faces straight afore going in.

"'Come in,' ses Reddish, and they follered 'im into the parler, where Mrs. Reddish was sitting in a armchair shaking 'er 'ead and looking at the carpet very sorrowful.

"'I was afraid you'd come,' she ses, in a low voice.

"'So was I,' ses Reddish.

"'What for?' ses old Sam. It didn't look much like money, and 'e felt cross.

"'We've 'ad a loss,' ses Mrs. Reddish. She touched 'erself, and then they see she was all in black, and that Ted Reddish was wearing a black tie and a bit o' crape round 'is arm.

"'Sorry to 'ear it, mum,' ses old Sam.

"'It was very sudden, too,' ses Mrs. Reddish, wiping 'er eyes.

"'That's better than laying long,' ses Peter Russet, comforting like.

"Ginger Dick gives a cough. 'Twenty-five pounds was wot *'e'd* come for; not to 'ear this sort o' talk.'

"'We've been in the wild-beast line seven-an'-twenty years,' ses Mrs. Reddish, 'and it's the fust time anythink of this sort 'as 'appened.'

"''Ealthy family, I s'pose,' ses Sam, staring.

"'Tell 'im, Ted,' ses Mrs. Reddish, in a 'usky whisper.

"'No, you,' ses Ted.

"'It's your place,' ses Mrs. Reddish.

"'A woman can break it better,' ses 'er 'usband.

"'Tell us wot?' ses Ginger, very snappish.

"Ted Reddish cleared 'is throat.

"'It wasn't our fault,' he ses, slowly, while Mrs. Reddish began to cry agin; 'gin'rally speakin', animals is afraid o' wild men, and night before last, as the wild man wot you left on approval didn't seem to like "'Appy Cottage," we took 'im out an' put 'im in with the tiger.'

"'Put him in with the WOT?' ses the unfort'nit man's uncle, jumping off 'is chair.

"'The tiger,' ses Reddish. 'We 'eard something in the night, but we thought they was only 'aving a little bit of a tiff, like. In the morning I went down with a bit o' cold meat for the wild man, and I thought at first he'd escaped; but looking a little bit closer——'

"'Don't, Ted,' ses 'is wife. 'I can't bear it.'

"'Do you mean to tell me that the tiger 'as eat 'im?' screams old Sam.

"'Most of 'im,' ses Ted Reddish; 'but 'e couldn't ha' been much of a wild man to let a tiger get the better of 'im. I must say I was surprised.'

"'We both was,' ses Mrs. Reddish, wiping 'er eyes.

"You might ha' 'eard a pin drop; old Sam's eyes was large and staring, Peter Russet was sucking 'is teeth, an' Ginger was wondering wot the law would say to it—if it 'eard of it.

"'It's an unfortunit thing for all parties,' ses Ted Reddish, at last, getting up and standing on the 'earthrug.

"''Orrible,' ses Sam, 'uskily. 'You ought to ha' known better than to put 'im in with a tiger. Wot could you expect? W'y, it was a mad thing to do.'

"'Crool thing,' ses Peter Russet.

"'You don't know the bisness properly,' ses Ginger, 'that's about wot it is. W'y, *I* should ha' known better than that.'

"'Well, it's no good making a fuss about it,' ses Reddish. 'It was only a wild man arter all, and he'd ha' died anyway, cos 'e wouldn't eat the raw meat we gave 'im, and 'is pan o' water was scarcely touched. He'd ha' starved himself anyhow. I'm sorry, as I said before, but I must be off; I've got an appointment down at the docks.'

"He moved towards the door; Ginger Dick gave Russet a nudge and whispered something, and Russet passed it on to Sam.

"'What about the 'undered quid?' ses pore Beauty's uncle, catching 'old o' Reddish as 'e passed 'im.

"'Eh?' ses Reddish, surprised—'Oh, that's off.'

"'Ho!' says Sam. 'Ho! is it? We want a 'undered quid off of you; an' wot's more, we mean to 'ave it.'

"'But the tiger's ate 'im,' says Mrs. Reddish, explaining.

"'I know that,' ses Sam, sharply. 'But 'e was our wild man, and we want to be paid for 'im. You should ha' been more careful. We'll give you five minutes; and if the money ain't paid by that time, we'll go straight off to the police-station.'

"'Well, go,' ses Ted Reddish.

"Sam got up, very stern, and looked at Ginger.

"'You'll be ruined if we do,' ses Ginger.

"'All right,' ses Ted Reddish, comfortably.

"'I'm not sure they can't 'ang you,' ses Russet.

"'I ain't sure either,' says Reddish; 'and I'd like to know 'ow the law stands, in case it 'appens agin.'

"'Come on, Sam,' ses Ginger; 'come straight to the police-station.'

"He got up, and moved towards the door. Ted Reddish didn't move a muscle, but Mrs Reddish flopped on her knees and caught old Sam round the legs, and 'eld him so's 'e couldn't move.

"'Spare 'im,' she ses, crying.

"'Lea' go o' my legs, mum,' ses Sam.

"'Come on, Sam,' ses Ginger; 'come to the police.'

"Old Sam made a desperit effort, and Mrs. Reddish called 'im a crool monster, and let go and 'id 'er face on 'er husband's shoulder as they all moved out of the parlour, larfing like a mad thing with hysterics.

"They moved off slowly, not knowing wot to do, as, of course they knew they daren't go to the police about it. Ginger Dick's temper was awful; but Peter Russet said they mustn't give up all 'ope—he'd write to Ted Reddish and tell 'im as a friend wot a danger 'e was in. Old Sam didn't say anything, the loss of his nevy and twenty-five pounds at the same time being almost more than 'is 'art could bear, and in a slow, melancholy fashion they walked back to old Sam's lodgings.

"'Well, what the blazes is up now?' ses Ginger Dick, as they turned the corner.

"There was three or four 'undered people standing in front of the 'ouse, and women's 'eads out of all the winders screaming their 'ardest for the police, and as they got closer they 'eard a incessant knocking. It took 'em nearly five minutes to force their way through the crowd, and then they nearly went crazy as they saw the wild man with 'alf the winder-blind missing, but otherwise well and 'arty, standing on the step and giving rat-a-tat-tats at the door for all 'e was worth.

"They never got to know the rights of it, Beauty getting so excited every time they asked 'im 'ow he got on that they 'ad to give it up. But they began to 'ave a sort of idea at last that Ted Reddish 'ad been 'aving a game with 'em, and that Mrs. Reddish was worse than wot 'e was."

A QUESTION OF HABIT

"WIMMIN aboard ship I don't 'old with," said the night-watchman, severely. "They'll arsk you all sorts o' silly questions, an' complain to the skipper if you don't treat 'em civil in answering 'em. If you do treat 'em civil, what's the result? Is it a bit o' bacca, or a shilling, or anything like that? Not a bit of it; just a 'thank you,' an' said in a way as though they've been giving you a perfect treat by talking to you.

"They're a contrary sects too. Ask a girl civil-like to stand off a line you want to coil up, and she'll get off an' look at you as though you ought to have waited until she 'ad offered to shift. Pull on it without asking her to step off fust, an' the ship won't 'old her 'ardly. A man I knew once—he's dead now, poor chap, and left three widders mourning their unrepairable loss—said that with all 'is experience wimmin was as much a riddle to 'im as when he fust married.

"O' course, sometimes you get a gal down the fo'c's'le pretending to be a man, shipping as ordinary seaman or boy, and nobody not a penny the wiser. It's happened before, an' I've no doubt it will again.

"We 'ad a queer case once on a barque I was on as steward, called the *Tower of London*, bound from the Albert Docks to Melbourne with a general cargo. We shipped a new boy just after we started as was entered in the ship's books as 'Enery Mallow, an' the fust thing we noticed about 'Enery was as 'e had a great dislike to work and was terrible sea-sick. Every time there was a job as wanted to be done, that lad 'ud go and be took bad quite independent of the weather.

"Then Bill Dowsett adopted 'im, and said he'd make a sailor of 'im. I believe if 'Enery could 'ave chose 'is father, he'd sooner 'ad any man than Bill, and I would sooner have been a orphan than a son to any of 'em. Bill relied on his langwidge mostly, but when

18

that failed he'd just fetch 'im a cuff. Nothing more than was good for a boy wot 'ad got 'is living to earn, but 'Enery used to cry until we was all ashamed of 'im.

"Bill got almost to be afraid of 'itting 'im at last, and used to try wot being sarcastic would do. Then we found as 'Enery was ten times as sarcastic as Bill—'e'd talk all round 'im so to speak, an' even take the words out of Bill's mouth to use agin 'im. Then Bill would turn to 'is great natural gifts, and the end of it was when we was about a fortnight out that the boy ran up on deck and went aft to the skipper and complained of Bill's langwidge.

"'Langwidge,' ses the old man, glaring at 'im as if 'e'd eat 'im— 'What sort o' langwidge?'

"'Bad langwidge, sir,' ses 'Enery.

"'Repeat it,' ses the skipper.

"'Enery gives a little shiver. 'I couldn't do it, sir,' he ses, very solemn; 'it's like—like you was talking to the bo'sen yesterday.'

"'Go to your duties,' roars the skipper; 'go to your duties at once, and don't let me 'ear any more of it. Why, you ought to be at a young ladies' school.'

"'I know I ought, sir,' 'Enery ses, with a w'imper, 'but I never thought it'd be like this.'

"The old man stares at him, and then he rubs his eyes and stares agin. 'Enery wiped his eyes and stood looking down at the deck.

"''Eavens above,' ses the old man, in a dazed voice, 'don't tell me you're a gal!'

"'I won't if you don't want me to,' ses 'Enery, wiping his eyes agin.

"'What's your name?' ses the old man, at last.

"'Mary Mallow, sir,' ses 'Enery, very soft.

"'What made you do it?' ses the skipper, at last.

"'My father wanted me to marry a man I didn't want to,' ses Miss Mallow. 'He used to admire my hair very much, so I cut it off. Then I got frightened at what I'd done, and as I looked like a boy I thought I'd go to sea.'

"'Well, it's a nice responsibility for me,' ses the skipper, and he called the mate, who 'ad just come on deck, and asked his advice. The mate was a very straitlaced man—for a mate—and at fust he was so shocked 'e couldn't speak.

"'She'll have to come aft,' he ses, at last.

"'O' course she will,' ses the skipper, and he called me up and told me to clear a spare cabin out for her—we carried a passenger or two sometimes—and to fetch her chest up.

"'I s'pose you've got some clothes in it?' he ses, anxious-like.

"'Only these sort o' things,' ses Miss Mallow, bashfully.

"'And send Dowsett to me,' ses the skipper, turning to me agin.

"We 'ad to shove pore Bill up on deck a'most, and the way the skipper went on at 'im, you'd thought 'e was the greatest rascal unhung. He begged the young lady's pardon over and over agin, and when 'e come back to us 'e was that upset that 'e didn't know what 'e was saying, and begged an ordinary seaman's pardon for treading on 'is toe.

"Then the skipper took Miss Mallow below to her new quarters, and to 'is great surprise caught the third officer, who was fond of female society, doing a step-dance in the saloon all on 'is own.

"That evening the skipper and the mate formed themselves into a committee to decide what was to be done. Everything the mate suggested the skipper wouldn't have, and when the skipper thought of anythink, the mate said it was impossible. After the committee 'ad been sitting for three hours it began to abuse each other; leastaways, the skipper abused the mate, and the mate kep' on saying if it wasn't for discipline he knew somebody as would tell the skipper a thing or two it would do 'im good to hear.

"'She must have a dress, I tell you, or a frock at any rate,' ses the skipper, very mad.

"'What's the difference between a dress and a frock?' ses the mate.

"'There is a difference,' ses the skipper.

"'Well, what is it?' ses the mate.

"'It wouldn't be any good if I was to explain to you,' ses the skipper; 'some people's heads are too thick.'

"'I know they are,' ses the mate.

"The committee broke up after that, but it got amiable agin over breakfast next morning, and made quite a fuss over Miss Mallow. It was wonderful what a difference a night aft had made in that gal. She'd washed herself beautiful, and had just frizzed 'er 'air, which was rather long, over 'er forehead, and the committee kept pursing its lips up and looking at each other as Mr. Fisher talked to 'er and kep' on piling 'er plate up.

"She went up on deck after breakfast and stood leaning against the side talking to Mr. Fisher. Pretty laugh she'd got, too, though I never noticed it when she was in the fo'c's'le. Perhaps she hadn't got much to laugh about then; and while she was up there enjoying 'erself watching us chaps work, the committee was down below laying its 'eads together agin.

"When I went down to the cabin agin it was like a dressmaker's shop. There was silk handkerchiefs and all sorts o' things on the table, an' the skipper was hovering about with a big pair of scissors in his hands, wondering how to begin.

"'I shan't attempt anything very grand,' he ses, at last; 'just something to slip over them boy's clothes she's wearing.'

"The mate didn't say anything. He was busy drawing frocks on a little piece of paper, and looking at 'em with his 'ead on one side to see whether they looked better that way.

"'By Jove! I've got it,' ses the old man, suddenly. 'Where's that dressing-gown your wife gave you?'

"The mate looked up. 'I don't know,' he ses, slowly. 'I've mislaid it.'

"'Well, it can't be far,' ses the skipper. 'It's just the thing to make a frock of.'

"'I don't think so,' ses the mate. 'It wouldn't hang properly. Do you know what I was thinking of?'

"'Well,' ses the skipper.

"'Three o' them new flannel shirts o' yours,' ses the mate. 'They're very dark an' they'd hang beautiful.'

"'Let's try the dressing-gown fust,' ses the skipper, hearty-like. 'That's easier. I'll help you look for it.'

"'I can't think what I've done with it,' ses the mate.

"'Well, let's try your cabin,' ses the old man.

"They went to the mate's cabin and, to his great surprise, there it was hanging just behind the door. It was a beautiful dressing-gown—soft, warm cloth trimmed with braid—and the skipper took up his scissors agin, and fairly gloated over it. Then he slowly cut off the top part with the two arms 'anging to it, and passed it over to the mate.

"'I shan't want that, Mr. Jackson,' he ses, slowly. 'I dare say you'll find it come in useful.'

"'While you're doing that, s'pose I get on with them three shirts,' ses Mr. Jackson.

"'What three shirts?' ses the skipper, who was busy cutting buttons off.

"'Why, yours,' ses Mr. Jackson. 'Let's see who can make the best frock.'

"'No, Mr. Jackson,' ses the old man. 'I'm sure you couldn't make anything o' them shirts. You're not at all gifted that way. Besides, I want 'em.'

"'Well, I wanted my dressing-gown, if you come to that,' ses the mate, in a sulky voice.

"'Well, what on earth did you give it to me for?' ses the skipper. 'I do wish you'd know your own mind, Mr. Jackson.'

"The mate didn't say any more. He sat and watched the old man, as he threaded his needle and stitched the dressing-gown together down the front. It really didn't look half bad when he'd finished it, and it was easy to see how pleased Miss Mallow was. She really looked quite fine in it, and with the blue guernsey she was wearing and a band made o' silk handkerchiefs round her waist, I saw at once it was a case with the third officer.

"'Now you look a bit more like the gal your father used to know,' ses the skipper. 'My finger's a bit sore just at present, but by and by I'll make you a bonnet.'

"'I'd like to see it,' ses the mate.

"'It's quite easy,' ses the skipper. 'I've seen my wife do 'em. She calls 'em tokes. You make the hull out o' cardboard and spread your canvas on that.'

"That dress made a wonderful difference in the gal. Wonderful! She seemed to change all at once and become the lady altogether. She just 'ad that cabin at her beck and call; and as for me, she seemed to think I was there a puppose to wait on 'er.

"I must say she 'ad a good time of it. We was having splendid weather, and there wasn't much work for anybody; consequently, when she wasn't receiving good advice from the skipper and the mate, she was receiving attention from both the second and third officers. Mr. Scott, the second, didn't seem to take much notice of her for a day or two, and the first I saw of his being in love was 'is being very rude to Mr. Fisher and giving up bad langwidge, so sudden it's a wonder it didn't do 'im a injury.

"I think the gal rather enjoyed their attentions at first, but arter a time she got fairly tired of it. She never 'ad no rest, pore thing. If she was up on deck looking over the side the third officer would come up and talk romantic to 'er about the sea and the lonely lives of sailor-men, and I actually 'eard Mr. Scott repeating poetry to her. The skipper 'eard it too, and being suspicious o' poetry, and not having heard clearly, called him up to 'im and made 'im say it all over agin to 'im. 'E didn't seem quite to know wot to make of it, so 'e calls up the mate for 'im to hear it. The mate said it was rubbish, and the skipper told Mr. Scott that if ever he was taken that way agin 'e'd 'ear more of it.

"There was no doubt about them two young fellers being genuine. She 'appened to say one day that she could never, never care for a man who drank and smoked, and I'm blest if both of 'em didn't give 'er their pipes to chuck overboard, and the agony those two chaps used to suffer when they saw other people smoking was pitiful to witness.

"It got to such a pitch at last that the mate, who, as I said afore, was a very particular man, called another committee meeting. It was a very solemn affair, and 'e made a long speech in which he said he was the father of a family, and that the second and third officers was far too attentive to Miss Mallow, and 'e asked the skipper to stop it.

"'How?' ses the skipper.

"'Stop the draught-playing and the card-playing and the poetry,' ses the mate; 'the gal's getting too much attention; she'll have 'er 'ead turned. Put your foot down, sir, and stop it.'

"The skipper was so struck by what he said, that he not only did that, but he went and forbid them two young men to speak to the gal except at meal times, or when the conversation was general. None of 'em liked it, though the gal pretended to, and for the matter of a week things was very quiet in the cabin, not to say sulky.

"Things got back to their old style agin in a very curious way. I'd just set the tea in the cabin one afternoon, and 'ad stopped at the foot of the companion-ladder to let the skipper and Mr. Fisher come down, when we suddenly 'eard a loud box on the ear. We all rushed into the cabin at once, and there was the mate looking fairly thunderstruck, with his hand to his face, and Miss Mallow glaring at 'im.

"'Mr. Jackson,' ses the skipper, in a awful voice, 'what's this?'

"'Ask her,' shouts the mate. 'I think she's gone mad or something.'

"'What does this mean, Miss Mallow?' ses the skipper.

"'Ask him,' ses Miss Mallow, breathing very 'ard.

"'Mr. Jackson,' ses the skipper, very severe, 'what have you been doing?'

"'Nothing,' roars the mate.

"'Was that a box on the ear I 'eard?' ses the skipper.

"'It was,' ses the mate, grinding his teeth.

"'Your ear?' ses the skipper.

"'Yes. She's mad, I tell you,' ses the mate. 'I was sitting here quite quiet and peaceable, when she came alongside me and slapped my face.'

"'Why did you box his ear?' ses the skipper to the girl again.

"'Because he deserved it,' ses Miss Mallow.

"The skipper shook his 'ead and looked at the mate so sorrowful that he began to stamp up and down the cabin and bang the table with his fist.

"'If I hadn't heard it myself, I couldn't have believed it,' ses the skipper; 'and you the father of a family, too. Nice example for the young men, I must say.'

"'Please don't say anything more about it,' ses Miss Mallow; 'I'm sure he's very sorry.'

"'Very good,' ses the skipper; 'but you understand, Mr. Jackson, that if I overlook your conduct, you're not to speak to this young lady agin. Also, you must consider yourself as removed from the committee.'

"'Curse the committee,' screamed the mate. 'Curse——'

"He looked all round, with his eyes starting out of 'is 'ead, and then suddenly shut his mouth with a snap and went up on deck. He never allooded to the affair again, and in fact for the rest of the voyage 'e hardly spoke to a soul. The young people got their cards and draughts agin, but he took no notice, and 'e never spoke to the skipper unless he spoke to 'im fust.

"We got to Melbourne at last, and the fust thing the skipper did was to give our young lady some money to go ashore and buy clothes with. He did it in a very delikit way by giving her the pay as boy, and I don't think I ever see anybody look so pleased and surprised as she did. The skipper went ashore with her, as she looked rather a odd figure to be going about alone, and comes back about a hour later without 'er.

"'I thought perhaps she'd have come aboard,' he ses to Mr. Fisher. 'I managed to miss her somehow while I was waiting outside a shop.'

"They fidgeted about a bit, and then went ashore to look for 'er, turning up again at eight o'clock quite worried. Nine o'clock came, and there was no signs of 'er. Mr. Fisher and Mr. Scott was in a dreadful state, and the skipper sent almost every man aboard ashore to search for 'er. They 'unted for 'er high and low, up and down and round about, and turned up at midnight so done up that they could 'ardly stand without holding on to somethink, and so upset that they couldn't speak. None of the officers got any sleep that night except Mr. Jackson, and the fust thing in the morning they was ashore agin looking for her.

'She'd disappeared as completely as if she'd gone overboard, and more than one of the chaps looked over the side half expecting to see 'er come floating by. By twelve o'clock most of us was convinced that she'd been made away with, and Mr. Fisher made some remarks about the police of Melbourne as would ha' done them good to hear.

"I was just going to see about dinner when we got the first news of her. Three of the most miserable and solemn-looking captains

I've ever seen came alongside and asked for a few words with our skipper. They all stood in a row looking as if they was going to cry.

"'Good morning, Captain Hart,' ses one of 'em, as our old man came up with the mate.

"'Good morning,' ses he.

"'Do you know this?' ses one of 'em, suddenly, holding out Miss Mallow's dressing-gown on a walking-stick.

"'Good 'eavens,' ses the skipper, 'I hope nothing's happened to that pore gal.'

"The three captains shook their heads all together.

"'She is no more,' ses another of 'em.

"'How did it happen?' ses the skipper, in a low voice.

"'She took this off,' ses the fust captain, shaking his head and pointing to the dressing-gown.

"'And took a chill?' ses the skipper, staring very 'ard.

"The three captains shook their 'eads agin, and I noticed that they seemed to watch each other and do it all together.

"'I don't understand,' ses the skipper.

"'I was afraid you wouldn't,' ses the first captain; 'she took this off.'

"'So you said before,' ses the skipper, rather short.

"'And became a boy agin,' ses the other; 'the wickedest and most artful young rascal that ever signed on with me.'

"He looked round at the others, and they all broke out into a perfect roar of laughter, and jumped up and down and slapped each other on the back, as if they was all mad. Then they asked which was the one wot had 'is ears boxed, and which was Mr. Fisher and which was Mr. Scott, and told our skipper what a nice fatherly man he was. Quite a crowd got round, an' wouldn't go away for all we could do to 'em in the shape o' buckets o' water and lumps o' coal. We was the laughing-stock o' the place, and the way they carried on when the steamer passed us two days later with the fust captain on the bridge, pretending not to see that imp of a boy standing in the bows blowing us kisses and dropping curtsies, nearly put the skipper out of 'is mind."

HARD LABOUR

POLICE-CONSTABLE C 49 paced slowly up Wapping High Street in the cool of the evening. The warehouses were closed, and the street almost denuded of traffic. He addressed a short and stern warning to a couple of youths struggling on the narrow pavement, and pointed out—with the toe of his boot—the undesirability of the curbstone as a seat to a small maiden of five. With his white gloves in his hand he swung slowly along, monarch of all he surveyed.

His complacency and the air with which he stroked his red moustache and side-whiskers were insufferable. Mr. Charles Pinner, ship's fireman, whose bosom friend C 49 had pinched—to use Mr. Pinner's own expressive phrase—a week before for causing a crowd to collect, eyed the exhibition with sneering wrath. The injustice of locking up Mr. Johnson, because a crowd of people whom he didn't know from Adam persisted in obstructing the pathway, had reduced Mr. Pinner to the verge of madness. For a time he kept behind C 49, and contented himself with insulting but inaudible remarks bearing upon the colour of his whiskers.

The constable turned up a little alley-way between two small pieces of waste ground, concerning the desirability and value of which as building sites a notice-board was lurid with adjectives. Mr. Pinner was still behind; he was a man who believed in taking what life could offer him at the moment, and something whispered to him that if he lived a hundred years he would never have such another chance of bonneting that red-whiskered policeman. There were two or three small houses at the end of the alley, but the only other living person in it was a boy of ten. He looked to be the sort of boy who might be trusted to smile approval on Mr Pinner's contemplated performance.

C 49's first thought was that a chimney had fallen, and his one idea was to catch it in the act. He made a desperate grab even before pushing his helmet up, and caught Mr. Pinner by the arm.

"Leggo," said that gentleman, struggling.

"Ho," said C 49, crimson with wrath, as he pushed his helmet up. "Now you come along o' me, my lad."

Mr. Pinner, regretting the natural impulse which had led to his undoing, wrenched himself free and staggered against the fence which surrounded the waste ground. Then he ducked sideways, and as C 49 renewed his invitation coupled with a warning concerning the futility of resistance, struck him full and square on the temple.

The constable went down as though he had been shot. His helmet rolled off as he fell, and his head struck the pavement. Mr. Pinner, his taste for bonneting policemen all gone, passed the admiring small boy at the double, and then, turning the corner rapidly, slackened his pace to something less conspicuous.

He reached his home, a small house in a narrow turning off Cable Street, safely, and, throwing himself into a chair, breathed heavily, while his wife, whose curiosity at seeing him home at that early hour would not be denied, plied him with questions.

"Spend a 'alf-hour with *me*?" she repeated, in a dazed voice. "Ain't you well, Charlie?"

"Well?" said the fireman, frowning, "o' course I'm well. But it struck me you ought to see a little of me sometimes when I'm ashore."

"That's generally what I do see," said Mrs. Pinner; "it's been a long time striking you, Charlie."

"Better late than never," murmured her husband, absently, as he listened in shuddering suspense to every footfall outside.

"Well, I'm glad you've turned over a new leaf," said Mrs. Pinner. "It ain't afore it was time, I'm sure. I'll go up and fetch the baby down."

"What for?" demanded her husband, shortly.

"So as it can see a little of you too," said his wife. "Up to the present it calls every man it sees 'farver'. It ain't its fault, pore little dear."

Mr. Pinner, still intent on footsteps, grumbled something beneath his breath, and the baby being awakened out of its first sleep and brought downstairs, they contemplated each other for some time with offensive curiosity.

Until next morning Mr. Pinner's odd reasons for his presence sufficed, but when he sat still after breakfast and showed clearly his intention to remain, his wife insisted upon others less insulting to her intelligence. Mr. Pinner, prefacing his remarks with an allusion to a life-long abhorrence of red whiskers, made a clean breast of it.

"It served him right," said his wife, judicially, "but it'll be six months for you if they nab you, Charlie. You'll 'ave to make up your mind to a quiet spell indoors with me and baby till the ship sails."

Mr. Pinner looked at his son and heir disparagingly, and emitted a groan.

"He 'ad no witnesses," he remarked, "except a boy, that is, and 'e didn't look the sort to be fond o' policemen."

"You can't tell by looks," replied his wife, in whose brain a little plan to turn this escapade to good account was slowly maturing. "You mustn't get nabbed for my sake."

"I won't get nabbed for my own sake," rejoined Mr. Pinner, explicitly. "I wonder whether it's got into the papers?"

"Sure to," said his wife, shaking her head.

"Go and buy one and see," said the fireman, glancing at the baby. "I'll look after it, but don't be long."

His wife went out and got a paper, and Mr. Pinner, who was unable to read, watched her anxiously as she looked through it. It was evident, at length, that his prowess of the previous evening had escaped being immortalised in print, and his spirits rose.

"I don't s'pose he was much 'urt," he said. "I dare say he wouldn't like to tell 'em at the station he'd been knocked down. Some of 'em don't. I'll just keep my eyes open when I'm out."

"I don't think you ought to go out," said his wife.

She picked up the paper again, and regarded him furtively. Then she bent over it, and slowly scanned the pages, until a sudden horrified gasp drove the roses from Mr. Pinner's cheek and prepared him for the worst.

"Wot is it?" he stammered.

Mrs. Pinner folded the paper back and, motioning him to silence, read as follows:—

"A violent assault was committed last night on a policeman down at Wapping, who was knocked down by a seafaring man until he got concussion of the brain. The injured constable states that he can identify the man what attacked him, and has given a full description of him at the police-station, where search is now being made for 'im. The public-houses are being watched."

"Ho, are they?" commented Mr. Pinner, much annoyed. "Ho, indeed."

"That's all," said his wife, putting down the paper.

"All!" echoed the indignant fireman. "'Ow much more do

you want? I'm in a nice 'ole, I don't think. Seems to me I might as well be in quod as 'ere."

"You don't know when you're well off," retorted his wife.

Mr. Pinner sighed, and moved aimlessly about the room; then he resumed his chair, and, shaking his head slowly, lit his pipe.

"You'll be quite safe indoors," said his wife, whose plan was now perfected. "The only thing is, people'll wonder what you're staying indoors all day for."

Mr. Pinner took his pipe out of his mouth and stared at her blankly.

"Seems to me you want a reason for staying indoors," she pursued.

"Well, I've got one, ain't I?" said the injured man.

"Yes, but you can't tell them that," said his wife. "You want a reason everybody can understand and keep 'em from talking."

"Yes, all very fine for you to talk," said Mr. Pinner; "if you could think of a reason it 'ud be more sensible."

Mrs. Pinner, who had got several ready, assumed an air of deep thoughtfulness, and softly scratched her cheek with her needle.

"Whitewash the kitchen ceiling," she said, suddenly.

"'Ow long would that take?' demanded her lord, who was not fond of whitewashing.

"Then you could put a bit of paper in this room," continued Mrs. Pinner, "and put them shelves in the corner what you said you'd do. That would take some time."

"It would," agreed Mr. Pinner, eyeing her disagreeably.

"And I was thinking," said his wife, "if I got a sugar-box from the grocer's and two pairs o' wheels you could make the baby a nice little perambulator."

"Seems to me——" began the astonished Mr. Pinner.

"While you're doing those things I'll try and think of some more," interrupted his wife.

Mr. Pinner stared at her for some time in silence; finally he said "Thank'ee," in a voice slightly tinged with emotion, and fell into a sullen reverie.

"It's the safest plan," urged his wife, seriously; "there's so many things want doing that it's the most natural thing in the world for you to stay indoors doing them. Nobody'll think it strange."

She stitched on briskly and watched her husband from the corner of her eye. He smoked on for some time, and rising at last with a sigh, sent her out for the materials, and spent the day whitewashing.

He was so fatigued with the unwonted exertion that he was almost content to stay in that evening and smoke; but the following morning was so bright and inviting that his confinement appeared more galling than ever. Hoping for some miracle that should rescue him from these sordid tasks, he sent out for another paper.

"It don't say much about it," said his wife.

The baby was crying, the breakfast things were not washed, and there were several other hindrances to journalistic work.

"Read it," said the fireman, sternly.

"The injured constable," read Mrs. Pinner, glibly, "is still going on satisfactory, and the public-houses are still being watched."

"They do seem fond o' them public-houses," remarked Mr. Pinner, impatiently. "I'm glad the chap's getting on all right, but I 'ope 'e won't be about afore I get to sea again."

"I shouldn't think he would," said his wife. "I'd better go out and get the wall-paper, 'adn't I? What colour would you like?"

Mr. Pinner said that all wall-papers were alike to him, and indulged in dreary speculations as to where the money was to come from. Mrs. Pinner, who knew that they were saving fast owing to his enforced seclusion, smiled at his misgivings.

He papered the room that day, after a few choice observations on the price of wall-paper, and expressed his opinion that in a properly governed country the birth of red-whiskered policemen would be rendered an impossibility. To the compliments on his workmanship bestowed by the gratified Mrs. Pinner he turned a deaf ear.

There was nothing in the paper next morning, Mrs. Pinner's invention being somewhat fatigued, but she promptly quelled her husband's joy by suggesting that the police authorities were lying low in the hope of lulling him into a sense of false security. She drew such an amusing picture of the police searching streets and public-houses, while Mr. Pinner was blithely making a perambulator indoors, that she was fain to wipe the tears of merriment from her eyes, while Mr. Pinner sat regarding her in indignant astonishment.

It was no source of gratification to Mr. Pinner to find that the other ladies in the house were holding him up as a pattern to their husbands, and trying to incite those reluctant gentlemen to follow in his footsteps. Mrs. Smith, of the first floor, praised him in terms which made him blush with shame, and Mrs. Hawk, of the second, was so complimentary that Mr. Hawk, who had not long been married, came downstairs and gave him a pressing invitation to step out into the back yard.

By the time the perambulator was finished his patience was at an end, and he determined at all hazards to regain his liberty. Never had the street as surveyed from the small window appeared so inviting. He filled his pipe and communicated to the affrighted Mrs. Pinner his intention of going for a stroll.

"Wait till I've seen the paper," she protested.

"Wot's the good of seeing the paper?" replied Mr. Pinner. "We know as 'e's in bed, and it seems to me while 'e's in bed is my time to be out. I shall keep a look-out. Besides, I've just 'ad an idea; I'm going to shave my moustache off. I ought to ha' thought of it before."

He went upstairs, leaving his wife wringing her hands below. So far from the red policeman being in bed, she was only too well aware that he was on duty in the district, with every faculty strained to the utmost to avenge the outrage of which he had been the victim. It became necessary to save her husband at all costs, and while he was busy upstairs with the razor she slipped out and bought a paper.

He had just come down by the time she returned, and turned to confront her with a conscious grin; but at the sight of her face the smile vanished from his own, and he stood waiting nervously for ill news.

"Oh, dear," moaned his wife.

"What's the matter?" said Mr. Pinner, anxiously.

Mrs. Pinner supported herself by the table and shook her head despondently.

"'Ave they found me out?" demanded Mr. Pinner.

"Worse than that," said his wife.

"Worse than that!" said her husband, whose imagination was not of a soaring description. "How can it be?"

"He's dead," said Mrs. Pinner, solemnly.

"*Dead!*" repeated her husband, starting violently.

Mrs. Pinner, with a little sniff, took up the paper and read slowly, interrupted only by the broken ejaculations of her husband.

"The unfortunate policeman who was assaulted the other day down at Wapping passed away peacefully yesterday evening. Lady Verax is prostrate with grief and refuses to leave the death-chamber. Several members of the Royal family have telegraphed their——"

"*Wot?*" interrupted the astounded listener.

"I was reading the wrong bit," said Mrs. Pinner, who was too engrossed in her reading of the death of a well-known nobleman to remember to make all the corrections necessary to render them suitable for a policeman. Here it is:—

"The unfortunate policeman who was assaulted the other day down at Wapping passed away peacefully yesterday evening in the arms of his wife and family. The ruffian is believed to be at sea."

"I wish 'e was," said Mr. Pinner, mournfully. "I wish 'e was anywhere but 'ere. The idea o' making a delikit man like that a policeman. Why, I 'ardly touched 'im."

"Promise me you won't go out," said his wife, tearfully.

"*Out?*" said Mr. Pinner, energetically; "*out?* D'ye think I'm mad, or wot? I'm going to stay 'ere till the ship sails, then I'm going down in a cab. Wot d'ye think I want to go out for?"

He sat in a frightened condition in the darkest corner of the room, and spoke only to his wife in terms of great bitterness concerning the extraordinary brittleness of members of the police force. "I'll never touch one on 'em agin as long as I live," he protested. "If you brought one to me asleep on a chair I wouldn't touch 'im."

"It's the drink as made you do it," said his wife.

"I'll never touch a drop agin," affirmed Mr. Pinner, shivering.

His pipe had lost its flavour, and he sat pondering in silence until the absolute necessity of finding more reasons for his continued presence in the house occurred to him. Mrs. Pinner agreed with the idea, and together they drew up a list of improvements which would occupy every minute of his spare time.

He worked so feverishly that he became a by-word in the mouths of the other lodgers, and the only moments of security and happiness he knew were when he was working in the bedroom with the door locked. Mr. Smith attributed it to disease, and for one panic-stricken hour discussed with Mr. Hawk the possibility of its being infectious.

Slowly the days passed until at length there were only two left, and he was in such a nervous and overwrought state that Mrs. Pinner was almost as anxious as he was for the day of departure. To comfort him she read a paragraph from the paper to the effect that the police had given up the search in despair. Mr. Pinner shook his head at this, and said it was a trap to get him out. He also, with a view of defeating the ends of justice, set to work upon a hood for the perambulator.

He was employed on this when his wife went out to do a little shopping. The house when she returned was quiet, and there were no signs of anything unusual having occurred; but when she entered the room she started back with a cry at the sight which met her eyes. Mr. Pinner was in a crouching attitude on the sofa, his face buried in the cushion, while one leg waved spasmodically in the air.

"Charlie," she cried; "Charlie."

There was a hollow groan from the cushion in reply.

"What's the matter?" she cried, in alarm. "What's the matter?"

"I've seen it," said Mr. Pinner, in trembling tones. "I've seen a ghost. I was just peeping out of the winder behind the blind when it went by."

"Nonsense," said his wife.

"*His* ghost," said Mr. Pinner, regaining a more natural attitude and shivering violently, "red whiskers, white gloves and all. It's doing a beat up and down this street. I shall go mad. It's been by twice."

"'Magination," said his wife, aghast at this state of affairs.

"I'm afraid of its coming for me," said Mr. Pinner, staring wildly. "Every minnit I expect to see it come to the door and beckon me to foller it to the station. Every minnit I expect to see it with its white face stuck up agin the winder-pane staring in at me."

"You mustn't 'ave such fancies," said his wife.

"I see it as plain as I see you," persisted the trembling fireman. "It was prancing up and down in just the same stuck-up way as it did when it was alive."

"I'll draw the blind down," said his wife.

She crossed over to the window, and was about to lower the blind when she suddenly drew back with an involuntary exclamation.

"Can you see it?" cried her husband.

"No," said Mrs. Pinner, recovering herself. "Shut your eyes."

The fireman sprang to his feet. "Keep back," said his wife, "don't look."

"I must," said her husband.

His wife threw herself upon him, but he pushed her out of the way and rushed to the window. Then his jaw dropped and he murmured incoherently, for the ghost of the red policeman was plainly visible. Its lofty carriage of the head and pendulum-like swing of the arms were gone, and it was struggling in a most fleshly manner to lead a recalcitrant costermonger to the station. In the intervals of the wrestling bout it blew loudly upon a whistle.

"Wonderful," said Mrs. Pinner, nervously. "Lifelike, I call it."

The fireman watched the crowd pass up the road, and then he turned and regarded her.

"Would you like to hear what I call it?" he thundered.

"Not before the baby, Charlie," quavered Mrs. Pinner, drawing back.

The fireman regarded her silently, and his demeanour was so alarming that she grabbed Charles Augustus Pinner suddenly from his cradle and held him in front of her.

"You've kep' me here," said Mr. Pinner, in a voice which trembled with self-pity, "for near three weeks. For three weeks I've wasted my time, my little spare time, and my money in making perambulators, and whitewashing and papering, and all sort of things. I've been the larfing-stock o' this house, and I've been worked like a convict. Wot 'ave you got to say for yourself?"

"Wot do you mean?" inquired Mrs. Pinner, recovering herself. "I ain't to blame for what's in the paper, am I? How was I to know that the policeman as died wasn't your policeman?"

Mr. Pinner eyed her closely, but she met his gaze with eyes honest and clear as those of a child. Then, realising that he was wasting precious time, he picked up his cap, and as C 49 turned the corner with his prize, set off in the opposite direction to spend in the usual manner the brief remnant of the leave which remained to him.

A GARDEN PLOT

THE able-bodied men of the village were at work, the children were at school singing the multiplication-table lullaby, while the wives and mothers at home nursed the baby with one hand and did the housework with the other. At the end of the village an old man past work sat at a rough deal table under the creaking sign-board of the "Cauliflower," gratefully drinking from a mug of ale supplied by a chance traveller who sat opposite him.

The shade of the elms was pleasant and the ale good. The traveller filled his pipe and, glancing at the dusty hedges and the white road baking in the sun, called for the mugs to be refilled, and pushed his pouch towards his companion. After which he paid a compliment to the appearance of the village.

"It ain't what it was when I was a boy," quavered the old man, filling his pipe with trembling fingers. "I mind when the grindstone was stuck just outside the winder o' the forge instead o' being one side as it now is; and as for the shop winder—it's twice the size it was when I was a young 'un."

He lit his pipe with the scientific accuracy of a smoker of sixty years' standing, and shook his head solemnly as he regarded his altered birthplace. Then his colour heightened and his dim eye flashed.

"It's the people about 'ere 'as changed more than the place 'as," he said, with sudden fierceness; "there's a set o' men about here nowadays as are no good to anybody; reg'lar raskels. And if you've the mind to listen I can tell you of one or two as couldn't be beat in London itself.

"There's Tom Adams for one. He went and started wot 'e called a Benevolent Club. Three-pence a week each we paid agin sickness or accident, and Tom was secretary. Three weeks arter the club was started he caught a chill and was laid up for a month. He got back to work a week, and then 'e sprained something in 'is leg; and arter that was well 'is inside went wrong. We didn't think

35

much of it at first, not understanding figures; but at the end o' six months the club hadn't got a farthing, and they was in Tom's debt one pound seventeen-and-six.

"He isn't the only one o' that sort in the place, either. There was Herbert Richardson. He went to town, and came back with the idea of a Goose Club for Christmas. We paid twopence a week into that for pretty near ten months, and then Herbert went back to town agin, and all we 'ear of im, through his sister, is that he's still there and doing well, and don't know when he'll be back.

"But the artfullest and worst man in this place—and that's saying a good deal, mind you—is Bob Pretty. Deep is no word for 'im. There's no way of being up to 'im. It's through 'im that we lost our Flower Show; and, if you'd like to 'ear the rights o' that, I don't suppose there's anybody in this place as knows as much about it as I do—barring Bob hisself that is, but 'e wouldn't tell it to you as plain as I can.

"We'd only 'ad the Flower Show one year, and little anybody thought that the next one was to be the last. The first year you might smell the place a mile off in the summer, and on the day of the show people came from a long way round, and brought money to spend at the 'Cauliflower' and other places.

"It was started just after we got our new parson, and Mrs. Pawlett, the parson's wife, 'is name being Pawlett, thought as she'd encourage men to love their 'omes and be better 'usbands by giving a prize every year for the best cottage garden. Three pounds was the prize, and a metal teapot with writing on it.

"As I said, we only 'ad it two years. The fust year the garden as got it was a picter, and Bill Chambers, 'im as won the prize, used to say as 'e was out o' pocket by it, taking 'is time and the money 'e spent on flowers. Not as we believed that, you understand, 'specially as Bill did 'is very best to get it the next year, too. 'E didn't get it, and though p'r'aps most of us was glad 'e didn't, we was all very surprised at the way it turned out in the end.

"The Flower Show was to be 'eld on the 5th o' July, just as a'most everything about here was at its best. On the 15th of June Bill Chambers's garden seemed to be leading, but Peter Smith and Joe Gubbins and Sam Jones and Henery Walker was almost as good, and it was understood that more than one of 'em had got a surprise which they'd produce at the last moment, too late for the others to copy. We used to sit up here of an evening at this 'Cauliflower' public-house and put money on it. I put mine on Henery Walker, and the time I spent in 'is garden 'elping 'im is a sin and a shame to think of.

"Of course some of 'em used to make fun of it, and Bob Pretty was the worst of 'em all. He was always a lazy, good-for-nothing man, and 'is garden was a disgrace. He'd chuck down any rubbish in it: old bones, old tins, bits of an old bucket, anything to make it untidy. He used to larf at 'em awful about their gardens and about being took up by the parson's wife. Nobody ever see 'im do any work, real 'ard work, but the smell from 'is place at dinner-time was always nice, and I believe that he knew more about game than the parson hisself did.

"It was the day arter this one I'm speaking about, the 16th o' June, that the trouble all began, and it came about in a very eggstrordinary way. George English, a quiet man getting into years, who used when 'e was younger to foller the sea, and whose only misfortin was that 'e was a brother-in-law o' Bob Pretty's, his sister marrying Bob while 'e was at sea and knowing nothing about it, 'ad a letter come from a mate of his who 'ad gone to Australia to live. He'd 'ad letters from Australia before, as we all knew from Miss Wicks at the post-office, but this one upset him altogether. He didn't seem like to know what to do about it.

"While he was wondering Bill Chambers passed. He always did pass George's 'ouse about that time in the evening, it being on 'is way 'ome, and he saw George standing at 'is gate with a letter in 'is 'and looking very puzzled.

"'Evenin', George,' ses Bill.

"'Evenin',' ses George.

"'Not bad news, I 'ope?' ses Bill, noticing 'is manner, and thinking it was strange.

"'No,' ses George. 'I've just 'ad a very eggstrordinary letter from Australia,' he ses, 'that's all.'

"Bill Chambers was always a very inquisitive sort o' man, and he stayed and talked to George until George, arter fust making him swear oaths that 'e wouldn't tell a soul, took 'im inside and showed 'im the letter.

"It was more like a story-book than a letter. George's mate, John Biggs by name, wrote to say that an uncle of his who had just died, on 'is deathbed told him that thirty years ago he 'ad been in this very village, staying at this 'ere very 'Cauliflower,' whose beer we're drinking now. In the night, when everybody was asleep, he got up and went quiet-like and buried a bag of five hundred and seventeen sovereigns and one half-sovereign in one of the cottage gardens till 'e could come for it agin. He didn't say 'ow he come by the money, and, when Bill spoke about that, George English said that, knowing the man, he was afraid 'e 'adn't come by it honest,

37

but anyway his friend John Biggs wanted it, and, wot was more, 'ad asked 'im in the letter to get it for 'im.

"'And wot I'm to do about it, Bill,' he ses, 'I don't know. All the directions he gives is, that 'e thinks it was the tenth cottage on the right-'and side of the road, coming down from the "Cauliflower." He thinks it's the tenth, but 'e's not quite sure. Do you think I'd better make it known and offer a reward of ten shillings, say, to any one who finds it?'

"'No,' ses Bill, shaking 'is 'ead. 'I should hold on a bit if I was you, and think it over. I shouldn't tell another single soul, if I was you.'

"'I b'lieve you're right,' ses George. 'John Biggs would never forgive me if I lost that money for 'im. You'll remember about keeping it secret, Bill?'

"Bill swore he wouldn't tell a soul, and 'e went off 'ome and 'ad his supper, and then 'e walked up the road to the 'Cauliflower' and back, and then up and back again, thinking over what George 'ad been telling 'im, and noticing, what 'e 'd never taken the trouble to notice before, that 'is very house was the tenth one from the 'Cauliflower.'

"Mrs. Chambers woke up at two o'clock next morning and told Bill to get up further, and then found 'e wasn't there. She was rather surprised at first, but she didn't think much of it, and thought, what happened to be true, that 'e was busy in the garden, it being a light night. She turned over and went to sleep again, and at five when she woke up she could distinctly 'ear Bill working 'is 'ardest. Then she went to the winder and nearly dropped as she saw Bill in his shirt and trousers digging away like mad. A quarter of the garden was all dug up, and she shoved open the winder and screamed out to know what 'e was doing.

"Bill stood up straight and wiped 'is face with his shirt-sleeve and started digging again, and then his wife just put something on and rushed downstairs as fast as she could go.

"'What on earth are you a-doing of, Bill?' she screams.

"'Go indoors,' ses Bill, still digging.

"'Have you gone mad?' she ses, half crying.

"Bill just stopped to throw a lump of mould at her, and then went on digging till Henery Walker who also thought 'e 'ad gone mad, and didn't want to stop 'im too soon, put 'is 'ead over the 'edge and asked 'im the same thing.

"'Ask no questions and you'll 'ear no lies, and keep your ugly face your own side of the 'edge,' ses Bill. 'Take it indoors and frighten the children with,' he ses. 'I don't want it staring at me.'

"Henery walked off offended, and Bill went on with his digging. He wouldn't go to work, and 'e 'ad his breakfast in the garden, and his wife spent all the morning in the front answering the neighbours' questions and begging of 'em to go in and say something to Bill. One of 'em did go, and came back a'most directly and stood there for hours telling diff'rent people wot Bill 'ad said to 'er, and asking whether 'e couldn't be locked up for it.

"By tea-time Bill was dead-beat, and that stiff he could 'ardly raise 'is bread and butter to his mouth. Several o' the chaps looked in in the evening, but all they could get out of 'im was, that it was a new way o' cultivating 'is garden 'e 'ad just 'eard of, and that those who lived the longest would see the most. By night-time 'e'd nearly finished the job, and 'is garden was just ruined.

"Afore people 'ad done talking about Bill, I'm blest if Peter Smith didn't go and cultivate 'is garden in exactly the same way. The parson and 'is wife was away on their 'oliday, and nobody could say a word. The curate who 'ad come over to take 'is place for a time, and who took the names of people for the Flower Show, did point out to 'im that he was spoiling 'is chances, but Peter was so rude to 'im that he didn't stay long enough to say much.

"When Joe Gubbins started digging up 'is garden people began to think they were all bewitched, and I went round to see Henery Walker to tell 'im wot a fine chance 'e'd got, and to remind 'im that I'd put another ninepence on 'im the night before. All 'e said was, 'More fool you,' and went on digging a 'ole in his garden big enough to put a 'ouse in.

"In a fortnight's time there wasn't a garden worth looking at in the place, and it was quite clear there'd be no Flower Show that year, and of all the silly, bad-tempered men in the place them as 'ad dug up their pretty gardens was the wust.

"It was just a few days before the day fixed for the Flower Show, and I was walking up the road when I see Joe and Henery Walker and one or two more leaning over Bob Pretty's fence and talking to 'im. I stopped, too, to see what they were looking at, and found they was watching Bob's two boys a-weeding of 'is garden. It was a disgraceful, untidy sort of place, as I said before, with a few marigolds and nasturtiums, and sich-like put in anywhere, and Bob was walking up and down smoking of 'is pipe and watching 'is wife hoe atween the plants and cut off dead marigold blooms.

"'That's a pretty garden you've got there, Bob,' ses Joe, grinning.

"'I've seen wuss,' ses Bob.

"'Going in for the Flower Show, Bob?' ses Henery, with a wink at us.

"'O' course I am,' ses Bob, 'olding 'is 'ead up; 'my marigolds ought to pull me through,' he ses.

"Henery wouldn't believe it at fust, but when he saw Bob show 'is missus 'ow to pat the path down with the back o' the spade and hold the nails for 'er while she nailed a climbing nasturtium to the fence, he went off and fetched Bill Chambers and one or two others, and they all leaned over the fence breathing their 'ardest and a-saying of all the nasty things to Bob they could think of.

"'It's the best-kep' garden in the place,' ses Bob. 'I ain't afraid o' your new way o' cultivating flowers, Bill Chambers. Old-fashioned ways suit me best; I learnt 'ow to grow flowers from my father.'

"'You ain't 'ad the cheek to give your name in, Bob?' ses Sam Jones, staring.

"Bob didn't answer 'im. 'Pick those bits o' grass out o' the path, old gal,' he ses to 'is wife; 'they look untidy, and untidiness I can't abear.'

"He walked up and down smoking 'is pipe and pretending not to notice Henery Walker, wot 'ad moved farther along the fence, and was staring at some drabble-tailed-looking geraniums as if 'e'd seen 'em afore but wasn't quite sure where.

"'Admiring my geraniums, Henery?' ses Bob, at last.

"'Where'd you get 'em?' ses Henery, 'ardly able to speak.

"'My florist's,' ses Bob, in a off-hand manner.

"'Your *wot*?' asks Henery.

"'My florist,' ses Bob.

"'And who might 'e be when 'e's at home?' asked Henery.

"''Tain't so likely I'm going to tell you that,' ses Bob. 'Be reasonable, Henery, and ask yourself whether it's likely I should tell you 'is name. Why, I've never seen sich fine geraniums afore. I've been nursing 'em inside all the summer, and just planted 'em out.'

"'About two days arter I threw mine over my back fence,' ses Henery Walker, speaking very slowly.

"'Ho,' ses Bob, surprised. 'I didn't know you 'ad any geraniums, Henery. I thought you was digging for gravel this year.'

"Henery didn't answer 'im. Not because 'e didn't want to, mind you, but because he couldn't.

"'That one,' ses Bob, pointing at a broken geranium with the stem of 'is pipe, 'is a "Dook o' Wellington," and that white one there is wot I'm going to call "Pretty's Pride." That fine marigold over there, wot looks like a sunflower, is called "Golden Dreams."'

"'Come along, Henery,' ses Bill Chambers, bursting, 'come and get something to take the taste out of your mouth.'

"'I'm sorry I can't offer you a flower for your button-'ole,' ses Bob, perlitely, 'but it's getting so near the Flower Show now I can't afford it. If you chaps only knew wot pleasure was to be 'ad sitting among your innercent flowers, you wouldn't want to go to the public-house so often.'

"He shook 'is 'ead at 'em, and telling his wife to give the 'Dook o' Wellington' a mug of water, sat down in the chair agin and wiped the sweat off 'is brow.

"Bill Chambers did a bit o' thinking as they walked up the road, and by and by 'e turns to Joe Gubbins and 'e ses—

"'Seen anything o' George English lately, Joe?'

"'*Yes*,' ses Joe.

"'Seems to me we all 'ave,' ses Sam Jones.

"None of 'em liked to say wot was in their minds, 'aving all seen George English and swore pretty strong not to tell his secret, and none of 'em liking to own up that they'd been digging up their gardens to get money as 'e'd told 'em about. But presently Bill Chambers ses—

"'Without telling no secrets or breaking no promises, Joe, supposing a certain 'ouse was mentioned in a certain letter from forrin parts, wot 'ouse was it?'

"'Supposing it was so,' ses Joe, careful too; 'the second 'ouse counting from the "Cauliflower."'

"'The ninth 'ouse, you mean,' ses Henery Walker, sharply.

"'Second 'ouse in Mill Lane, you mean,' ses Sam Jones, wot lived there.

"Then they all see 'ow they'd been done, and that they wasn't, in a manner o' speaking, referring to the same letter. They came up and sat 'ere where we're sitting now, all dazed-like. It wasn't only the chance o' losing the prize that upset 'em, but they'd wasted their time and ruined their gardens and got called mad by the other folks. Henery Walker's state o' mind was dreadful for to see, and he kep' thinking of 'orrible things to say to George English, and then being afraid they wasn't strong enough.

"While they was talking who should come along but George English hisself! He came right up to the table, and they all sat back on the bench and stared at 'im fierce, and Henery Walker crinkled 'is nose at him.

41

"'Evening,' he ses, but none of 'em answered 'im; they all looked at Henery to see wot 'e was going to say.

"'Wot's up?' ses George, in surprise.

"'*Gardens*,' ses Henery.

"'So I've 'eard,' ses George.

"He shook 'is 'ead and loked at them sorrowful and severe at the same time.

"'So I 'eard, and I couldn't believe my ears till I went and looked for myself,' he ses, 'and wot I want to say is this: you know wot I'm referring to. If any man 'as found wot don't belong to him 'e knows who to give it to. It ain't wot I should 'ave expected of men wot's lived in the same place as *me* for years. Talk about honesty,' 'e ses, shaking 'is 'ead agin, 'I should like to see a little of it.'

"Peter Smith opened his mouth to speak, and 'ardly knowing wot 'e was doing took a pull at 'is beer at the same time, and if Sam Jones 'adn't been by to thump 'im on the back I b'lieve he'd ha' died there and then.

"'Mark my words,' ses George English, speaking very slow and solemn, 'there'll be no blessing on it. Whoever's made 'is fortune by getting up and digging 'is garden over won't get no real benefit from it. He may wear a black coat and new trousers on Sunday, but 'e won't be 'appy. I'll go and get my little taste o' beer somewhere else,' 'e ses. 'I can't breathe here.'

"He walked off before any one could say a word; Bill Chambers dropped 'is pipe and smashed it, Henery Walker sat staring after 'im with 'is mouth wide open, and Sam Jones, who was always one to take advantage, drank 'is own beer under the firm belief that it was Joe's.

"'I shall take care that Mrs. Pawlett 'ears o' this,' ses Henery, at last.

"'And be asked wot you dug your garden up for,' ses Joe, 'and 'ave to explain that you broke your promise to George. Why, she'd talk at us for years and years.'

"'And parson 'ud preach a sermon about it,' ses Sam; 'where's your sense, Henery?'

"'We should be the larfing-stock for miles round,' ses Bill Chambers. 'If anybody wants to know, I dug my garden up to enrich the soil for next year, and also to give some other chap a chance of the prize.'

"Peter Smith 'as always been a unfortunit man; he's got the name for it. He was just 'aving another drink as Bill said that, and this time we all thought 'e'd gorn. He did hisself.

"Mrs. Pawlett and the parson came 'ome next day, an' 'er voice got that squeaky with surprise it was painful to listen to her. All the chaps stuck to the tale that they'd dug their garden up to give the others a chance, and Henery Walker, 'e went further and said it was owing to a sermon on unselfishness wot the curate 'ad preached three weeks afore. He 'ad a nice little red-covered 'ymn-book the next day with 'From a friend' wrote in it.

"All things considered, Mrs. Pawlett was for doing away with the Flower Show that year and giving two prizes next year instead, but one or two other chaps, encouraged by Bob's example, 'ad given in their names too, and they said it wouldn't be fair to their wives. All the gardens but one was worse than Bob's, the men not having started till later than wot 'e did, and not being able to get their geraniums from 'is florist. The only better garden was Ralph Thomson's, who lived next door to 'im, but two nights afore the Flower Show 'is pig got walking in its sleep. Ralph said it was a mystery to 'im 'ow the pig could ha' got out; it must ha' put its foot through a hole too small for it, and turned the button of its door, and then climbed over a four-foot fence. He told Bob 'e wished the pig could speak, but Bob said that that was sinful and unchristian of 'im, and that most likely if it could, it would only call 'im a lot o' bad names, and ask 'im why he didn't feed it properly.

"There was quite a crowd on Flower Show day following the judges. First of all, to Bill Chambers's astonishment and surprise, they went to 'is place and stood on the 'eaps in is garden judging 'em, while Bill peeped at 'em through the kitchen winder 'arf crazy. They went to every garden in the place, until one of the young ladies got tired of it, and asked Mrs. Pawlett whether they was there to judge cottage-gardens or earthquakes.

"Everybody 'eld their breaths that evening in the schoolroom when Mrs. Pawlett got up on the platform and took a slip of paper from one of the judges. She stood a moment waiting for silence, and then 'eld up her 'and to stop what she thought was clapping at the back, but which was two or three wimmen who 'ad 'ad to take their crying babies out, trying to quiet 'em in the porch. Then Mrs. Pawlett put 'er glasses on her nose and just read out, short and sweet, that the prize of three sovereigns and a metal teapot for the best-kept cottage garden 'ad been won by Mr. Robert Pretty.

"One or two people patted Bob on the back as 'e walked up the middle to take the prize; then one or two more did, and Bill Chambers's pat was the 'eartiest of 'em all. Bob stopped and spoke to 'im about it.

"You would 'ardly think that Bob 'ud have the cheek to stand up there and make a speech, but 'e did. He said it gave 'im great pleasure to take the teapot and the money, and the more pleasure because 'e felt that 'e had earned 'em. He said that if 'e told 'em all 'e'd done to make sure o' the prize they'd be surprised. He said that 'e'd been like Ralph Thomson's pig, up early and late.

"He stood up there talking as though 'e was never going to leave off, and said that 'e hoped as 'is example would be of benefit to 'is neighbours. Some of 'em seemed to think that digging was everything, but 'e could say with pride that 'e 'adn't put a spade to 'is garden for three years until a week ago, and then not much.

"He finished 'is remarks by saying that 'e was going to give a tea-party up at the 'Cauliflower' to christen the teapot, where 'e'd be pleased to welcome all friends. Quite a crowd got up and followed 'im out then, instead o' waiting for the dissolving views, and came back 'arf an hour arterwards, saying that until they'd got as far as the 'Cauliflower' they'd no idea as Bob was so pertickler who 'e mixed with.

"That was the last Flower Show we ever 'ad in Claybury, Mrs. Pawlett and the judges meeting the tea-party coming 'ome, and 'aving to get over a gate into a field to let it pass. What with that and Mrs. Pawlett tumbling over something further up the road, which turned out to be the teapot, smelling strong of beer, the Flower Show was given up, and the parson preached three Sundays running on the sin of beer-drinking to children who'd never 'ad any and wimmen who couldn't get it."

PRIVATE CLOTHES

AT half-past nine the crew of the *Merman* were buried in slumber, at nine thirty-two three of the members were awake with heads protruding out of their bunks, trying to peer through the gloom, while the fourth dreamt that a tea-tray was falling down a never-ending staircase. On the floor of the forecastle something was cursing prettily and rubbing itself.

"Did you 'ear anything, Ted?" inquired a voice in an interval of silence.

"Who is it?" demanded Ted, ignoring the question. "Wot d'yer want?"

"I'll let you know who I am," said a thick and angry voice. "I've broke my blarsted back."

"Light the lamp, Bill," said Ted.

Bill struck a tandsticker match, and carefully nursing the sulphurous flame with his hand, saw dimly some high-coloured object on the floor. He got out of his bunk and lit the lamp, and an angry and very drunken member of His Majesty's foot forces became visible.

"Wot are you doin' 'ere?" inquired Ted, sharply, "this ain't the guard-room."

"Who knocked me over?" demanded the soldier, sternly; "take your co—coat off lik' a man."

He rose to his feet and swayed unsteadily to and fro.

"If you keep your li'l' 'eads still," he said gravely, to Bill, "I'll punch 'em."

By a stroke of good fortune he selected the real head, and gave it a blow which sent it crashing against the woodwork. For a moment the seaman stood gathering his scattered senses, then with an oath he sprang forward, and in the lightest of fighting trim waited until his adversary, who was by this time on the floor again, should have regained his feet.

"He's drunk, Bill," said another voice, "don't 'urt 'im. He's a

45

chap wot said 'e was coming aboard to see me—I met 'im in the 'Green Man' this evening. You was coming to see me, mate, wasn't you?"

The soldier looked up stupidly, and gripping hold of the injured Bill by the shirt, staggered to his feet again, and advancing towards the last speaker let fly suddenly in his face.

"Sort man I am," he said, autobiographically. "Feel my arm."

The indignant Bill took him by both, and throwing himself upon him suddenly fell with him to the floor. The intruder's head met the boards with a loud crash, and then there was silence.

"You ain't killed 'im, Bill?" said an old seaman, stooping over him anxiously.

"Course not," was the reply; "give us some water."

He threw some in the soldier's face, and then poured some down his neck, but with no result. Then he stood upright, and exchanged glances of consternation with his friends.

"I don't like the way he's breathing," he said, in a trembling voice.

"You always was pertickler, Bill," said the cook, who had thankfully got to the bottom of his staircase. "If I was you——"

He was not allowed to proceed any further; footsteps and a voice were heard above, and as old Thomas hastily extinguished the lamp, the mate's head was thrust down the scuttle, and the mate's voice sounded a profane *reveille*.

"Wot are we goin' to do with it?" inquired Ted, as the mate walked away.

"'*Im*, Ted," said Bill, nervously. "He's alive all right."

"If we put 'im ashore an' 'e's dead," said old Thomas, "there'll be trouble for somebody. Better let 'im be, and if 'e's dead, why we don't none of us know nothing about it."

The men ran up on deck, and Bill, being the last to leave, put a boot under the soldier's head before he left. Ten minutes later they were under way, and standing about the deck, discussed the situation in thrilling whispers as opportunity offered.

At breakfast, by which time they were in a dirty tumbling sea, with the *Nore* lightship, a brown forlorn-looking object, on their beam, the soldier, who had been breathing stertorously, raised his heavy head from the boot, and with glassy eyes and tightly compressed lips gazed wonderingly about him.

"Wot cheer, mate?" said the delighted Bill. "'Ow goes it?"

"Where am I?" inquired Private Harry Bliss, in a weak voice.

"Brig *Merman*," said Bill; "bound for Bystermouth."

"Well, I'm damned," said Private Bliss; "it's a blooming miracle

Open the winder, it's a bit stuffy down here. Who—who brought me here?"

"You come to see me last night," said Bob, "an' fell down, I s'pose; then you punched Bill 'ere in the eye and me in the jor."

Mr. Bliss, still feeling very sick and faint, turned to Bill, and after critically glancing at the eye turned on him for inspection, transferred his regards to the other man's jaw.

"I'm a devil when I'm boozed," he said, in a satisfied voice. "Well, I must get ashore; I shall get cells for this, I expect."

He staggered to the ladder, and with unsteady haste gained the deck and made for the side. The heaving waters made him giddy to look at, and he gazed for preference at a thin line of coast stretching away in the distance.

The startled mate, who was steering, gave him a hail, but he made no reply. A little fishing-boat was jumping about in a way to make a sea-sick man crazy, and he closed his eyes with a groan. Then the skipper, aroused by the mate's hail, came up from below, and walking up to him put a heavy hand on his shoulder.

"What are you doing aboard this ship?" he demanded, austerely.

"Go away," said Private Bliss, faintly; "take your paw off my tunic; you'll spoil it."

He clung miserably to the side, leaving the incensed skipper to demand explanations from the crew. The crew knew nothing about him, and said that he must have stowed himself away in an empty bunk; the skipper pointed out coarsely that there were no empty bunks, whereupon Bill said that he had not occupied his the previous evening, but had fallen asleep sitting on the locker, and had injured his eye against the corner of a bunk in consequence. In proof whereof he produced the eye.

"Look here, old man," said Private Bliss, who suddenly felt better. He turned and patted the skipper on the back. "You just turn to the left a bit and put me ashore, will you?"

"I'll put you ashore at Bystermouth," said the skipper, with a grin. "You're a deserter, that's what you are, and I'll take care you're took care of."

"You put me ashore now!" roared Private Bliss, with a very fine imitation of the sergeant-major's parade voice.

"Get out and walk," said the skipper contemptuously, over his shoulder, as he walked off.

"Here," said Mr. Bliss, unbuckling his belt, "hold my tunic one of you. I'll learn 'im."

Before the paralysed crew could prevent him he had flung his coat into Bill's arms and followed the master of the *Merman* aft.

47

As a light-weight he was rather fancied at the gymnasium, and in the all too brief exhibition which followed he displayed fine form and a knowledge of anatomy which even the skipper's tailor was powerless to frustrate.

The frenzy of the skipper as Ted assisted him to his feet and he saw his antagonist struggling in the arms of the crew was terrible to behold. Strong men shivered at his words, but Mr. Bliss, addressing him as "Whiskers," told him to call his crew off and to come on, and shaping as well as two pairs of brawny arms round his middle would permit, endeavoured in vain to reach him.

"This," said the skipper, bitterly, as he turned to the mate, "is what you an' me have to pay to keep up. I wouldn't let you go now, my lad, not for a fi'pun' note. Deserter, that's what you are!"

He turned and went below, and Private Bliss, after an insulting address to the mate, was hauled forward, struggling fiercely, and seated on the deck to recover. The excitement passed, he lost his colour again, and struggling into his tunic, went and brooded over the side.

By dinner-time his faintness had passed, and he sniffed with relish at the smell from the galley. The cook emerged bearing dinner to the cabin, then he returned and took a fine smoking piece of boiled beef flanked with carrots down to the forecastle. Private Bliss eyed him wistfully and his mouth watered.

For a time pride struggled with hunger, then pride won a partial victory and he descended carelessly to the forecastle.

"Can any o' you chaps lend me a pipe o' baccy?" he asked, cheerfully.

Bill rummaged in his pocket and found a little tobacco in a twist of paper.

"Bad thing to smoke on a empty stomach," he said, with his mouth full.

"'Tain't my fault it's empty," said Private Bliss, pathetically.

"'Tain't mine," said Bill.

"I've 'eard," said the cook, who was a tender-hearted man, "as 'ow it's a good thing to go for a day or so without food some-times."

"Who said so?" inquired Private Bliss, hotly.

"Diff'rent people," replied the cook.

"You can tell 'em from me they're blamed fools," said Mr. Bliss.

There was an uncomfortable silence; Mr. Bliss lit his pipe, but it did not seem to draw well.

"Did you like that pot o' six-half I stood you last night?" he inquired somewhat pointedly of Bob.

Bob hesitated, and looked at his plate.

"No, it was a bit flat," he said, at length.

"Well, I won't stop you chaps at your grub," said Private Bliss, bitterly, as he turned to depart.

"You're not stopping us," said Ted, cheerfully. "I'd offer you a bit, only——"

"Only what?" demanded the other.

"Skipper's orders," said Ted. "He ses we're not to. He ses if we do it's helping a deserter, and we'll all get six months."

"But you're helping me by having me on board," said Private Bliss; "besides, I don't want to desert."

"We couldn't 'elp you coming aboard," said Bill, "that's wot the old man said, but 'e ses we can 'elp giving of him vittles, he ses."

"Well, have I got to starve?" demanded the horror-stricken Mr. Bliss.

"Look 'ere," said Bill, frankly, "go and speak to the old man. It's no good talking to us. Go and have it out with him."

Private Bliss thanked him and went on deck. Old Thomas was at the wheel, and a pleasant clatter of knives and forks came up through the open skylight of the cabin. Ignoring the old man, who waved him away, he raised the open skylight still higher, and thrust his head in.

"Go away," bawled the skipper, pausing with his knife in his fist, as he caught sight of him.

"I want to know where I'm to have my dinner," bawled back the thoroughly roused Mr. Bliss.

"Your *dinner!*" said the skipper, with an air of surprise; "why, I didn't know you 'ad any."

Private Bliss took his head away, and holding it very erect, took in his belt a little and walked slowly up and down the deck. Then he went to the water-cask and took a long drink, and an hour later a generous message was received from the skipper that he might have as many biscuits as he liked.

On this plain fare Private Bliss lived the whole of that day and the next, snatching a few hours' troubled sleep on the locker at nights. His peace of mind was by no means increased by the information of Ted that Bystermouth was a garrison town, and feeling that in spite of any explanation he would be treated as a deserter, he resolved to desert in good earnest at the first opportunity that offered.

By the third day nobody took any notice of him, and his

presence on board was almost forgotten, until Bob, going down to the forecastle, created a stir by asking somewhat excitedly what had become of him.

"He's on deck, I s'pose," said the cook, who was having a pipe.

"He's not," said Bob, solemnly.

"He's not gone overboard, I s'pose?" said Bill, starting up.

Touched by this morbid suggestion they went up on deck and looked round; Private Bliss was nowhere to be seen, and Ted, who was steering, had heard no splash. He seemed to have disappeared by magic, and the cook, after a hurried search, ventured aft, and, descending to the cabin, mentioned his fears to the skipper.

"Nonsense!" said that gentleman, sharply. "I'll lay I'll find him."

He came on deck and looked round, followed at a respectful distance by the crew, but there was no sign of Mr. Bliss. Then an idea, a horrid idea, occurred to the cook. The colour left his cheeks and he gazed helplessly at the skipper.

"What is it?" bawled the latter.

The cook, incapable of speech, raised a trembling hand and pointed to the galley. The skipper started, and, rushing to the door, drew it hastily back.

Mr. Bliss had apparently finished, though he still toyed languidly with his knife and fork as though loth to put them down. A half-emptied saucepan of potatoes stood on the floor by his side, and a bone, with a small fragment of meat adhering, was between his legs on a saucepan lid which served as a dish.

"Rather underdone, cook," he said, severely, as he met that worthy's horror-stricken gaze.

"Is that the cabin's or the men's he's eaten?" vociferated the skipper.

"Cabin's," replied Mr. Bliss, before the cook could speak; "it looked the best. Now has anybody got a nice see-gar?"

He drew back the door the other side of the galley as he spoke, and went out that way. A move was made towards him, but he backed, and picking up a handspike swung it round his head.

"Let him be," said the skipper in a choking voice, "let him be. He'll have to answer for stealing my dinner when I get 'im ashore. Cook, take the men's dinner down into the cabin. I'll talk to you by and by."

He walked aft and disappeared below, while Private Bliss, still fondling the handspike, listened unmoved to a lengthy vituperation which Bill called a plain and honest opinion of his behaviour.

"It's the last dinner you'll 'ave for some time," he concluded, spitefully; "it'll be skilly for you when you get ashore."

Mr. Bliss smiled, and, fidgeting with his tongue, asked him for the loan of his toothpick.

"You won't be using it yourself," he urged. "Now you go below all of you and start on the biscuits, there's good men. It's no use standing there saying a lot o' bad words what I left off when I was four years old."

He filled his pipe with some tobacco he had thoughtfully borrowed from the cook before dinner, and dropping into a negligent attitude on the deck, smoked placidly with his eyes half closed. The brig was fairly steady and the air hot and slumberous, and with an easy assurance that nobody would hit him while in that position, he allowed his head to fall on his chest and dropped off into a light sleep.

It became evident to him the following afternoon that they were nearing Bystermouth. The skipper contented himself with eyeing him with an air of malicious satisfaction, but the crew gratified themselves by painting the horrors of his position in strong colours. Private Bliss affected indifference, but listened eagerly to all they had to say, with the air of a general considering his enemy's plans.

It was a source of disappointment to the crew that they did not arrive until after nightfall, and the tide was already too low for them to enter the harbour. They anchored outside, and Private Bliss, despite his position, felt glad as he smelt the land again, and saw the twinkling lights and houses ashore. He could even hear the clatter of a belated vehicle driving along the seafront. Lights on the summits of the heights in the background indicated, so Bill said, the position of the fort.

To the joy of the men he partly broke down in the forecastle that night; and, in tropical language, severally blamed his parents, the School Board, and the Army for not having taught him to swim. The last thing that Bill heard, ere sleep closed his lids, was a pious resolution on the part of Mr. Bliss to the effect that all his children should be taught the art of natation as soon as they were born.

Bill woke up just before six; and, hearing a complaining voice, thought at first that his military friend was still speaking. The voice got more and more querulous with occasional excursions into the profane, and the seaman, rubbing his eyes, turned his head, and saw old Thomas groping about the forecastle.

"Wot's the matter with you, old 'un?" he demanded.

"I can't find my trousis," grumbled the old man.

"Did you 'ave 'em on larst night?" inquired Bill, who was still half asleep.

"Course I did, you fool," said the other, snappishly.

"Be civil," said Bill, calmly, "be civil. Are you sure you haven't got 'em on now?"

The old man greeted this helpful suggestion with such a volley of abuse that Bill lost his temper.

"P'r'aps somebody's got 'em on their bed, thinking they was a patchwork quilt," he said, coldly; "it's a mistake anybody might make. Have you got the jacket?"

"I ain't got nothing," replied the bewildered old man, "'cept wot I stand up in."

"That ain't much," said Bill, frankly. "Where's that blooming sojer?" he demanded, suddenly.

"I don't know where 'e is, and I don't care," replied the old man. "On deck, I s'pose."

"P'r'aps 'e's got 'em on," said the unforgiving Bill; "'e didn't seem a very pertickler sort of chap."

The old man started, and hurriedly ascended to the deck. He was absent two or three minutes, and, when he returned, consternation was writ large upon his face.

"He's gone," he spluttered; "there ain't a sign of 'im about, and the life-belt wot hangs on the galley 'as gone too. Wot am I to do?"

"Well, they was very old cloes," said Bill, soothingly, "an' you ain't a bad figger, not for your time o' life, Thomas."

"There's many a wooden-legged man 'ud be glad to change with you," affirmed Ted, who had been roused by the noise. "You'll soon get over the feeling o' shyness, Thomas."

The forecastle laughed encouragingly, until Thomas, who had begun to realise the position, joined in. He laughed till the tears ran down his cheeks, and his excitement began to alarm his friends.

"Don't be a fool, Thomas," said Bob, anxiously.

"I can't help it," said the old man, struggling hysterically; "it's the best joke I've heard."

"He's gone dotty," said Ted, solemnly. "I never 'eard of a man larfing like that a 'cos he'd lorst 'is cloes."

"I'm not larfing at that," said Thomas, regaining his composure by a great effort. "I'm larfing at a joke wot you don't know of yet."

A deadly chill struck at the hearts of the listeners at these words, then Bill, after a glance at the foot of his bunk, where he usually kept his clothes, sprang out and began a hopeless search. The other men followed suit, and the air rang with lamentations and profanity. Even the spare suits in the men's chests had gone; and Bill, a prey to acute despair, sat down, and in a striking passage consigned the entire British Army to perdition.

"'E's taken one suit and chucked the rest overboard, I expect, so as we shan't be able to go arter 'im," said Thomas. "I expect he could swim arter all, Bill."

Bill, still busy with the British Army, paid no heed.

"We must go an' tell the old man," said Ted.

"Better be careful," cautioned the cook. "'Im an' the mate 'ad a go at the whisky last night, an' you know wot 'e is next morning."

The men went up slowly on deck. The morning was fine, but the air, chill with a breeze from the land, had them at a disadvantage. Ashore, a few people were early astir.

"You go down, Thomas, you're the oldest," said Bill..

"I was thinking o' Ted going," said Thomas, "'e's the youngest."

Ted snorted derisively. "Oh, was you?" he remarked, helpfully.

"Or Bob," said the old man, "don't matter which."

"Toss up for it," said the cook.

Bill, who was keeping his money in his hand as the only safe place left to him, produced a penny and spun it in the air.

"Wait a bit," said Ted, earnestly. "Wot time was you to call the old man?" he asked, turning to the cook.

"Toss up for it," repeated that worthy, hurriedly.

"Six o'clock," said Bob, speaking for him; "it's that now, cookie. Better go an' call 'im at once."

"I dassent go like this," said the trembling cook.

"Well, you'll 'ave to," said Bill. "If the old man misses the tide, you know wot you've got to expect."

"Let's follow 'im down," said Ted. "Come along, cookie, we'll see you righted."

The cook thanked him, and, followed by the others, led the way down to interview the skipper. The clock ticked on the mantel-piece, and heavy snoring proceeded both from the mate's bunk and the state-room. On the door of the latter the cook knocked gently; then he turned the handle and peeped in.

The skipper, raising a heavy head, set in matted hair and disordered whiskers, glared at him fiercely.

"What d'ye want?" he roared.

"If you please, sir——" began the cook.

He opened the door as he spoke, and disclosed the lightly-clad crowd behind. The skipper's eyes grew large and his jaw dropped, while inarticulate words came from his parched and astonished throat; and the mate, who was by this time awake, sat up in his bunk and cursed them roundly for their indelicacy.

"Get out," roared the skipper, recovering his voice.

"We came to tell you," interposed Bill, "as 'ow——"

"Get out," roared the skipper again. "How dare you come to my state-room, and like this, too."

"All our clothes 'ave gone and so 'as the sojer chap," said Bill.

"Serve you damned well right for letting him go," cried the skipper, angrily. "Hurry up, George, and get alongside," he called to the mate, "we'll catch him yet. Clear out, you—you—ballet girls."

The indignant seamen withdrew slowly, and, reaching the foot of the companion, stood there in mutinous indecision. Then, as the cook placed his foot on the step, the skipper was heard calling to the mate again.

"George?" he said, in an odd voice.

"Well?" was the reply.

"I hope you're not forgetting yourself and playing larks," said the skipper, with severity.

"Larks?" repeated the mate, as the alarmed crew fled silently on deck and stood listening open-mouthed at the companion. "Of course I ain't. You don't mean to tell me——"

"All my clothes have gone, every stitch I've got," replied the skipper, desperately, as the mate sprang out. "I shall have to borrow some of yours. If I catch that infernal——"

"You're quite welcome," said the mate, bitterly, "only somebody has borrowed 'em already. That's what comes of sleeping too heavy."

The *Merman* sailed bashfully into harbour half an hour later, the uniforms of its crew evoking severe comment from the people on the quay. At the same time, Mr. Harry Bliss, walking along the road some ten miles distant, was trying to decide upon his future career, his present calling of "shipwrecked sailor" being somewhat too hazardous even for his bold spirit.

THE BULLY OF THE "CAVENDISH"

"Talking of prize-fighters, sir," said the night-watchman, who had nearly danced himself over the edge of the wharf in illustrating one of Mr. Corbett's most trusted blows, and was now sitting down taking in sufficient air for three, "they ain't wot they used to be when I was a boy. They advertise in the papers for months and months about their fights, and when it does come off, they do it with gloves, and they're all right agin a day or two arter.

"I saw a picter the other day o' one punching a bag wot couldn't punch back, for practice. Why, I remember as a young man Sinker Pitt, as used to 'ave the 'King's Arms' 'ere in 'is old age; when 'e wanted practice 'is plan was to dress up in a soft 'at and black coat like a chapel minister or something, and go in a pub and contradict people; sailor-men for choice. He'd ha' no more thought o' hitting a pore 'armless bag than I should ha' thought of hitting 'im.

"The strangest prize-fighter I ever come acrost was one wot shipped with me on the *Cavendish*. He was the most eggstrordinry fighter I've ever seen or 'eard of, and 'e got to be such a nuisance afore 'e'd done with us that we could 'ardly call our souls our own. He shipped as an ordinary seaman—a unfair thing to do, as 'e was anything but ordinary, and 'ad no right to be there at all.

"We'd got one terror on board afore he come, and that was Bill Bone, one o' the biggest and strongest men I've ever seen down a ship's fo'c's'le, and that's saying a good deal. Built more like a bull than a man, 'e was, and when he was in his tantrums the best thing to do was to get out of 'is way or else get into your bunk and keep quiet. Oppersition used to send 'im crazy a'most, an' if 'e said a red shirt was a blue one, you 'ad to keep quiet. It didn't do to agree with 'im and call it blue even, cos if you did he'd call you a liar and punch you for telling lies.

"He was the only drawback to that ship. We 'ad a nice old man, good mates, and good grub. You may know it was A1 when I tell you that most of us 'ad been in 'er for several v'y'ges.

"But Bill was a drawback, and no mistake. In the main he was a 'earty, good-tempered sort o' shipmate as you'd wish to see, only, as I said afore, oppersition was a thing he could not and would not stand. It used to fly to his 'ead direckly.

"The v'y'ge I'm speaking of—we used to trade between Australia and London—Bill came aboard about an hour afore the ship sailed. The rest of us was already aboard and down below, some of us stowing our things away and the rest sitting down and telling each other lies about wot we'd been doing. Bill came lurching down the ladder, and Tom Baker put 'is 'and to 'im to steady 'im as he got to the bottom.

"'Who are you putting your 'ands on?' ses Bill, glaring at 'im.

"'Only 'olding you up, Bill,' ses Tom, smiling.

"'Oh,' ses Bill.

"He put 'is back up agin a bunk and pulled hisself together.

"''Olding of me—up—was you?' he ses; 'whaffor, if I might be so bold as to arsk?'

"'I thought your foot 'ad slipped, Bill, old man,' ses Tom; 'but I'm sorry if it 'adn't.'

"Bill looks at 'im agin, 'ard.

"'Sorry if my foot didn't slip?' he ses.

"'You know wot I mean, Bill,' ses Tom, smiling a uneasy smile.

"'Don't laugh at me,' roars Bill.

"'I wasn't laughing, Bill, old pal,' ses Tom.

"''E's called me a liar,' ses Bill, looking round at us; 'called me a liar. 'Old my coat, Charlie, and I'll split 'im in halves.'

"Charlie took the coat like a lamb, though he was Tom's pal, and Tom looked round to see whether he couldn't nip up the ladder and get away, but Bill was just in front of it. Then Tom found out that one of 'is bootlaces was undone and he knelt down to do it up, and this young ordinary seaman, Joe Simms by name, put his 'ead out of his bunk and he ses, quiet-like—

"'You ain't afraid of that thing, mate, are you?'

"'*Wot?*' screams Bill, starting.

"'Don't make such a noise when I'm speaking,' ses Joe; 'where's your manners, you great 'ulking rascal?'

"I thought Bill would ha' dropped with surprise at being spoke to like that. His face was purple all over and 'e stood staring at Joe as though 'e didn't know wot to make of 'im. And we stared too, Joe being a smallish sort o' chap and not looking at all strong.

"'Go easy, mate,' whispers Tom; 'you don't know who you're talking to.'

"'Bosh,' ses Joe, 'he's no good. He's too fat and too silly to do any 'arm. He shan't 'urt you while I'm 'ere.'

"He just rolled out of 'is bunk and, standing in front of Bill, put 'is fists up at 'im and stared 'im straight in the eye.

"'You touch that man,' he ses, quietly, pointing to Tom, 'and I'll give you such a dressing-down as you've never 'ad afore. Mark my words, now.'

"'I wasn't going to 'it him,' ses Bill, in a strange, mild voice.

"'You'd better not,' ses the young 'un, shaking his fist at 'im; 'you'd better not, my lad. If there's any fighting to be done in this fo'c's'le I'll do it. Mind that.'

"It's no good me saying we was staggered; becos staggered ain't no word for it. To see Bill put 'is hands in 'is pockets and try and whistle, and then sit down on a locker and scratch 'is 'ead, was the most amazing thing I've ever seen. Presently 'e begins to sing under his breath.

"'Stop that 'umming,' ses Joe; 'when I want you to 'um I'll tell you.'

"Bill left off 'umming, and then he gives a little cough behind the back of 'is 'and, and, arter fidgeting about a bit with 'is feet, went up on deck again.

"''Strewth,' ses Tom, looking round at us, ''ave we shipped a bloomin' prize-fighter?'

"'Wot did you call me?' ses Joe, looking at 'im.

"'Nothing, mate,' ses Tom, drawing back.

"'You keep a quiet tongue in your 'ead,' ses Joe, 'and speak when you're spoken to, my lad.'

"He was a ordinary seaman, mind, talking to A.B.'s like that. Men who'd been up aloft and doing their little bit when 'e was going about catching cold in 'is little petticuts. Still, if Bill could stand it, we supposed as we'd better.

"Bill stayed up on deck till we was under way, and 'is spirit seemed to be broke. He went about 'is work like a man wot was walking in 'is sleep, and when breakfast come 'e 'ardly tasted it.

"Joe made a splendid breakfast, and when he'd finished 'e went to Bill's bunk and chucked the things out all over the place and said 'e was going to 'ave it instead of his own. And Bill sat there and took it all quiet, and by and by he took 'is things up and put them in Joe's bunk without a word.

"It was the most peaceful fust day we 'ad ever 'ad down that fo'c's'le, Bill usually being in 'is tantrums the fust day or two at

sea, and wanting to know why 'e'd been born. If you talked you
was noisy and worriting, and if you didn't talk you was sulky; but
this time 'e sat quite still and didn't interfere a bit. It was such a
pleasant change that we all felt a bit grateful, and at tea-time Tom
Baker patted Joe on the back and said he was one o' the right old
sort.

"'You've been in a scrap or two in your time, I know,' he ses,
admiring like. 'I knew you was a bit of a one with your fists
direckly I see you.'

"'Oh, 'ow's that?' asks Joe.

"'I could see by your nose,' ses Tom.

"You never know how to take people like that. The words 'ad
'ardly left Tom's lips afore the other ups with a basin of 'ot tea and
heaves it all over 'im.

"'Take that, you insulting rascal,' he ses, as Tom jumped up
spluttering and wiping 'is face with his coat. 'How dare you insult
me?'

"'Get up,' ses Tom, dancing with rage. 'Get up; prize-fighter or
no prize-fighter, I'll mark you.'

"'Sit down,' ses Bill, turning round.

"'I'm going to 'ave a go at 'im, Bill,' ses Tom; 'if you're afraid of
'im, I ain't.'

"'Sit down,' ses Bill, starting up. ''Ow dare you insult me like
that?'

"'Like wot?' ses Tom, staring.

"'If I can't lick 'im you can't,' ses Bill; 'that's 'ow it is, mate.'

"'But I can try,' ses Tom.

"'All right,' ses Bill. 'Me fust, then if you lick me, you can 'ave
a go at 'im. If you can't lick me, 'ow can you lick 'im?'

"'Sit down both of you,' ses young Joe, drinking Bill's tea to
make up for 'is own. 'And mind you, I'm cock o' this fo'c's'le, and
don't you forget it. Sit down, both of you, afore I start on you.'

"They both sat down, but Tom wasn't quick enough to please
Bill, and he got a wipe o' the side o' the 'ead that made it ring for
an hour afterwards.

"That was the beginning of it, and instead of 'aving one master
we found we'd got two, owing to the eggstordinry way Bill had o'
looking at things. He gave Joe best without even 'aving a try at
him, and if anybody else wanted to 'ave a try, it was a insult to Bill.
We couldn't make 'ead or tail of it, and all we could get out of Bill
was that 'e had one time 'ad a turn-up with Joe Simms ashore,
which he'd remember all 'is life. It must ha' been something of a
turn, too, the way Bill used to try and curry favour with 'im.

"In about three days our life wasn't worth living, and the fo'c's'le was more like a Sunday-school class than anything else. In the fust place Joe put down swearing. He wouldn't 'ave no bad langwidge, he said, and he didn't neither. If a man used a bad word Joe would pull 'im up the fust time, and the second he'd order Bill to 'it 'im, being afraid of 'urting 'im too much 'imself. 'Arf the men 'ad to leave off talking altogether when Joe was by, but the way they used to swear when he wasn't was something shocking. Harry Moore got clergyman's sore throat one arternoon through it.

"Then Joe objected to us playing cards for money, and we 'ad to arrange on the quiet that brace buttons was ha'-pennies and coat buttons pennies, and that lasted until one evening Tom Baker got up and danced and nearly went off 'is 'ead with joy through havin' won a few dozen. That was enough for Joe, and Bill by his orders took the cards and pitched 'em over the side.

"Sweet-'earting and that sort o' thing Joe couldn't abear, and Ned Davis put his foot into it finely one arternoon through not knowing. He was lying in 'is bunk smoking and thinking, and by and by he looked across at Bill, who was 'arf asleep, and 'e ses:—

"'I wonder whether you'll see that little gal at Melbourne agin this trip, Bill.'

"Bill's eyes opened wide and he shook 'is fist at Ned, as Ned thought, playful-like.

"'All right, I'm a-looking at you, Bill,' 'e ses. 'I can see you.'

"'What gal is that, Ned?' ses Joe, who was in the next bunk to him, and I saw Bill's eyes screw up tight, and e' suddenly fell fast asleep.

"'I don't know 'er name,' ses Ned, 'but she was very much struck on Bill; they used to go to the theayter together.'

"'Pretty gal?' ses Joe, leading 'im on.

"'*Rather*,' ses Ned. 'Trust Bill for that, 'e always gets the prettiest gal in the place—I've known as many as six and seven to——'

'WOT!' screams Bill, waking up out of 'is sleep, and jumping out of 'is bunk.

"'Keep still, Bill, and don't interfere when I'm talking,' ses Joe, very sharp.

"'E's insulted me,' ses Bill; 'talking about gals when everybody knows I 'ate 'em worse than pison.'

"'Hold your tongue,' ses Joe. 'Now, Ned, what's this about this little gal? What's 'er name?'

"'It was only a little joke o' mine,' ses Ned, who saw 'e'd put 'is foot in it. 'Bill 'ates 'em worse than—worse than—pison.'

"'You're telling me a lie,' ses Joe, sternly. 'Who was it?'

"'It was only my fun, Joe,' ses Ned.

"'Oh, very well then, I'm going to 'ave a bit of fun now,' ses Joe. 'Bill!'

"'Yes,' ses Bill.

"'I won't 'it Ned myself for fear I shall do 'im a lasting injury,' ses Joe, 'so you just start on 'im and keep on till 'e tells all about your goings on with that gal.'

"'Hit *'im* to make 'im tell about *me*?' ses Bill, staring 'is 'ardest.

"'You 'eard wot I said,' ses Joe; 'don't repeat my words. You a married man, too; I've got sisters of my own, and I'm going to put this sort o' thing down. If you don't down 'im, I will.'

"Ned wasn't much of a fighter, and I 'alf expected to see 'im do a bolt up on deck and complain to the skipper. He did look like it for a moment, then he stood up, looking a bit white as Bill walked over to 'im, and the next moment 'is fist flew out, and afore we could turn round I'm blest if Bill wasn't on the floor. 'E got up as if 'e was dazed like, struck out wild at Ned and missed 'im, and the next moment was knocked down agin. We could 'ardly believe our eyes, and as for Ned, 'e looked as though 'e'd been doing miracles by mistake.

"When Bill got up the second time 'e was that shaky 'e could 'ardly stand, and Ned 'ad it all 'is own way, until at last 'e got Bill's 'ead under 'is arm and punched at it till they was both tired.

"'All right,' ses Bill; 'I've 'ad enough. I've met my master.'

"'*Wot?*' ses Joe, staring.

"'I've met my master,'' ses Bill, going and sitting down. 'Ned 'as knocked me about crool.'

"Joe looked at 'im, speechless, and then without saying another word, or 'aving a go at Ned himself, as we expected, 'e went up on deck, and Ned crossed over and sat down by Bill.

"'I 'ope I didn't hurt you, mate,' he ses, kindly.

"'Hurt me?' roars Bill. 'You! You 'urt me? You, you little bag o' bones. Wait till I get you ashore by yourself for five minits, Ned Davis, and then you'll know what 'urting means.'

"'I don't understand you, Bill,' ses Ned; 'you're a mystery, that's what you are; but I tell you plain when you go ashore you don't have me for a companion.'

"It was a mystery to all of us, and it got worse and worse as time went on. Bill didn't dare to call 'is soul 'is own, although Joe only hit 'im once the whole time, and then not very hard, and he excused 'is cowardice by telling us of a man Joe 'ad killed in a fight down in one o' them West-end clubs.

"Wot with Joe's Sunday-school ways and Bill backing 'em up, we was all pretty glad by the time we got to Melbourne. It was like getting out o' pris'n to get away from Joe for a little while. All but Bill, that is, and Joe took 'im to hear a dissolving views on John Bunyan. Bill said 'e'd be delighted to go, but the language he used about 'im on the quiet when he came back showed what 'e thought of it. I don't know who John Bunyan is, or wot he's done, but the things Bill said about 'im I wouldn't soil my tongue by repeating.

"Arter we'd been there two or three days we began to feel a'most sorry for Bill. Night arter night, when we was ashore, Joe would take 'im off and look arter im, and at last, partly for 'is sake, but more to see the fun, Tom Baker managed to think o' something to put things straight.

"'You stay aboard to-night, Bill,' he ses one morning, 'and you'll see something that'll startle you.'

"'Worse than you?' ses Bill, whose temper was getting worse and worse.

"'There'll be an end o' that bullying Joe,' ses Tom, taking 'im by the arm. 'We've arranged to give 'im a lesson as'll lay 'im up for a time.'

"'Oh,' ses Bill, looking 'ard at a boat wot was passing.

"'We've got Dodgy Pete coming to see us to-night,' ses Tom, in a whisper; 'there'll only be the second officer aboard, and he'll likely be asleep. Dodgy's one o' the best light-weights in Australia, and if 'e don't fix up Mister Joe, it'll be a pity.'

"'You're a fair treat, Tom,' ses Bill, turning round; 'that's what you are. A fair treat.'

"'I thought you'd be pleased, Bill,' ses Tom.

"'Pleased ain't no name for it, Tom,' answers Bill. 'You've took a load off my mind.'

"The fo'c's'le was pretty full that evening, everybody giving each other a little grin on the quiet, and looking over to where Joe was sitting in 'is bunk putting a button or two on his coat. At about ha'-past six Dodgy comes aboard, and the fun begins to commence.

"He was a nasty, low-looking little chap, was Dodgy, very fly-looking and very conceited. I didn't like the look of 'im at all, and unbearable as Joe was, it didn't seem to be quite the sort o' thing to get a chap aboard to 'ammer a shipmate you couldn't 'ammer yourself.

"'Nasty stuffy place you've got down 'ere,' ses Dodgy, who was smoking a big cigar; 'I can't think 'ow you can stick it.'

"'It ain't bad for a fo'c's'le,' ses Charlie.

"'An' what's that in that bunk over there?' ses Dodgy, pointing with 'is cigar at Joe.

"'Hush, be careful,' ses Tom, with a wink; 'that's a prize-fighter.'

"'Oh,' ses Dodgy, grinning, 'I thought it was a monkey.'

"You might 'ave heard a pin drop, and there was a pleasant feeling went all over us at the thought of the little fight we was going to see all to ourselves, as Joe lays down the jacket he was stitching at and just puts 'is little 'ead over the side o' the bunk.

"'Bill,' he ses, yawning.

"'Well,' ses Bill, all on the grin like the rest of us.

"'Who is that 'andsome, gentlemanly-looking young feller over there smoking a half-crown cigar?' ses Joe.

"'That's a young gent wot's come down to 'ave a look round,' ses Tom, as Dodgy takes 'is cigar out of 'is mouth and looks round, puzzled.

"'Wot a terror 'e must be to the gals, with them lovely little peepers of 'is,' ses Joe, shaking 'is 'ead. '*Bill!*'

"'Well,' ses Bill, agin, as Dodgy got up.

"'Take that lovely little gentleman and kick 'im up the fo'c's'le ladder,' ses Joe, taking up 'is jacket agin; 'and don't make too much noise over it, cos I've got a bit of a 'eadache, else I'd do it myself.'

"There was a laugh went all round then, and Tom Baker was near killing himself, and then I'm blessed if Bill didn't get up and begin taking off 'is coat.

"'Wot's the game?' ses Dodgy, staring.

"'I'm obeying orders,' ses Bill. 'Last time I was in London, Joe 'ere half killed me one time, and 'e made me promise to do as 'e told me for six months. I'm very sorry, mate, but I've got to kick you up that ladder.'

"'You kick me up?' ses Dodgy, with a nasty little laugh.

"'I can try, mate, can't I?' ses Bill, folding 'is things up very neat and putting 'em on a locker.

"''Old my cigar,' ses Dodgy, taking it out of 'is mouth and sticking it in Charlie's. 'I don't need to take my coat off to 'im.'

"'E altered 'is mind, though, when he saw Bill's chest and arms, and not only took off his coat, but his waistcoat too. Then, with a nasty look at Bill, 'e put up 'is fists and just pranced up to 'im.

"The fust blow Bill missed, and the next moment 'e got a tap on the jaw that nearly broke it, and that was followed up by one in the eye that sent 'im staggering up agin the side, and when 'e was there Dodgy's fists were rattling all round 'im.

"I believe it was that that brought Bill round, and the next moment Dodgy was on 'is back with a blow that nearly knocked his 'ead off. Charlie grabbed at Tom's watch and began to count, and after a little bit called out 'Time.' It was a silly thing to do, as it would 'ave stopped the fight then and there if it 'adn't been for Tom's presence of mind, saying it was two minutes slow. That gave Dodgy a chance, and he got up again and walked round Bill very careful, swearing 'ard at the small size of the fo'c's'le.

"He got in three or four at Bill afore you could wink a'most, and when Bill 'it back 'e wasn't there. That seemed to annoy Bill more than anything, and he suddenly flung out 'is arms, and grabbing 'old of 'im flung 'im right across the fo'c's'le to where, fortunately for 'im—Dodgy, I mean—Tom Baker was sitting.

"Charlie called 'Time' again, and we let 'em 'ave five minutes while we 'elped Tom to bed, and then wot 'e called the 'disgusting exhibishun' was resoomed. Bill 'ad dipped 'is face in a bucket and 'ad rubbed 'is great arms all over and was as fresh as a daisy. Dodgy looked a bit tottery, but 'e was game all through and very careful, and, try as Bill might, he didn't seem to be able to get 'old of 'im agin.

"In five minutes more, though, it was all over, Dodgy not being able to see plain—except to get out o' Bill's way—and hitting wild. He seemed to think the whole fo'c's'le was full o' Bills sitting on a locker and waiting to be punched, and the end of it was a knock-out blow from the real Bill which left 'im on the floor without a soul offering to pick 'im up.

"Bill 'elped 'im up at last and shook hands with 'im, and they rinsed their faces in the same bucket, and began to praise each other up. They sat there purring like a couple o' cats, until at last we 'eard a smothered voice coming from Joe Simms's bunk.

"'Is it all over?' he asks.

"'Yes,' ses somebody.

"'How is Bill?' ses Joe's voice again.

"'Look for yourself,' ses Tom.

"Joe sat up in 'is bunk then and looked out, and he no sooner saw Bill's face than he gave a loud cry and fell back agin, and, as true as I'm sitting here, fainted clean away. We was struck all of a 'eap, and then Bill picked up the bucket and threw some water over 'im, and by and by he comes round agin and in a dazed sort o' way puts his arm round Bill's neck and begins to cry.

"*'Mighty Moses!'* ses Dodgy Pete, jumping up, 'it's a woman!'
"'It's my *wife!*' ses Bill.

"We understood it all then, leastways the married ones among us did. She'd shipped aboard partly to be with Bill and partly to keep an eye on 'im, and Tom Baker's mistake about a prize-fighter had just suited 'er book better than anything. How Bill was to get 'er home 'e couldn't think, but it 'appened the second officer had been peeping down the fo'c's'le, waiting for ever so long for a suitable opportunity to stop the fight, and the old man was so tickled about the way we'd all been done 'e gave 'er a passage back as stewardess to look arter the ship's cat."

THE RESURRECTION OF MR. WIGGETT

MR. SOL KETCHMAID, landlord of the "Ship," sat in his snug bar, rising occasionally from his seat by the taps to minister to the wants of the customers who shared this pleasant retreat with him.

Forty years at sea before the mast had made Mr. Ketchmaid an authority on affairs maritime; five years in command of the Ship Inn, with the nearest other licensed house five miles off, had made him an autocrat.

From his cushioned Windsor-chair he listened pompously to the conversation. Sometimes he joined in and took sides, and on these occasions it was a foregone conclusion that the side he espoused would win. No matter how reasonable the opponent's argument or how gross his personalities, Mr. Ketchmaid, in his capacity of host, had one unfailing rejoinder—the man was drunk. When Mr. Ketchmaid had pronounced that opinion the argument was at an end. A nervousness about his licence—conspicuous at other times by its absence—would suddenly possess him, and, opening the little wicket which gave admission to the bar, he would order the offender in scathing terms to withdraw.

Twice recently had he found occasion to warn Mr. Ned Clark, the village shoemaker, the strength of whose head had been a boast in the village for many years. On the third occasion the indignant shoemaker was interrupted in the middle of an impassioned harangue on free speech and bundled into the road by the ostler. After this nobody was safe.

To-night Mr. Ketchmaid, meeting his eye as he entered the bar, nodded curtly. The shoemaker had stayed away three days as a protest, and the landlord was naturally indignant at such contumacy.

"Good evening, Mr. Ketchmaid," said the shoemaker, screwing up his little black eyes; "just give me a small bottle o' lemonade, if you please."

Mr. Clark's cronies laughed, and Mr. Ketchmaid, after glancing at him to make sure that he was in earnest, served him in silence.

"There's one thing about lemonade," said the shoemaker, as he sipped it gingerly; "nobody could say you was drunk, not if you drank bucketsful of it."

There was an awkward silence, broken at last by Mr. Clark smacking his lips.

"Any news since I've been away, chaps?" he inquired; "or 'ave you just been sitting round as usual listening to the extra-ordinary adventures what happened to Mr. Ketchmaid whilst a-follering of the sea?"

"Truth is stranger than fiction, Ned," said Mr. Peter Smith, the tailor, reprovingly.

The shoemaker assented. "But I never thought so till I heard some o' the things Mr. Ketchmaid 'as been through," he remarked.

"Well, you know now," said the landlord, shortly.

"And the truthfullest of your yarns are the most wonderful of the lot, to my mind," said Mr. Clark.

"What do you mean by the truthfullest?" demanded the landlord, gripping the arms of his chair.

"Why, the strangest," grinned the shoemaker.

"Ah, he's been through a lot, Mr. Ketchmaid has," said the tailor.

"The truthfullest one to my mind," said the shoemaker, regarding the landlord with spiteful interest, "is that one where Henry Wiggett, the boatswain's mate, 'ad his leg bit off saving Mr. Ketchmaid from the shark, and 'is shipmate Sam Jones, the nigger cook, was wounded saving 'im from the South Sea Highlanders."

"I never get tired o' hearing that yarn," said the affable Mr. Smith.

"I do," said Mr. Clark.

Mr. Ketchmaid looked up from his pipe and eyed him darkly; the shoemaker smiled serenely.

"Another small bottle o' lemonade, landlord," he said, slowly.

"Go and get your lemonade somewhere else," said the bursting Mr. Ketchmaid.

"I prefer to 'ave it here," rejoined the shoemaker, "and you've got to serve me, Ketchmaid. A licensed publican is compelled to serve people whether he likes to or not, else he loses of 'is licence."

"Not when they're the worse for licker he ain't," said the landlord.

"Certainly not," said the shoemaker; "that's why I'm sticking to lemonade, Ketchmaid."

The indignant Mr. Ketchmaid removing the wire from the cork discharged the missile at the ceiling. The shoemaker took the glass from him and looked round with offensive slyness.

"Here's the 'ealth of Henry Wiggett what lost 'is leg to save Mr. Ketchmaid's life," he said, unctuously. "Also the 'ealth of Sam Jones, who let hisself be speared through the chest for the same noble purpose. Likewise the 'ealth of Captain Peters, who nursed Mr. Ketchmaid like 'is own son when he got knocked up doing the work of five men as was drownded; likewise the 'ealth o' Dick Lee, who helped Mr. Ketchmaid capture a Chinese junk full of pirates and killed the whole seventeen of 'em by—— 'Ow did you say you killed 'em, Ketchmaid?"

The landlord, who was busy with the taps, affected not to hear.

"Killed the whole seventeen of 'em by first telling 'em yarns till they fell asleep and then choking 'em with Henry Wiggett's wooden leg," resumed the shoemaker.

"Kee—hee," said a hapless listener, explosively. "Kee—hee—kee—"

He checked himself suddenly, and assumed an air of great solemnity as the landlord looked his way.

"You'd better go 'ome, Jem Summers," said the fuming Mr. Ketchmaid. "You're the worse for licker."

"I'm not," said Mr. Summers, stoutly.

"Out you go," said Mr. Ketchmaid, briefly. "You know my rules. I keep a respectable house, and them as can't drink in moderation are best outside."

"You should stick to lemonade, Jem," said Mr. Clark. "You can say what you like then."

Mr Summers looked round for support, and then, seeing no pity in the landlord's eye, departed, wondering inwardly how he was to spend the remainder of the evening. The company in the bar gazed at each other soberly and exchanged whispers.

"Understand, Ned Clark," said the indignant Mr. Ketchmaid, "I don't want your money in this public-house. Take it some-where else."

"Thank'ee, but I prefer to come here," said the shoemaker, ostentatiously sipping his lemonade. "I like to listen to your tales of the sea. In a quiet way I get a lot of amusement out of 'em."

"Do you disbelieve my word?" demanded Mr. Ketchmaid, hotly.

"Why o' course I do," replied the shoemaker; "we all do. You'd see how silly they are yourself if you only stopped to think. You and your sharks!—no shark would want to eat you unless it was blind."

Mr. Ketchmaid allowed this gross reflection on his personal appearance to pass unnoticed, and for the first time of many evenings sat listening in torment as the shoemaker began the narration of a series of events which he claimed had happened to a seafaring nephew. Many of these bore a striking resemblance to Mr. Ketchmaid's own experiences, the only difference being that the nephew had no eye at all for the probabilities.

In this fell work Mr. Clark was ably assisted by the offended Mr. Summers. Side by side they sat and quaffed lemonade, and burlesqued the landlord's autobiography, the only consolation afforded to Mr. Ketchmaid consisting in the reflection that they were losing a harmless pleasure in good liquor. Once, and once only, they succumbed to the superior attractions of alcohol, and Mr. Ketchmaid, returning from a visit to his brewer at the large seaport of Burnsea, heard from the ostler the details of a carouse with which he had been utterly unable to cope.

The couple returned to lemonade the following night, and remained faithful to that beverage until an event transpired which rendered further self-denial a mere foolishness.

It was about a week later; Mr. Ketchmaid had just resumed his seat after serving a customer, when the attention of all present was attracted by an odd and regular tapping on the brick-paved passage outside. It stopped at the tap-room, and a murmur of voices escaped at the open door. Then the door was closed, and a loud penetrating voice called on the name of Sol Ketchmaid.

"Good heavens!" said the amazed landlord, half rising from his seat and falling back again, "I ought to know that voice."

"Sol Ketchmaid," bellowed the voice again; "where are you, shipmate?"

"Hennery Wig-gett!" gasped the landlord, as a small man with ragged whiskers appeared at the wicket, "it can't be!"

The new-comer regarded him tenderly for a moment without a word, and then, kicking open the door with an unmistakable wooden leg, stumped into the bar, and grasping his outstretched hand shook it fervently.

"I met Cap'n Peters in Melbourne," said the stranger, as his friend pushed him into his own chair, and questioned him breathlessly. "He told me where you was."

"The sight o' you, Hennery Wiggett, is better to me than

68

diamonds," said Mr. Ketchmaid, ecstatically. "How did you get here?"

"A friend of his, Cap'n Jones, of the barque *Venus*, gave me a passage to London," said Mr. Wiggett, "and I've tramped down from there without a penny in my pocket."

"And Sol Ketchmaid's glad to see you, sir," said Mr. Smith, who, with the rest of the company, had been looking on in a state of great admiration. "He's never tired of telling us 'ow you saved him from the shark and 'ad your leg bit off in so doing."

"I'd 'ave my other bit off for 'im, too," said Mr. Wiggett, as the landlord patted him affectionately on the shoulder and thrust a glass of spirits into his hands. "Cheerful, I would. The kindest-'earted and the bravest man that ever breathed, is old Sol Ketchmaid."

He took the landlord's hand again, and, squeezing it affectionately, looked round the comfortable bar with much approval. They began to converse in the low tones of confidence, and names which had figured in many of the landlord's stories fell continuously on the listeners' ears.

"You never 'eard anything more o' pore Sam Jones, I s'pose?" said Mr. Ketchmaid.

Mr Wiggett put down his glass.

"I ran up agin a man in Rio Janeiro two years ago," he said, mournfully. "Pore old Sam died in 'is arms with your name upon 'is honest black lips."

"Enough to kill any man," muttered the discomfited Mr. Clark, looking round defiantly upon his murmuring friends.

"Who is this putty-faced swab, Sol?" demanded Mr. Wiggett, turning a fierce glance in the shoemaker's direction.

"He's our cobbler," said the landlord, "but you don't want to take no notice of 'im. Nobody else does. He's a man who as good as told me I'm a liar."

"Wot!" said Mr. Wiggett, rising and stumping across the bar; "take it back, mate. I've only got one leg, but nobody shall run down Sol while I can draw breath. The finest sailor-man that ever trod a deck is Sol, and the best-'earted."

"Hear, hear," said Mr. Smith; "own up as you're in the wrong, Ned."

"When I was lying in my bunk in the fo'c's'le being nursed back to life," continued Mr. Wiggett, enthusiastically, "who was it that set by my side 'olding my 'and and telling me to live for his sake? —why, Sol Ketchmaid. Who was it that said that he'd stick to me for life?—why, Sol Ketchmaid. Who was it said that so long as 'e 'ad a crust I should have first bite at it, and so long as 'e 'ad a bed I should 'ave first half of it?—why, Sol Ketchmaid!"

He paused to take breath, and a flattering murmur arose from his listeners, while the subject of his discourse looked at him as though his eloquence was in something of the nature of a surprise even to him.

"In my old age and on my beam-ends," continued Mr. Wiggett, "I remembered them words of old Sol, and I knew if I could only find 'im my troubles were over. I knew that I could creep into 'is little harbour and lay snug. I knew that what Sol said he meant. I lost my leg saving 'is life, and he is grateful."

"So he ought to be," said Mr. Clark, "and I'm proud to shake 'ands with a hero."

He gripped Mr. Wiggett's hand, and the others followed suit. The wooden-legged man wound up with Mr. Ketchmaid, and, disdaining to notice that that veracious mariner's grasp was somewhat limp, sank into his chair again, and asked for a cigar.

"Lend me the box, Sol," he said, jovially, as he took it from him. "I'm going to 'and 'em round. This is my treat, mates. Pore old Henry Wiggett's treat."

He passed the box round, Mr. Ketchmaid watching in helpless indignation as the customers, discarding their pipes, thanked Mr. Wiggett warmly, and helped themselves to a threepenny cigar apiece. Mr. Clark was so particular that he spoilt at least two by undue pinching before he could find one to his satisfaction.

Closing time came all too soon, Mr. Wiggett, whose popularity was never for a moment in doubt, developing gifts to which his friend had never even alluded. He sang comic songs in a voice which made the glasses rattle on the shelves, asked some really clever riddles, and wound up with a conjuring trick which consisted in borrowing half a crown from Mr. Ketchmaid and making it pass into the pocket of Mr. Peter Smith. This last was perhaps not quite so satisfactory, as the utmost efforts of the tailor failed to discover the coin, and he went home under a cloud of suspicion which nearly drove him frantic.

"I 'ope you're satisfied," said Mr. Wiggett, as the landlord, having shot the bolts of the front door, returned to the bar.

"You went a bit too far," said Mr. Ketchmaid, shortly; "you should ha' been content with doing what I told you to do. And who asked you to 'and my cigars round?"

"I got a bit excited," pleaded the other.

"And you forgot to tell 'em you're going to start to-morrow to live with that niece of yours in New Zealand," added the landlord.

"So I did," said Mr. Wiggett, smiting his forehead; "so I did. I'm very sorry; I'll tell 'em to-morrow night."

"Mention it casual like, to-morrow morning," commanded Mr. Ketchmaid, "and get off in the arternoon, then I'll give you some dinner besides the five shillings as arranged."

Mr. Wiggett thanked him warmly, and, taking a candle, withdrew to the unwonted luxury of clean sheets and a soft bed. For some time he lay awake in deep thought and then, smothering a laugh with the bed-clothes, he gave a sigh of content and fell asleep.

To the landlord's great annoyance his guest went for a walk next morning and did not return until the evening, when he explained that he had walked too far for his crippled condition and was unable to get back. Much sympathy was manifested for him in the bar, but in all the conversation that ensued Mr. Ketchmaid llistened in vain for any hint of his departure. Signals were of no use, Mr. Wiggett merely nodding amiably and raising his glass in response; and when, by considerable strategy, he brought the conversation from pig-killing to nieces, Mr. Wiggett deftly transferred it to uncles and discoursed on pawnbroking.

The helpless Mr. Ketchmaid suffered in silence, with his eye on the clock, and almost danced with impatience at the tardiness of his departing guests. He accompanied the last man to the door, and then, crimson with rage, returned to the bar to talk to Mr. Wiggett.

"Wot d' y'r mean by it?" he thundered.

"Mean by what, Sol?" inquired Mr. Wiggett, looking up in surprise.

"Don't you call me Sol, 'cos I won't have it," vociferated the landlord, standing over him with his fist clenched. "First thing to-morrow morning off you go."

"Off?" repeated the other in amazement. "Off? Where to?"

"Anywhere," said the overwrought landlord; "so long as you get out of here, I don't care where you go."

Mr. Wiggett, who was smoking a cigar, the third that evening, laid it carefully on the table by his side, and regarded him with tender reproach.

"You ain't yourself, Sol," he said, with conviction; "don't say another word else you might say things you'll be sorry for."

His forebodings were more than justified, Mr. Ketchmaid indulging in a few remarks about his birth, parentage, and character which would have shocked an East-end policeman.

"First thing to-morrow morning you go," he concluded,

fiercely. "I've a good mind to turn you out now. You know the arrangement I made with you."

"Arrangement!" said the mystified Mr. Wiggett; "what arrangement? Why, I ain't seen you for ten years and more. If it 'adn't been for meeting Cap'n Peters——"

He was interrupted by frenzied and incoherent exclamations from Mr. Ketchmaid.

"Sol Ketchmaid," he said, with dignity, "I 'ope you're drunk. I 'ope it's the drink and not Sol Ketchmaid, wot I saved from the shark by aving my leg bit off, taking. I saved your life, Sol, an' I 'ave come into your little harbour and let go my little anchor to stay there till I go aloft to join poor Sam Jones wot died with your name on 'is lips."

He sprang suddenly erect as Mr. Ketchmaid, with a loud cry, snatched up a bottle and made as though to brain him with it.

"You rascal," said the landlord, in a stifled voice. "You infernal rascal. I never set eyes on you till I saw you the other day on the quay at Burnsea, and, just for an innercent little joke like with Ned Clark, asked you to come in and pretend."

"Pretend!" repeated Mr. Wiggett, in a horror-stricken voice. "Pretend! Have you forgotten me pushing you out of the way and saying, 'Save yourself, Sol,' as the shark's jaw clashed together over my leg? Have you forgotten 'ow——?"

"Look 'ere," said Mr. Ketchmaid, thrusting an infuriated face close to his, "there never was a Henery Wiggett; there never was a shark; there never was a Sam Jones!"

"Never—was—a—Sam Jones!" said the dazed Mr. Wiggett, sinking into his chair. "Ain't you got a spark o' proper feeling left, Sol?"

He fumbled in his pocket, and producing the remains of a dirty handkerchief wiped his eyes to the memory of the faithful black.

"Look here," said Mr. Ketchmaid, putting down the bottle and regarding him intently, "you've got me fair. Now, will you go for a pound?"

"Got you?" said Mr. Wiggett, severely; "I'm ashamed of you, Sol. Go to bed and sleep off the drink, and in the morning you can take Henry Wiggett's 'and, but not before."

He took a box of matches from the bar and, relighting the stump of his cigar, contemplated Mr. Ketchmaid for some time in silence, and then, with a serious shake of his head, stumped off to bed. Mr. Ketchmaid remained below, and for at least an hour sat thinking of ways and means out of the dilemma into which his ingenuity had led him.

He went to bed with the puzzle still unsolved, and the morning yielded no solution. Mr. Wiggett appeared to have forgotten the previous night's proceedings altogether, and steadfastly declined to take umbrage at a manner which would have chilled a rhinoceros. He told several fresh anecdotes of himself and Sam Jones that evening; anecdotes which, at the imminent risk of choking, Mr. Ketchmaid was obliged to indorse.

A week passed, and Mr. Wiggett still graced with his presence the bar of the "Ship." The landlord lost flesh, and began seriously to consider the advisability of making a clean breast of the whole affair. Mr. Wiggett watched him anxiously, and with a skill born of a life-long study of humanity, realised that his visit was drawing to an end. At last, one day, Mr. Ketchmaid put the matter bluntly.

"I shall tell the chaps to-night that it was a little joke on my part," he announced, with grim decision; "then I shall take you by the collar and kick you into the road."

Mr Wiggett sighed and shook his head.

"It'll be a terrible show-up for you," he said, softly. "You'd better make it worth my while, and I'll tell 'em this evening that I'm going to New Zealand to live with a niece of mine there, and that you've paid my passage for me. I don't like telling any more lies, but, seeing it's for you, I'll do it for a couple of pounds."

"Five shillings," snarled Mr. Ketchmaid.

Mr. Wiggett smiled comfortably and shook his head. Mr. Ketchmaid raised his offer to ten shillings, to a pound, and finally, after a few remarks which prompted Mr. Wiggett to state that hard words broke no bones, flung into the bar and fetched the money.

The news of Mr. Wiggett's departure went round the village at once, the landlord himself breaking the news to the next customer, and an overflow meeting assembled that evening to bid the emigrant farewell.

The landlord noted with pleasure that business was brisk. Several gentlemen stood drink to Mr. Wiggett, and in return he put his hand in his own pocket and ordered glasses round. Mr. Ketchmaid, in a state of some uneasiness, took the order, and then Mr. Wiggett, with the air of one conferring inestimable benefits, produced a lucky halfpenny, which had once belonged to Sam Jones, and insisted upon his keeping it.

"This is my last night, mates," he said, mournfully, as he acknowledged the drinking of his health. "In many ports I've been, and many snug pubs I 'ave visited, but I never in all my days come across a nicer, kinder-'earted lot o' men than wot you are."

"Hear, hear," said Mr. Clark.

Mr. Wiggett paused, and, taking a sip from his glass to hide his emotion, resumed.

"In my lonely pilgrimage through life, crippled, and 'aving to beg my bread," he said, tearfully, "I shall think o' this 'appy bar and these friendly faces. When I am wrestlin' with the pangs of 'unger and being moved on by the 'eartless police, I shall think of you as I last saw you."

"But," said Mr. Smith, voicing the general consternation, "you're going to your niece in New Zealand?"

Mr. Wiggett shook his head and smiled a sad, sweet smile.

"I 'ave no niece," he said, simply; "I'm alone in the world."

At these touching words his audience put their glasses down and stared in amaze at Mr. Ketchmaid, while that gentleman in his turn gazed at Mr. Wiggett as though he had suddenly developed horns and a tail.

"Ketchmaid told me hisself as he'd paid your passage to New Zealand," said the shoemaker; "he said as 'e'd pressed you to stay, but that you said as blood was thicker even than friendship."

"All lies," said Mr. Wiggett, sadly. "I'll stay with pleasure if he'll give the word. I'll stay even now if 'e wishes it."

He paused a moment as though to give his bewildered victim time to acept this offer, and then addressed the scandalised Mr. Clark again.

"He don't like my being 'ere," he said, in a low voice. "He grudges the little bit I eat, I s'pose. He told me I'd got to go, and that for the look o' things 'e was going to pretend I was going to New Zealand. I was too broken-'earted at the time to care wot he said—I 'ave no wish to sponge on no man—but, seeing your 'onest faces round me, I couldn't go with a lie on my lips—Sol Ketchmaid, old shipmate—good-bye."

He turned to the speechless landlord, made as though to shake hands with him, thought better of it, and then, with a wave of his hand full of chastened dignity, withdrew. His stump rang with pathetic insistence upon the brick-paved passage, paused at the door, and then, tapping on the hard road, died slowly away in the distance. Inside the "Ship" the shoemaker gave an ominous order for lemonade.

A MARKED MAN

"Tattooing is a gift," said the night-watchman, firmly. "It 'as to be a gift, as you can well see. A man 'as to know wot 'e is going to tattoo an' 'ow to do it; there's no rubbing out or altering. It's a gift, an' it can't be learnt. I knew a man once as used to tattoo a cabin-boy all over every v'y'ge trying to learn. 'E was a slow, painstaking sort o' man, and the langwidge those boys used to use while 'e was at work would 'ardly be believed, but 'e 'ad to give up trying arter about fifteen years and take to crochet-work instead.

"Some men won't be tatooed at all, being proud o' their skins or sich-like, and for a good many years Ginger Dick, a man I've spoke to you of before, was one o' that sort. Like many red-'aired men 'e 'ad a very white skin, which 'e was very proud of, but at last, owing to a unfortnit idea o' making 'is fortin, 'e let hisself be done.

"It come about in this way: Him and old Sam Small and Peter Russet 'ad been paid off from their ship and was 'aving a very 'appy, pleasant time ashore. They was careful men in a way, and they 'ad taken a room down East India Road way, and paid up the rent for a month. It came cheaper than a lodging-'ouse, besides being a bit more private and respectable, a thing old Sam was always very pertickler about.

"They 'ad been ashore about three weeks when one day old Sam and Peter went off alone becos Ginger said 'e wasn't going with 'em. He said a lot more things, too: 'ow 'e was going to see wot it felt like to be in bed without 'aving a fat old man groaning 'is 'eart out, and another one knocking on the mantelpiece all night with twopence and wanting to know why he wasn't being served.

"Ginger Dick fell into a quiet sleep arter they'd gone; then 'e woke up and 'ad a sip from the water-jug—he'd 'a had more, only somebody 'ad dropped the soap in it—and then dozed off agin. It was late in the afternoon when 'e woke, and then 'e see Sam and Peter Russet standing by the side o' the bed looking at 'im.

"'Where've you been?' ses Ginger, stretching hisself and yawning.

"'Bisness,' ses Sam, sitting down an' looking very important. 'While you've been laying on your back all day me an' Peter Russet 'as been doing a little 'ead-work.'

"'Oh!' ses Ginger. 'Wot with?'

Sam coughed and Peter began to whistle, an' Ginger he laid still and smiled up at the ceiling, and began to feel good-tempered agin.

"'Well, wot's the bisness?' he ses, at last.

Sam looked at Peter, but Peter shook 'is 'ead at him.

"'It's just a little bit o' bisness we 'appened to drop on,' ses Sam, at last, 'me an' Peter, and I think that, with luck and management, we're in a fair way to make our fortunes. Peter, 'ere, ain't given to looking on the cheerful side o' things, but 'e thinks so, too.'

"'I do,' ses Peter, 'but it won't be managed right if you go blabbing it to everybody.'

"'We must 'ave another man in it, Peter,' ses Sam; 'and, wot's more, 'e must 'ave ginger-coloured 'air. That being so, it's only right and proper that our dear old pal Ginger should 'ave the fust offer.'

"It wasn't often that Sam was so affeckshunate, and Ginger couldn't make it out at all. Ever since 'e'd known 'im the old man 'ad been full o' plans o' making money without earning it. Stupid plans they was, too, but the stupider they was the more old Sam liked 'em.

"'Well, wot is it?' asks Ginger, agin.

"Old Sam walked over to the door and shut it; then 'e sat down on the bed and spoke low so that Ginger could hardly 'ear 'im.

"'A little public-'ouse,' he ses, 'to say nothing of 'ouse property, and a red-'aired old landlady wot's a widder. As nice a old lady as any one could wish for, for a mother.'

"'For a mother!' ses Ginger, staring.

"'And a lovely barmaid with blue eyes and yellow 'air, wot ud be the red-'edded man's cousin,' ses Peter Russet.

"'Look 'ere,' ses Ginger, 'are you going to tell me in plain English wot it's all about, or are you not?'

"'We've been in a little pub down Bow way, me an' Peter,' ses Sam, 'and we'll tell you more about it if you promise to join us an' go shares. It's kep' by a widder woman whose on'y son—*red-'aired son*—went to sea twenty-three years ago, at the age o' fourteen, an' was never 'eard of arterwards. Seeing we was sailor-men, she told us all about it, an' 'ow she still 'opes for him to walk into 'er arms afore she dies.'

"'She dreamt a fortnit ago that 'e turned up safe and sound, with red whiskers,' ses Peter.

"Ginger Dick sat up and looked at 'em without a word; then 'e got up out o' bed, an' pushing old Sam out of the way began to dress, and at last 'e turned round and asked Sam whether he was drunk or only mad.

"'All right,' ses Sam; 'if you won't take it on we'll find somebody as will, that's all; there's no call to get huffy about it. You ain't the on'y red-'edded man in the world.'

"Ginger didn't answer 'im; he went on dressing, but every now and then 'e'd look at Sam and give a little larf wot made Sam's blood boil.

"'You've got nothin' to larf at, Ginger,' he ses, at last; 'the landlady's boy 'ud be about the same age as wot you are now; 'e 'ad a scar over the left eyebrow same as wot you've got, though I don't suppose *he* got it by fighting a chap three times 'is size. 'E 'ad bright blue eyes, a small, well-shaped nose, and a nice mouth.'

"'Same as you, Ginger,' ses Peter, looking out of the winder.

"Ginger coughed and looked thoughtful.

"'It sounds all right, mates,' 'e ses, at last, 'but I don't see 'ow we're to go to work. I don't want to get locked up for deceiving.'

"'You can't get locked up,' ses Sam; 'if you let 'er discover you and claim you, 'ow can you get locked up for it? We shall go in an' see her agin, and larn all there is to larn, especially about the tattoo marks, and then——'

"'*Tattoo marks!*' ses Ginger.

"'That's the strong p'int,' ses Sam. ''Er boy 'ad a sailor dancing a 'ornpipe on 'is left wrist, an' a couple o' dolphins on his right. On 'is chest 'e 'ad a full-rigged ship, and on 'is back between 'is shoulder-blades was the letters of 'is name—C.R.S.: Charles Robert Smith.'

"'Well, you silly old fool,' ses Ginger, starting up in a temper, 'that spiles it all. I ain't got a mark on me.'

"Old Sam smiles at 'im and pats him on the shoulder. 'That's where you show your want of intelleck, Ginger,' he ses, kindly. 'Why don't you think afore you speak? Wot's easier than to 'ave 'em put on?'

"'*Wot?*' screams Ginger. 'Tattoo *me*! Spile my skin with a lot o' beastly blue marks! Not me, not if I know it. I'd like to see anybody try it, that's all.'

"He was that mad 'e wouldn't listen to reason, and, as old Sam said, 'e couldn't have made more fuss if they'd offered to skin 'im alive, an' Peter Russet tried to prove that a man's skin was made to be tattooed on, or else there wouldn't be tattooers; same as a man 'ad been given two legs so as 'e could wear trousers. But reason was chucked away on Ginger, an' 'e wouldn't listen to 'em.

"They started on 'im agin next day, but all Sam and Peter could say didn't move 'im, although Sam spoke so feeling about the joy of a pore widder woman getting 'er son back agin arter all these years that 'e nearly cried.

"They went down agin to the pub that evening, and Ginger, who said 'e was curious to see, wanted to go too. Sam, who still 'ad 'opes of 'im, wouldn't 'ear of it, but at last it was arranged that 'e wasn't to go inside, but should take a peep through the door. They got on a tram at Aldgate, and Ginger didn't like it becos Sam and Peter talked it over between theirselves in whispers and pointed out likely red-'aired men in the road.

"And 'e didn't like it when they got to the 'Blue Lion,' and Sam and Peter went in and left 'im outside, peeping through the door. The landlady shook 'ands with them quite friendly, and the barmaid, a fine-looking girl, seemed to take a lot o' notice of Peter. Ginger waited about outside for nearly a couple of hours, and at last they came out, talking and larfing, with Peter wearing a white rose wot the barmaid 'ad given 'im.

"Ginger Dick 'ad a good bit to say about keeping 'im waiting all that time, but Sam said that they'd been getting valuable information, an' the more 'e could see of it the easier the job appeared to be, an' then him an' Peter wished for to bid Ginger good-bye, while they went and 'unted up a red-'aired friend o' Peter's named Charlie Bates.

"They all went in somewhere and 'ad a few drinks fust, though, and arter a time Ginger began to see things in a different light to wot 'e 'ad before, an' to be arf ashamed of 'is selfishness, and 'e called Sam's pot a loving-cup, an' kep' on drinking out of it to show there was no ill-feeling, although Sam kep' telling him there wasn't. Then Sam spoke up about tattooing agin, and Ginger said that every man in the country ought to be tattooed to prevent the smallpox. He got so excited about it that old Sam 'ad to promise 'im that he should be tattooed that very night, before he could pacify 'im.

"They all went off 'ome with their arms round each other's necks, but arter a time Ginger found that Sam's neck wasn't there, an' 'e stopped and spoke serious to Peter about it. Peter said 'e couldn't account for it, an' 'e had such a job to get Ginger 'ome that 'e thought they would never ha' got there. He got 'im to bed at last an' then 'e sat down and fell asleep waiting for Sam.

"Ginger was the last one to wake up in the morning, an' before 'e woke he kept making a moaning noise. His 'ead felt as though it was going to bust, 'is tongue felt like a brick, and 'is chest was so sore 'e could 'ardly breathe. Then at last 'e opened 'is eyes and looked up and saw Sam an' Peter and a little man with a black moustache.

"'Cheer up, Ginger,' ses Sam, in a kind voice, 'it's going on beautiful.'

"'My 'ead's splittin',' ses Ginger, with a groan, 'an' I've got pins an' needles all over my chest.'

"'Needles,' ses the man with the black moustache. 'I never use pins; they'd pison the flesh.'

"Ginger sat up in bed and stared at 'im; then 'e bent 'is 'ead down and squinted at 'is chest, and next moment 'e was out of bed and all three of 'em was holding 'im down on the floor to prevent 'im breaking the tattooer's neck which 'e'd set 'is 'eart upon doing, and explaining to 'im that the tattooer was at the top of 'is profession, and that it was only by a stroke of luck 'e had got 'im. And Sam reminded 'im of wot 'e 'ad said the night before, and said he'd live to thank 'im for it.

"''Ow much is there done?' ses Ginger, at last, in a desprit voice.

"Sam told 'im, and Ginger lay still and called the tattooer all the names he could think of; which took 'im some time.

"'It's no good going on like that, Ginger,' ses Sam. 'Your chest is quite spiled at present, but if you on'y let 'im finish it'll be a perfeck picter.'

"'I take pride in it,' ses the tattooer; 'working on your skin, mate, is like painting on a bit o' silk.'

"Ginger gave in at last, and told the man to go on with the job and finish it, and 'e even went so far as to do a little bit o' tattooing 'imself on Sam when he wasn't looking. 'E only made one mark, becos the needle broke off, and Sam made such a fuss that Ginger said any one would ha' thought 'e'd hurt 'im.

"It took three days to do Ginger altogether, and he was that sore 'e could 'ardly move or breathe, and all the time 'e was laying on 'is bed of pain Sam and Peter Russet was round at the 'Blue Lion' enjoying theirselves and picking up information. The second day was the worst, owing to the tattooer being the worse for licker. Drink affects different people in different ways, and Ginger said

79

the way it affected that chap was to make 'im think 'e was sewing buttons on instead o' tattooing.

"'Owever 'e was done at last; his chest and 'is arms and 'is shoulders, and he nearly broke down when Sam borrowed a bit o' looking-glass and let 'im see hisself. Then the tattooer rubbed in some stuff to make 'is skin soft agin, and some more stuff to make the marks look a bit old.

"Sam wanted to draw up an agreement, but Ginger Dick and Peter Russet wouldn't 'ear of it. They both said that that sort o' thing wouldn't look well in writing, not if anybody else happened to see it, that is; besides which Ginger said it was impossible for 'im to say 'ow much money he would 'ave the handling of. Once the tattooing was done 'e began to take a'most kindly to the plan, an' being an orfin, so far as 'e knew, he almost began to persuade hisself that the red-'aired landlady *was* 'is mother.

"They 'ad a little call over in their room to see 'ow Ginger was to do it, and to discover the weak p'ints. Sam worked up a squeaky voice, and pretended to be the landlady, and Peter pretended to be the good-looking barmaid.

"They went all through it over and over agin, the only un-pleasantness being caused by Peter Russet letting off a screech every time Ginger alluded to 'is chest wot set 'is teeth on edge, and old Sam as the landlady offering Ginger pots o' beer which made 'is mouth water.

"'We shall go round to-morrow for the last time,' ses Sam, 'as we told 'er we're sailing the day arter. Of course me an' Peter, 'aving made your fortin, drop out altogether, but I dessay we shall look in agin in about six months' time, and then perhaps the landlady will interduce us to you.'

"'Meantime,' ses Peter Russet, 'you mustn't forget that you've got to send us Post Office money-orders every week.'

"Ginger said 'e wouldn't forget, and they shook 'ands all round and 'ad a drink together, and the next arternoon Sam and Peter went to the 'Blue Lion' for a last visit.

"It was quite early when they came back. Ginger was surprised to see 'em, and he said so, but 'e was more surprised when 'e heard their reasons.

"'It come over us all at once as we'd bin doing wrong,' Sam ses, setting down with a sigh.

"'Come over us like a chill, it did,' ses Peter.

"'Doing wrong?' ses Ginger Dick, staring. 'Wot are you talking about?'

"'Something the landlady said showed us as we was doin'

wrong,' ses old Sam, very solemn; 'it come over us in a flash.'

"'Like lightning,' ses Peter.

"'All of a sudden we see wot a cruel, 'ard thing it was to go and try and deceive a poor widder woman,' ses Sam, in a 'usky voice; 'we both see it at once.'

"Ginger Dick looks at 'em 'ard, 'e did, and then, 'e ses, jeering like:—

"'I s'pose you don't want any Post Office money-orders sent you, then?' he ses.

"'No,' says Sam and Peter, both together.

"'You may have 'em all,' ses Sam; 'but if you'll be ruled by us, Ginger, you'll give it up, same as wot we 'ave—you'll sleep the sweeter for it.'

"'Give it up!' shouts Ginger, dancing up an' down the room, 'arter being tattooed all over? Why, you must be crazy, Sam— wot's the matter with you?'

"'It ain't fair play agin a woman,' says old Sam, 'three strong men agin one poor old woman; that's wot we feel, Ginger.'

"'Well, *I* don't feel like it,' ses Ginger; 'you please yourself, and I'll please myself.'

"'E went off in a huff, an' next morning 'e was so disagreeable that Sam an' Peter went and signed on board a steamer called the *Penguin*, which was to sail the day arter. They parted bad friends all round, and Ginger Dick gave Peter a nasty black eye, and Sam said that when Ginger came to see things in a proper way agin he'd be sorry for wot 'e'd said. And 'e said that 'im and Peter never wanted to look on 'is face again.

"Ginger Dick was a bit lonesome arter they'd gone, but 'e thought it better to let a few days go by afore 'e went and adopted the red-'aired landlady. He waited a week, and at last, unable to wait any longer, 'e went out and 'ad a shave and smartened hisself up, and went off to the 'Blue Lion.'

"It was about three o'clock when 'e got there, and the little public-'ouse was empty except for two old men in the jug-and-bottle entrance. Ginger stopped outside a minute or two to try and stop 'is trembling, and then 'e walks into the private bar and raps on the counter.

"'Glass o' bitter, ma'am, please,' he ses to the old lady as she came out o' the little parlour at the back o' the bar.

"The old lady drew the beer, and then stood with one 'and holding the beer-pull and the other on the counter, looking at Ginger Dick in 'is new blue jersey and cloth cap.

"'Lovely weather, ma'am,' ses Ginger, putting his left arm on the counter and showing the sailor-boy dancing the hornpipe.

"'Very nice,' ses the landlady, catching sight of 'is wrist an' staring at it. 'I suppose you sailors like fine weather?'

"'Yes, ma'am,' ses Ginger, putting his elbows on the counter so that the tattoo marks on both wrists was showing. 'Fine weather an' a fair wind suits us.'

"'It's a 'ard life, the sea,' ses the old lady.

"She kept wiping down the counter in front of 'im over an' over agin, an' 'e could see 'er staring at 'is wrists as though she could 'ardly believe her eyes. Then she went back into the parlour, and Ginger 'eard her whispering, and by and by she came out agin with the blue-eyed barmaid.

"'Have you been at sea long?' ses the old lady.

"'Over twenty-three years, ma'am,' ses Ginger, avoiding the barmaid's eye wot was fixed on 'is wrists, 'and I've been ship-wrecked four times; the fust time when I was a little nipper o' fourteen.'

"'Pore thing,' ses the landlady, shaking 'er 'ead. 'I can feel for you; my boy went to sea at that age, and I've never seen 'im since.'

"'I'm sorry to 'ear it, ma'am,' ses Ginger, very respectful-like. 'I suppose I've lost my mother, so I can feel for you.'

"'Suppose you've lost your mother!' ses the barmaid; 'don't you know whether you have?'

"'No,' ses Ginger Dick, very sad. "When I was wrecked the fust time I was in a open boat for three weeks, and, wot with the exposure and 'ardly any food, I got brain-fever and lost my memory.'

"'Pore thing,' ses the landlady agin.

"'I might as well be a orfin,' ses Ginger, looking down; 'sometimes I seem to see a kind, 'andsome face bending over me, and fancy it's my mother's, but I can't remember 'er name, or my name, or anythink about 'er.'

"'You remind me o' my boy very much,' ses the landlady, shaking 'er 'ed; 'you've got the same coloured 'air, and, wot's extraordinary, you've got the same tattoo marks on your wrists. Sailor-boy dancing on one and a couple of dolphins on the other. And 'e 'ad a little scar on 'is eyebrow, much the same as yours.'

"'Good 'evins,' ses Ginger Dick, starting back and looking as though 'e was trying to remember something.

"'I s'pose they're common among seafaring men?' ses the landlady, going off to attend to a customer.

"Ginger Dick would ha' liked to ha' seen 'er a bit more excited, but 'e ordered another glass o' bitter from the barmaid, and tried to think 'ow he was to bring out about the ship on his chest and the letters on 'is back. The landlady served a couple o' men, and by and by she came back and began talking agin.

"'I like sailors,' she ses; 'one thing is, my boy was a sailor; and another thing is, they've got such feelin' 'earts. There was two of 'em in 'ere the other day, who'd been in 'ere once or twice, and one of 'em was that kind 'earted I thought he would ha' 'ad a fit at something I told him.'

"'Ho,' ses Ginger, pricking up his ears, 'wot for?'

"'I was just talking to 'im about my boy, same as I might be to you,' ses the old lady, 'and I was just telling 'im about the poor child losing 'is finger——'

"'Losing 'is *wot?*' ses Ginger, turning pale and staggering back.

"'Finger,' ses the landlady. ''E was only ten years old at the time, and I'd sent 'im out to——Wot's the matter? Ain't you well?'

"Ginger didn't answer 'er a word; he couldn't. 'E went on going backwards until 'e got to the door, and then 'e suddenly fell through it into the street, and tried to think.

"Then 'e remembered Sam and Peter, and when 'e thought of them safe and sound aboard the *Penguin* he nearly broke down altogether, as 'e thought how lonesome he was.

"All 'e wanted was 'is arms round both their necks as same as they was the night afore they 'ad 'im tattooed."

TO HAVE AND TO HOLD

THE old man sat outside the Cauliflower Inn, looking crossly up the road. He was fond of conversation, but the pedestrian who had stopped to drink a mug of ale beneath the shade of the doors was not happy in his choice of subjects. He would only talk of the pernicious effects of beer on the constitutions of the aged, and he listened with ill-concealed impatience to various points which the baffled ancient opposite urged in its favour.

Conversation languished; the traveller rapped on the table and had his mug refilled. He nodded courteously to his companion and drank.

"Seems to me," said the latter, sharply, "you like it for all your talk."

The other shook his head gently, and, leaning back, bestowed a covert wink upon the signboard. He then explained that it was the dream of his life to give up beer.

"You're another Job Brown," said the old man, irritably, "that's wot you are; another Job Brown. I've seen your kind afore."

He shifted farther along the seat, and, taking up his long clay pipe from the table, struck a match and smoked the few whiffs which remained. Then he heard the traveller order a pint of ale with gin in it and a paper of tobacco. His dull eyes glistened, but he made a feeble attempt to express surprise when these luxuries were placed before him.

"Wot I said just now about you being like Job Brown was only in joke like," he said, anxiously, as he tasted the brew. "If Job 'ad been like you he'd ha' been a better man."

The philanthropist bowed. He also manifested a little curiosity concerning one to whom he had, for however short a time, suggested a resemblance.

"He was one o' the 'ardest drinkers in these parts," began the old man, slowly, filling his pipe.

The traveller thanked him.

"Wot I meant was"—said the old man, hastily—"that all the time 'e was drinking 'e was talking agin beer same as you was just now, and he used to try all sorts o' ways and plans of becoming a teetotaller. He used to sit up 'ere of a night drinking 'is 'ardest and talking all the time of ways and means by which 'e could give it up. He used to talk about hisself as if 'e was somebody else 'e was trying to do good to.

"The chaps about 'ere got sick of 'is talk. They was poor men mostly, same as they are now, and they could only drink a little ale now and then; an' while they was doing of it they 'ad to sit and listen to Job Brown, who made lots o' money dealing, drinking pint arter pint o' gin and beer and calling it pison, an' saying they was killing theirselves.

"Sometimes 'e used to get pitiful over it, and sit shaking 'is ead at 'em for drowning theirselves in beer, as he called it, when they ought to be giving the money to their wives and families. He sat down and cried one night over Bill Chambers's wife's toes being out of 'er boots. Bill sat struck all of a 'eap, and it might 'ave passed off, only Henery Walker spoke up for 'im, and said that he scarcely ever 'ad a pint but wot somebody else paid for it. There was unpleasantness all round then, and in the row somebody knocked one o' Henery's teeth out.

"And that wasn't the only unpleasantness, and at last some of the chaps put their 'eads together and agreed among theirselves to try and help Job Brown to give up the drink. They kep' it secret from Job, but the next time 'e came in and ordered a pint, Joe Gubbins—'aving won the toss—drank it by mistake, and went straight off 'ome as 'ard as 'e could, smacking 'is lips.

"He 'ad the best of it, the other chaps 'aving to 'old Job down in 'is chair, and trying their 'ardest to explain that Joe Gubbins was only doing him a kindness. He seemed to understand at last, and arter a long time 'e said as 'e could see Joe meant to do 'im a kindness, but 'e'd better not do any more.

"He kept a very tight 'old o' the next pint, and as 'e set down at the table he looked round nasty like and asked 'em whether there was any more as would like to do 'im a kindness, and Henery Walker said there was, and he went straight off 'ome arter fust dropping a handful o' sawdust into Job's mug.

"I'm an old man, an' I've seen a good many rows in my time, but I've never seen anything like the one that 'appened then. It was no good talking to Job, not a bit, he being that unreasonable that even when 'is own words was repeated to 'im he wouldn't listen. He behaved like a madman, an' the langwidge 'e used was that fearful and that wicked that Smith the landlord said 'e wouldn't 'ave it in 'is house.

"Arter that you'd ha' thought that Job Brown would 'ave left off 'is talk about being a teetotaller, but he didn't. He said they was quite right in trying to do 'im a kindness, but he didn't like the way they did it. He said there was a right way and a wrong way of doing everything, and they'd chose the wrong.

"It was all very well for 'im to talk, but the chaps said 'e might drink hisself to death for all they cared. And instead of seeing 'im safe 'ome as they used to when 'e was worse than usual he 'ad to look arter hisself and get 'ome as best he could.

"It was through that at last 'e came to offer five pounds reward to anybody as could 'elp 'im to become a teetotaller. He went off 'ome one night as usual, and arter stopping a few seconds in the parlour to pull hisself together, crept quietly upstairs for fear of waking 'is wife. He saw by the crack under the door that she'd left a candle burning, so he pulled hisself together agin and then turned the 'andle and went in and began to try an' take off 'is coat.

"He 'appened to give a 'alf-look towards the bed as 'e did so, and then 'e started back and rubbed 'is eyes and told 'imself he'd be better in a minute. Then 'e looked agin, for 'is wife was nowhere to be seen, and in the bed all fast and sound asleep and snoring their 'ardest was little Dick Weed the tailor and Mrs. Weed and the baby.

"Job Brown rubbed 'is eyes agin, and then 'e drew hisself up to 'is full height, and putting one 'and on the chest o' drawers to steady hisself, stood there staring at 'em and getting madder and madder every second. Then 'e gave a nasty cough, and Dick and Mrs. Weed an' the baby all woke up and stared at 'im as though they could 'ardly believe their eyesight.

"'Wot do you want?' ses Dick Weed, starting up.

"'Get up,' ses Job, 'ardly able to speak. 'I'm surprised at you. Get up out o' my bed direckly.'

"'Your bed?' screams little Dick; 'you're the worse for licker, Job Brown. Can't you see you've come into the wrong house?'

"'Eh?' ses Job, staring. 'Wrong 'ouse? Well, where's mine, then?'

"'Next door but one, same as it always was,' ses Dick. 'Will you go?'

"'A' right,' ses Job, staring. 'Well, goo'-night, Dick. Goo'-night, Mrs. Weed. Goo'-night, baby.'

"'Good-night,' ses Mrs. Weed from under the bedclothes.

"'Goo'-night, baby,' ses Job, agin.

"'It can't talk yet,' ses Dick. 'Will you *go*?'

"'Can't talk—why not?' ses Job.

"Dick didn't answer 'im.

"'Well, goo'-night, Dick,' he ses agin.

"'Good-night,' ses Dick from between 'is teeth.

"'Goo'-night, Mrs. Weed,' ses Job.

"Mrs. Weed forced herself to say 'Good-night' agin.

"'Goo'-night, baby,' ses Job.

"'Look 'ere,' ses Dick, raving, 'are you going' to stay 'ere all night, Job Brown?'

"Job didn't answer 'im, but began to go downstairs, saying 'goo'-night' as 'e went, and he'd got pretty near to the bottom when he suddenly wondered wot 'e was going downstairs for instead of up, and larfing gently at 'is foolishness for making sich a mistake 'e went upstairs agin. His surprise when 'e see Dick Weed and Mrs. Weed and the baby all in 'is bed pretty near took 'is breath away.

"'Wot are you doing in my bed?' he ses.

"'It's our bed,' ses Dick, trembling all over with rage. 'I've told you afore you've come into the wrong 'ouse.'

"'Wrong 'ouse,' ses Job, staring round the room. 'I b'leeve you're right. Goo'-night, Dick; goo'-night, Mrs. Weed; goo'-night, baby.'

"Dick jumped out of bed then and tried to push 'im out of the room, but 'e was a very small man, and Job just stood there and wondered wot he was doing. Mrs. Weed and the baby both started screaming one against the other, and at last Dick pushed the window open and called out for help.

"They 'ad the neighbours in then, and the trouble they 'ad to get Job downstairs wouldn't be believed. Mrs. Pottle went for 'is wife at last, and then Job went 'ome with 'er like a lamb, asking 'er where she'd been all the evening, and saying 'e'd been looking for 'er everywhere.

"There was such a to-do about it in the village next morning that Job Brown was fairly scared. All the wimmen was out at their doors talking about it, and saying wot a shame it was and 'ow silly Mrs. Weed was to put up with it. Then old Mrs. Gumm, 'er grandmother, who was eighty-eight years old, stood outside Job's 'ouse nearly all day, shaking 'er stick at 'im and daring of 'im to come out. Wot with Mrs. Gumm and the little crowd watching 'er all day and giving 'er good advice, which she wouldn't take, Job was afraid to show 'is nose outside the door.

"He wasn't like hisself that night up at the 'Cauliflower.' 'E sat up in the corner and wouldn't take any notice of anybody, and it was easy to see as he was thoroughly ashamed of hisself.

"'Cheer up, Job,' says Bill Chambers, at last; 'you ain't the fust man as has made a fool of hisself.'

"'Mind your own business,' ses Job Brown, 'and I'll mind mine.'

"'Why don't you leave 'im alone, Bill?' ses Henery Walker; 'you can see the man is worried because the baby can't talk.'

"'Oh,' ses Bill, 'I thought 'e was worried because 'is wife could.'

"All the chaps, except Job, that is, laughed at that; but Job 'e got up and punched the table, and asked whether there was anybody as would like to go outside with him for five minutes. Then 'e sat down agin, and said 'ard things agin the drink, which 'ad made 'im the larfing-stock of all the fools in Claybury.

"'I'm going to give it up, Smith,' he ses.

"'Yes, I know you are,' ses Smith.

"'If I could on'y lose the taste of it for a time I could give it up,' ses Job, wiping 'is mouth, 'and to prove I'm in earnest I'll give five pounds to anybody as'll prevent me tasting intoxicating licker for a month.'

"'You may as well save your breath to bid people "good-night" with, Job,' ses Bill Chambers; 'you wouldn't pay up if anybody did keep you off it.'

"Job swore honour bright he would, but nobody believed 'im, and at last he called for pen and ink and wrote it all down on a sheet o' paper and signed it, and then he got two other chaps to sign it as witnesses.

"Bill Chambers wasn't satisfied then. He pointed out that earning the five pounds, and then getting it out o' Job Brown arterwards, was two such entirely different things, that there was no likeness between 'em at all. Then Job Brown got so mad 'e didn't know wot 'e was doing, and 'e 'anded over five pounds to Smith the landlord and wrote on the paper that he was to give it to anybody who should earn it, without consulting 'im at all. Even Bill couldn't think of anything to say agin that, but he made a point of biting all the sovereigns.

"There was quite a excitement for a few days. Henery Walker 'e got a 'eadache with thinking, and Joe Gubbins, 'e got a 'eadache for drinking Job Brown's beer agin. There was all sorts o' wild ways mentioned to earn that five pounds, but they didn't come to anything.

"Arter a week had gone by Job Brown began to get restless like, and once or twice 'e said in Smith's hearing 'ow useful five pounds would be. Smith didn't take any notice, and at last Job told 'im there didn't seem any likelihood of the five pounds being earned, and he wanted it to buy pigs with. The way 'e went on when Smith said 'e 'adn't got the power to give it back, and 'e'd got to keep it in trust for anybody as might earn it, was disgraceful.

"He used to ask Smith for it every night, and Smith used to give 'im the same answer, until at last Job Brown said as he'd go an' see a lawyer about it. That frightened Smith a bit, and I b'lieve he'd ha' 'anded it over, but two days arterwards Job was going upstairs so careful that he fell down to the bottom and broke 'is leg.

"It was broken in two places, and the doctor said it would be a long job, owing to 'is drinking habits, and 'e gave Mrs. Brown strict orders that Job wasn't to 'ave a drop of anything, even if 'e asked for it.

"There was a lot o' talk about it up at the 'Cauliflower' 'ere, and Henery Walker, arter a bad 'eadache, thought of a plan by which 'e and Bill Chambers could 'ave that five pounds atween 'em. The idea was that Bill Chambers was to go with Henery to see Job, and take 'im a bottle of beer, and jist as Job was going to drink it Henery should knock it out of 'is 'ands, at the same time telling Bill Chambers 'e ought to be ashamed o' hisself.

"It was a good idea, and, as Henery Walker said, if Mrs. Brown was in the room so much the better, as she'd be a witness. He made Bill swear to keep it secret for fear of other chaps doing it arterwards, and then they bought a bottle o' beer and set off up the road to Job's. The annoying part of it was, arter all their trouble and Henery Walker's 'eadache, Mrs. Brown wouldn't let 'em in. They begged and prayed of 'er to let 'em go up and just 'ave a peep at 'im, but she wouldn't. She said she'd go upstairs and peep for 'em, and she came down agin and said that 'e was a little bit flushed, but sleeping like a lamb.

"They went round the corner and drank the ale up, and Bill Chambers said it was a good job Henery thought 'e was clever, because nobody else did. As for 'is 'eadaches, he put 'em down to over-eating.

"Several other chaps called to see Job, but none of them was allowed to go up, and for seven weeks that unfortunit man never touched a drop of anything. The doctor tried to persuade 'im now that 'e 'ad got the start to keep it, and 'e likewise pointed out that as 'e had been without liquor for over a month, he could go and get that five pounds back out o' Smith.

"Job promised that 'e would give it up; but the fust day 'e felt able to crawl on 'is crutches he made up 'is mind to go up to the 'Cauliflower' and see whether gin and beer tasted as good as it used to. The only thing was 'is wife might stop 'im.

"'You're done up with nursing me, old gal,' he ses to is wife.

"'I am a bit tired,' ses she.

"'I could see it by your eyes,' ses Job. 'What you want is a change, Polly. Why not go and see your sister at Wickham?'

"'I don't like leaving you alone,' ses Mrs. Brown, 'else I'd like to go. I want to do a little shopping.'

"'You go, my dear,' ses Job. 'I shall be quite 'appy sitting at the gate in the sun with a glass o' milk an' a pipe.'

"He persuaded 'er at last, and, in a fit o' generosity, gave 'er three shillings to go shopping with, and as soon as she was out o' sight he went off with a crutch and a stick, smiling all over 'is face. He met Dick Weed in the road and they shook 'ands quite friendly, and Job asked 'im to 'ave a drink. Then Henery Walker and some more chaps came along, and by the time they got to the 'Cauliflower' they was as merry a party as you'd wish to see.

"Every man 'ad a pint o' beer, which Job paid for, not forgetting Smith 'isself, and Job closed 'is eyes with pleasure as 'e took his. Then they began to talk about 'is accident, and Job showed 'em 'is leg and described wot it felt like to be a teetotaller for seven weeks.

"'And I'll trouble you for that five pounds, Smith,' 'e ses, smiling. 'I've been without anything stronger than milk for seven weeks. I never thought when I wrote that paper I was going to earn my own money.'

"'None of us did,' Job,' ses Smith. 'D'ye think that leg'll be all right agin? As good as the other, I mean?'

"'Doctor ses so,' ses Job.

"'It's wonderful wot they can do nowadays,' ses Smith, shaking 'is 'ead.

"''Strordinary,' ses Job; 'where's that five pounds, Smith?'

"'You don't want to put any sudden weight or anything like that on it for a time, Job,' ses Smith; 'don't get struggling or fighting, whatever you do, Job.'

"''Taint so likely,' ses Job; 'd'ye think I'm a fool? Where's that five pounds, Smith?'

"'Ah, yes,' ses Smith, looking as though 'e'd just remembered something. 'I wanted to tell you about that, to see if I've done right. I'm glad you've come in.'

"'Eh?' ses Job Brown, staring at 'im.

"'Has your wife gone shopping to-day?' ses Smith, looking at 'im very solemn.

"Job Brown put 'is mug down on the table and turned as pale as ashes. Then 'e got up and limped over to the bar.

"'Wot d'yer mean?' he ses, choking.

"'She said she thought o' doing so,' ses Smith, wiping a glass; 'she came in yesterday and asked for that five pounds she'd won. The doctor came in with 'er and said she'd kept you from licker for seven weeks, let alone a month; so, according to the paper, I 'ad to give it to 'er. I 'ope I done right, Job?'

"Job didn't answer 'im a word, good or bad. He just turned 'is back on him, and, picking up 'is crutch and 'is stick, hobbled off 'ome. Henery Walker tried to make 'im stop and 'ave another pint, but he wouldn't. He said he didn't want 'is wife to find 'im out when she returned."

BREVET RANK

THE crew of the *Elizabeth Hopkins* sat on deck in the gloaming, gazing idly at the dusky shapes of the barges as they dropped silently down on the tide, or violently discussing the identity of various steamers as they came swiftly past. Even with these amusements the time hung heavily, and they thought longingly of certain cosy bars by the riverside to which they were wont to betake themselves in their spare time.

To-night, in deference to the wishes of the skipper, wishes which approximated closely to those of Royalty in their effects, they remained on board. A new acquaintance of his, a brother captain, who dabbled in mesmerism, was coming to give them a taste of his quality, and the skipper, sitting on the side of the schooner in the faint light which streamed from the galley, was condescendingly explaining to them the marvels of hypnotism.

"I never 'eard the likes of it," said one, with a deep breath, as the skipper concluded a marvellous example.

"There's a lot you ain't 'eard of, Bill," said another, whose temper was suffering from lack of beer. "But 'ave you seen all this, sir?"

"Everything," said the skipper, impressively. "He wanted to mesmerise me, an' I said, 'All right,' I ses, 'do it an' welcome—if you can, but I expect my head's a bit too strong for you.'"

"And it was, sir, I'll bet," said the man who had been so candid with Bill.

"He tried everything," said the skipper, "then he give it up; but he's coming aboard to-night, so any of you that likes can come down the cabin and be mesermised free."

"Why can't he do it on deck?" said the mate, rising from the hatches and stretching his gigantic form.

"'Cos he must have artificial light, George," said the skipper. "He lets me a little bit into the secret, you know, an' he told me he likes to have the men a bit dazed-like first."

Voices sounded from the wharf, and the nightwatchman appeared piloting Captain Zingall to the schooner. The crew noticed that he came aboard quite like any other man, descending the ladder with even more care than usual. He was a small man, of much dignity, with light grey eyes which had been so strained by the exercise of his favourite hobby that they appeared to be starting from his head. He chatted agreeably about freights for some time, and then, at his brother skipper's urgent entreaty, consented to go below and give them a taste of his awful powers.

At first he was not very successful. The men stared at the discs he put into their hands until their eyes ached, but for some time without effect. Bill was the first to yield, and to the astonishment of his friends passed into a soft magnetic slumber, from which he emerged to perform the usual idiotic tricks peculiar to mesmerised subjects.

"It's wonderful what power you 'ave over 'em," said Captain Bradd, respectfully.

Captain Zingall smiled affably. "At the present moment," he said, "that man is my unthinkin' slave, an' whatever I wish him to do he does. Would any of you like him to do anything?"

"Well, sir," said one of the men, "'e owes me 'arf a dollar, an' I think it would be a 'ighly interestin' experiment if you could get 'im to pay me. If anything 'ud make me believe in mesmerism, that would."

"An' he owes me eighteenpence, sir," said another seaman, eagerly.

"One at a time," said the first speaker, sharply.

"An' 'e's owed me five shillin's since I don't know when," said the cook, with dishonest truthfulness.

Captain Zingall turned to his subject. "You owe that man half a crown," he said, pointing, "that one eighteenpence, and that one five shillings. Pay them."

In the most matter-of-fact way in the world, Bill groped in his pockets, and, producing some greasy coins, paid the sums mentioned, to the intense delight of everybody concerned.

"Well, I'm blest," said the mate, staring. "I thought mesmerism was all rubbish. Now bring him to again."

"But don't tell 'im wot 'e's been doin'," said the cook.

Zingall with a few passes brought his subject round, and with a subdued air he took his place with the others.

"What'd it feel like, Bill?" asked Joe. "Can you remember what you did?"

Bill shook his head.

"Don't try to," said the cook, feelingly.

"I should like to put you under the influence," said Zingall, eyeing the mate.

"You couldn't," said that gentleman, promptly.

"Let me try," said Zingall, persuasively.

"Do," said the skipper, "to oblige me, George."

"Well, I don't mind much," said the mate, hesitating; "but no making *me* give those chaps money, you know."

"No, no," said Zingall.

"Wot does 'e mean? Give the chaps money?" said Bill, turning with a startled air to the cook.

"I dunno," said the cook, airily. "Just watch 'im, Bill," he added, anxiously.

But Bill had something better to do, and feeling in his pockets hurriedly strove to balance his cash account. It was impossible to do anything else while he was doing it, and the situation became so strained and his language so weird that the skipper was compelled in the interests of law and morality to order him from the cabin.

"Look at me," said Zingall to the mate after quiet had been restored.

The mate complied, and everybody gazed spellbound at the tussle for supremacy between brute force and occult science. Slowly, very slowly, science triumphed, being interrupted several times by the blood-curdling threats of Bill, as they floated down the companion-way. Then the mate suddenly lurched forward, and would have fallen but that strong hands caught him and restored him to his seat.

"I'm going to show you something now, if I can," said Zingall, wiping his brow; "but I don't know how it'll come off, because I'm only a beginner at this sort of thing, and I've never tried this before. If you don't mind, cap'n, I'm going to tell him he is Cap'n Bradd, and that you are the mate."

"Go ahead," said the delighted Bradd.

Captain Zingall went ahead full speed. With a few rapid passes he roused the mate from his torpor and fixed him with his glittering eye.

"You are Cap'n Bradd, master o' this ship," he said, slowly.

"Ay, ay," said the mate, earnestly.

"And that's your mate, George," said Zingall, pointing to the deeply interested Bradd.

"Ay, ay," said the mate again, with a sigh.

"Take command, then," said Zingall, leaving him with a satisfied air and seating himself on the locker.

The mate sat up and looked about him with an air of quiet authority.

"George," he said, turning suddenly to the skipper with a very passable imitation of his voice.

"Sir," said the skipper, with a playful glance at Zingall.

"A friend o' mine named Cap'n Zingall is coming aboard to-night," said the mate, slowly. "Get a little whisky for him out o' my state-room."

"Ay, ay, sir," said the amused Bradd.

"Just a little in the bottom of the bottle'll do," continued the mate; "don't put more in, for he drinks like a fish."

"I never said such a thing, cap'n," said Bradd, in an agitated whisper. "I never thought o' such a thing."

"No, I know you wouldn't," said Zingall, who was staring hard at a nearly empty whisky bottle on the table.

"And don't leave your baccy pouch lying about, George," continued the mate, in a thrilling whisper.

The skipper gave a faint, mirthless little laugh, and looked at him uneasily.

"If ever there was a sponger for baccy, George, it's him," said the mate, in a confidential whisper.

Captain Zingall, who was at that very moment filling his pipe from the pouch which the skipper had himself pushed towards him, laid it carefully on the table again, and gazing steadily at his friend, took out the tobacco already in his pipe and replaced it. In the silence which ensued the mate took up the whisky bottle, and pouring the contents into a tumbler, added a little water, and drank it with relish.

He leaned back on the locker and smacked his lips. There was a faint laugh from one of the crew, and looking up smartly he seemed to be aware for the first time of their presence. "What are you doin' down here?" he roared. "What do you want?"

"Nothin', sir," said the cook. "Only we thought——"

"Get out at once," vociferated the mate, rising.

"Stay where you are," said the skipper, sharply.

"George!" said the mate, in the squeaky voice in which he chose to personate the skipper.

"Bring him round, Zingall," said the skipper, irritably. "I've had enough o' this. I'll let 'im know who's who."

With a confident smile Zingall got up quietly from the locker, and fixed his terrible gaze on the mate. The mate fell back and gazed at him open-mouthed.

"Who the devil are you staring at?" he demanded, rudely.

Still holding him with his gaze, Zingall clapped his hands together, and stepping up to him blew strongly in his face. The mate, with a perfect scream of rage, picked him up by the middle, and dumping him heavily on the floor, held him there and worried him.

"Help!" cried Zingall, in a smothered voice; "take him off!"

"Why don't you bring him round?" yelled the skipper, excitably. "What's the good of playing with him?"

Zingall's reply, which was quite irrelevant, consisted almost entirely of impious reflections upon his friend's understanding.

"Blow in 'is face agin, sir," said the cook, bending down kindly.

"Take him off!" yelled Zingall; "he's killing me!"

The skipper flew to the assistance of his friend, but the mate, who was of gigantic strength and stature, simply backed, and crushed him against a bulkhead. Then, as if satisfied, he released the crestfallen Zingall, and stood looking at him.

"Why—don't—you—bring—him—round?" panted the skipper.

"He's out of my control," said Zingall, rising nimbly to his feet. "I've heard of such cases before. I'm only new at the work, you know, but I dare say, in a couple of years' time——"

The skipper howled at him, and the mate suddenly alive again to the obnoxious presence of the crew, drove them up the companion ladder, and pursued them to the forecastle.

"This is a pretty kettle o' fish," said Bradd, indignantly. "Why don't you bring him round?"

"Because I can't," said Zingall, shortly. "It'll have to wear off."

"Wear off!" repeated the skipper.

"He's under a delusion now," said Zingall, "an' o' course I can't say how long it'll last, but whatever you do don't cross him in any way."

"Oh, don't cross him," repeated Bradd, with sarcastic inflection, "and you call yourself a mesmerist."

Zingall drew himself up with a little pride. "Well, see what I've done," he said. "The fact is, I was charged full with electricity when I came aboard, and he's got it all now. It's left me weak, and until my will wears off him he's captain o' this ship."

"And what about me?" said Bradd.

"You're the mate," said Zingall, "and mind, for your own sake, you act up to it. If you don't cross him I haven't any doubt it'll be all right, but if you do he'll very likely murder you in a fit of frenzy, and—he wouldn't be responsible. Good-night."

"You're not going?" said Bradd, clutching him by the sleeve.

"I am," said the other. "He seems to have took a violent dislike to me, and if I stay here it'll only make him worse."

He ran lightly up on deck, and avoiding an ugly rush on the part of the mate, who had been listening, sprang on to the ladder and hastily clambered ashore.

The skipper, worn and scared, looked up as the bogus skipper came below.

"I'm going to bed, George," said the mate, staring at him. "I feel a bit heavy. Give me a call just afore high water."

"Where are you goin' to sleep?" demanded the skipper.

"Goin' to sleep?" said the mate, "why, in my state-room, to be sure."

He took the empty bottle from the table, and opening the door of the state-room, closed it in the face of its frenzied owner, and turned the key in the lock. Then he leaned over the berth, and, cramming the pillow against his mouth, gave way to his feelings until he was nearly suffocated.

Any idea that the skipper might have had of the healing effects of sleep were rudely dispelled when the mate came on deck next morning, and found that they had taken the schooner out without arousing him. His delusion seemed to be stronger than ever, and pushing the skipper from the wheel he took it himself, and read him a short and sharp lecture on the virtues of obedience.

"I know you're a good sort, George Smith," he said, leniently, "nobody could wish for a better, but while I'm master of this here ship it don't become you to take things upon yourself in the way you do."

"But you don't understand," said the skipper, trying to conquer his temper. "Now look me in the eye, George."

"Who are you calling George?" said the mate, sharply.

"Well, look me in the eye, then," said the skipper, waiving the point.

"I'll look at you in a way you won't like in a minute," said the mate, ferociously.

"I want to explain the position of affairs to you," said the skipper. "Do you remember Cap'n Zingall what was aboard last night?"

"Little dirty-looking man what kept staring at me?" demanded the mate.

"Well, I don't know about 'is being dirty," said the skipper, "but that's the man. Do you know what he did to you, Geo——"

"Eh!" said the mate, sharply.

"He mesmerised you," said the skipper, hastily. "Now keep

quite calm. You say you're Benjamin Bradd, master o' this vessel, don't you?"

"I do," said the mate. "Let me hear anybody say as I ain't."

"Yesterday," said the skipper, plucking up courage and speaking very slowly and impressively, "you were George Smith, the mate, but my friend, Captain Zingall, mesmerised you and made you think you were me."

"I see what it is," said the mate, severely. "You've been drinking; you've been up to my whisky."

"Call the crew up and ask 'em, then," said Bradd, desperately.

"Call 'em up yourself, you lunatic," said the mate, loudly enough for the men to hear. "If anybody dares to play the fool with me I won't leave a whole bone in his body, that's all."

In obedience to the summons of Captain Bradd the crew came up, and being requested by him to tell the mate that he was the mate, and that he was at present labouring under a delusion, stood silently nudging each other and eyeing him uneasily.

"Well," said the latter at length, "why don't you speak and tell George he's gone off his 'ead a bit?"

"It ain't nothing to do with us, sir," said Bill, very respectfully.

"But, damn it all, man," said the mate, taking a mighty grip of his collar, "you know I'm the cap'n, don't you?"

"O' course I do, sir," said Bill.

"There you are, George," said the mate, releasing him, and turning to the frantic Bradd: "you hear that? Now, look here, you listen to me. Either you've been drinking, or else your 'ead's gone a little bit off. You go down and turn in, and if you don't give me any more of your nonsense I'll overlook it for this once."

He ordered the crew forward again, and being desirous of leaving some permanent mark of his command on the ship, had the galley fresh painted in red and blue, and a lot of old stores, which he had vainly condemned when mate, thrown overboard. The skipper stood by helplessly while it was done, and then went below of his own accord and turned in, as being the only way to retain his sanity, or, at any rate, the clearness of head which he felt to be indispensable at this juncture.

Time, instead of restoring the mate to his senses, only appeared to confirm him in his folly, and the skipper, after another attempt to convince him, let things drift, resolving to have him put under restraint as soon as they got to port.

They reached Tidescroft in the early afternoon, but before they entered the harbour the mate, as though he had had some subtle intuition that this would be his last command, called the crew to him, and read them a touching little homily upon their behaviour when they should land. He warned them of public-houses and other dangers, and reminded them affectingly of their duties as husbands and fathers. "Always go home to your wife and children, my lads," he continued with some emotion, "as I go home to mine."

"Why, he ain't got none," whispered Bill, staring.

"Don't be a fool, Bill," said the cook, "he means the cap'n's. Don't you see he's the cap'n now."

It was clear as noonday, and the agitation of the skipper—a perfect Othello in his way—was awful. He paced the deck incessantly, casting fretful glances ashore, and, as the schooner touched the side of the quay, sprang on to the bulwarks and jumped ashore. The mate watched him with an ill-concealed grin, and then, having made the vessel snug, went below to strengthen himself with a drop of the skipper's whisky for the crowning scene of his play. He came on deck again, and taking no heed of the whispers of the crew, went ashore.

Meantime, Captain Bradd had reached his house, and was discussing the situation with his astonished spouse. She pooh-poohed the idea of the police and the medical faculty as being likely to cause complications with the owners, and, despite the remonstrances of her husband, insisted upon facing the mate alone.

"Now you go in the kitchen," she said, looking from the window. "Here he comes. You see how I'll settle him."

The skipper looked out of the window and saw the unhappy victim of Captain Zingall slowly approaching. His wife drew him away, and, despite his remonstrances, pushed him into the next room and closed the door.

She sat on the sofa calmly sewing, as the mate, whose hardi-hood was rapidly failing him, entered. Her manner gave him no assistance whatever, and coming sheepishly in he took a chair.

"I've come home," he said at last.

"So I see, Ben," said Mrs. Bradd, calmly.

"He's told her," said the mate to himself.

"Children all right?" he inquired, after another pause.

"Yes," said Mrs. Bradd, simply. "Little Joe's boots are almost off his feet, though."

"Ah," said the mate, blankly.

"I've been waiting for you to come, Ben," said Mrs. Bradd after a pause. "I want you to change a five-pound note Uncle Dick gave me."

"Can't do it," said the mate, briefly. The absence of Captain Bradd was disquieting to a bashful man in such a position, and he had looked forward to a stormy scene which was to bring him to his senses again.

"Show me what you've got," said Mrs. Bradd, leaning forward. The mate pulled out an old leather purse and counted the contents, two pounds and a little silver.

"There isn't five pounds there," said Mrs. Bradd, "but I may as well take last week's housekeeping while you've got it out."

Before the mate could prevent her she had taken the two pounds and put it in her pocket. He looked at her placid face in amazement, but she met his gaze calmly and drummed on the table with her thimble.

"No, no, I want the money myself," said the mate at last. He put his hands to his head and began to prepare for the grand transformation scene. "My head's gone," he said, in a gurgling voice. "What am I doing here? Where am I?"

"Good gracious, what's the matter with the man?" said Mrs. Bradd, with a scream. She snatched up a bowl of flowers and flung the contents in his face as her husband burst into the room. The mate sprang to his feet, spluttering.

"What am I doing here, Cap'n Bradd?" he said in his usual voice.

"He's come round!" said Bradd, ecstatically. "He's come round. Oh, George, you have been playing the fool. Don't you know what you've been doing?"

The mate shook his head, and stared round the room. "I thought we were in London," he said, putting his hand to his head. "You said Cap'n Zingall was coming aboard. How did we get here? Where am I?"

In a hurried, breathless fashion the skipper told him, the mate regarding him the while with a stare of fixed incredulity.

"I can't understand it," he said at length. "My mind's a perfect blank."

"A perfect blank," said Mrs. Bradd, cheerfully. It might have been accident, but she tapped her pocket as she spoke, and the outwitted mate bit his lip as he realised his blunder, and turned to the door. The couple watched him as he slowly passed up the street.

"It's most extraordinary," said the skipper; "the most extraordinary case I ever heard of."

"So it is," said his wife, "and what's more extraordinary still for you, Ben, you're going to church on Sunday, and what's more

extraordinary even than that, you are going to put two golden
sovereigns in the plate."

TWIN SPIRITS

THE "Terrace," consisting of eight gaunt houses, faced the sea, while the back rooms commanded a view of the ancient little town some half-mile distant. The beach, a waste of shingle, was desolate and bare except for a ruined bathing-machine and a few pieces of linen drying in the winter sunshine. In the offing tiny steamers left a trail of smoke, while sailing-craft, their canvas glistening in the sun, slowly melted from the sight. On all these things the "Terrace" turned a stolid eye, and, counting up its gains of the previous season, wondered whether it could hold on to the next. It was a discontented "Terrace," and had become prematurely soured by a Board which refused them a pier, a band-stand, and illuminated gardens.

From the front windows of the third story of No. 1 Mrs. Cox, gazing out to sea, sighed softly. The season had been a bad one, and Mr. Cox had been even more troublesome than usual owing to tightness in the money market and the avowed preference of local publicans for cash transactions, to assets in chalk and slate. In Mr. Cox's memory there never had been such a drought, and his crop of patience was nearly exhausted.

He had in his earlier days attempted to do a little work, but his health had suffered so much that his wife had become alarmed for his safety. Work invariably brought on a cough, and as he came from a family whose lungs had formed the staple conversation of their lives, he had been compelled to abandon it, and at last it came to be understood that if he would only consent to amuse himself, and not get into trouble, nothing more would be expected of him. It was not much of a life for a man of spirit, and at times it became so unbearable that Mr. Cox would disappear for days together in search of work, returning unsuccessful after many days with nerves shattered in the pursuit.

Mrs. Cox's meditations were disturbed by a knock at the front door, and, the servants having been discharged for the season, she hurried downstairs to open it, not without a hope of belated lodgers—invalids in search of an east wind. A stout, middle-aged woman in widow's weeds stood on the door-step.

"Glad to see you, my dear," said the visitor, kissing her loudly.

Mrs. Cox gave her a subdued caress in return, not from any lack of feeling, but because she did everything in a quiet and spiritless fashion.

"I've got my Uncle Joseph from London staying with us," continued the visitor, following her into the hall, "so I just got into the train and brought him down for a blow at the sea."

A question on Mrs. Cox's lips died away as a very small man who had been hidden by his niece came into sight.

"My Uncle Joseph," said Mrs. Berry; "Mr. Joseph Piper," she added.

Mr. Piper shook hands, and after a performance on the door-mat, protracted by reason of a festoon of hemp, followed his hostess into the faded drawing-room.

"And Mr. Cox?" inquired Mrs. Berry, in a cold voice.

Mrs. Cox shook her head. "He's been away this last three days," she said, flushing slightly.

"Looking for work?" suggested the visitor.

Mrs. Cox nodded, and, placing the tips of her fingers together, fidgeted gently.

"Well, I hope he finds it," said Mrs. Berry, with more venom than the remark seemed to require. "Why, where's your marble clock?"

Mrs. Cox coughed. "It's being mended," she said, confusedly.

Mrs. Berry eyed her anxiously. "Don't mind him, my dear," she said, with a jerk of her head in the direction of Mr. Piper, "he's nobody. Wouldn't you like to go out on the beach a little while, uncle?"

"No," said Mr. Piper.

"I suppose Mr. Cox took the clock for company," remarked Mrs. Berry, after a hostile stare at her relative.

Mrs. Cox sighed and shook her head. It was no use pretending with Mrs. Berry.

"He'll pawn the clock and anything else he can lay his hands on, and when he's drunk it up come home to be made a fuss of," continued Mrs. Berry, heatedly; "that's you men."

Her glance was so fiery that Mr. Joseph Piper was unable to allow the remark to pass unchallenged.

"*I* never pawned a clock," he said, stroking his little grey head.

"That's a lot to boast of, isn't it?" demanded his niece; "if I hadn't got anything better than that to boast of I wouldn't boast at all."

Mr. Piper said that he was not boasting.

"It'll go on like this, my dear, till you're ruined," said the sympathetic Mrs. Berry, turning to her friend again; "what'll you do then?"

"Yes, I know," said Mrs. Cox. "I've had a bad season, too, and I'm so anxious about him in spite of it all. I can't sleep at nights for fearing that he's in some trouble. I'm sure I laid awake half last night crying."

Mrs. Berry sniffed loudly, and Mr. Piper making a remark in a low voice, turned on him with ferocity.

"What did you say?" she demanded.

"I said it does her credit," said Mr. Piper, firmly.

"I might have known it was nonsense," retorted his niece, hotly. "Can't you get him to take the pledge, Mary?"

"I couldn't insult him like that," said Mrs. Cox, with a shiver; "you don't know his pride. He never admits that he drinks; he says that he only takes a little for his indigestion. He'd never forgive me. When he pawns the things he pretends that somebody has stolen them, and the way he goes on at me for my carelessness is alarming. He gets worked up to such a pitch that sometimes I almost think he believes it himself."

"Rubbish," said Mrs. Berry, tartly, "you're too easy with him."

Mrs. Cox sighed, and, leaving the room, returned with a bottle of wine which was port to the look and red-currant to the taste, and a seed-cake of formidable appearance. The visitors attacked these refreshments mildly, Mr. Piper sipping his wine with an obtrusive carefulness which his niece rightly regarded as a reflection upon her friend's hospitality.

"What Cox wants is a shock," she said; "you've dropped some crumbs on the carpet, uncle."

Mr. Piper apologised and said he had got his eye on them, and would pick them up when he had finished and pick up his niece's at the same time to prevent her stooping. Mrs. Berry, in an aside to Mrs. Cox, said that her Uncle Joseph's tongue had got itself disliked on both sides of the family.

"And I'd give him one," said Mrs. Berry, returning again to the subject of Mr. Cox and shocks. "He has a gentleman's life of it here, and he would look rather silly if you were sold up and he had to do something for his living."

"It's putting away the things that is so bad," said Mrs. Cox, shaking her head; "that clock won't last him out, I know; he'll come back and take some of the other things. Every spring I have to go through his pockets for the tickets and get the things out again, and I mustn't say a word for fear of hurting his feelings. If I do he goes off again."

"If I were you," said Mrs. Berry, emphatically, "I'd get behind with the rent or something and have the brokers in. He'd look rather astonished if he came home and saw a broker's man sitting in a chair——"

"He'd look more astonished if he saw him sitting in a flower-pot," suggested the caustic Mr. Piper.

"I couldn't do that," said Mrs. Cox. "I couldn't stand the disgrace, even though I knew I could pay him out. As it is, Cox is always setting his family above mine."

Mrs. Berry, without ceasing to stare Mr. Piper out of countenance, shook her head, and, folding her arms, again stated her opinion that Mr. Cox wanted a shock, and expressed a great yearning to be the humble means of giving him one.

"If you can't have the brokers in, get somebody to pretend to be one," she said, sharply; "that would prevent him pawning any more things at any rate. Why wouldn't he do?" she added, nodding at her uncle.

Anxiety on Mrs. Cox's face was exaggerated on that of Mr. Piper.

"Let uncle pretend to be a broker's man in for the rent," continued the excitable lady, rapidly. "When Mr. Cox turns up after his spree, tell him what his doings have brought you to, and say you'll have to go to the workhouse."

"I look like a broker's man, don't I?" said Mr. Piper, in a voice more than tinged with sarcasm.

"Yes," said his niece, "that's what put it into my head."

"It's very kind of you, dear, and very kind of Mr. Piper," said Mrs. Cox, "but I couldn't think of it, I really couldn't.

"Uncle would be delighted," said Mrs. Berry, with a wilful blinking of plain facts. "He's got nothing better to do; it's a nice house and good food, and he could sit at the open window and sniff at the sea all day long."

Mr. Piper sniffed even as she spoke, but not at the sea.

"And I'll come for him the day after tomorrow," said Mrs. Berry.

It was the old story of the stronger will: Mrs. Cox after a feeble stand gave way altogether, and Mr. Piper's objections were demolished before he had given them full utterance. Mrs. Berry went off alone after dinner, secretly glad to have got rid of Mr.

Piper, who was making a self-invited stay at her house of indefinite duration; and Mr. Piper, in his new *rôle* of broker's man, essayed the part with as much help as a clay pipe and a pint of beer could afford him.

That day and the following he spent amid the faded grandeurs of the drawing-room, gazing longingly at the wide expanse of beach and the tumbling sea beyond. The house was almost uncannily quiet, an occasional tinkle of metal or crash of china from the basement giving the only indication of the industrious Mrs. Cox; but on the day after the quiet of the house was broken by the return of its master, whose annoyance, when he found the drawing-room clock stolen and a man in possession, was alarming in its vehemence. He lectured his wife severely on her mismanagement, and after some hesitation announced his intention of going through her books. Mrs. Cox gave them to him, and, armed with pen and ink and four square inches of pink blotting-paper, he performed feats of balancing which made him a very Blondin of finance.

"I shall have to get something to do," he said, gloomily, laying down his pen.

"Yes, dear," said his wife.

Mr. Cox leaned back in his chair and, wiping his pen on the blotting-paper, gazed in a speculative fashion round the room. "Have you any money?" he inquired.

For reply his wife rummaged in her pocket and after a lengthy search produced a bunch of keys, a thimble, a needle-case, two pocket-handkerchiefs, and a halfpenny. She put this last on the table, and Mr. Cox, whose temper had been mounting steadily, threw it to the other end of the room.

"I can't help it," said Mrs. Cox, wiping her eyes. "I'm sure I've done all I could to keep a home together. I can't even raise money on anything."

Mr. Cox, who had been glancing round the room again, looked up sharply.

"Why not?" he inquired.

"The broker's man" said Mrs. Cox, nervously; "he's made an inventory of everything, and he holds us responsible."

Mr. Cox leaned back in his chair. "This is a pretty state of things," he blurted, wildly. "Here have I been walking my legs off looking for work, any work so long as it's honest labour, and I come back to find a broker's man sitting in my own house and drinking up my beer."

He rose and walked up and down the room, and Mrs. Cox,

whose nerves were hardly equal to the occasion, slipped on her bonnet and announced her intention of trying to obtain a few necessaries on credit. Her husband waited in indignant silence until he heard the front-door close behind her, and then stole softly upstairs to have a look at the fell destroyer of his domestic happiness.

Mr. Piper, who was already very tired of his imprisonment, looked up curiously as he heard the door pushed open, and discovered an elderly gentleman with an appearance of great stateliness staring at him. In the ordinary way he was one of the meekest of men, but the insolence of this stare was outrageous. Mr. Piper, opening his mild blue eyes wide, stared back. Whereupon Mr. Cox, fumbling in his vest-pocket, found a pair of folders, and putting them astride his nose, gazed at the pseudo-broker's man with crushing effect.

"What do you want here?" he asked, at length. "Are you the father of one of the servants?"

"I'm the father of all the servants in the house," said Mr. Piper, sweetly.

"Don't answer me, sir," said Mr. Cox, with much pomposity; "you're an eyesore to an honest man, a vulture, a harpy."

Mr. Piper pondered.

"How do you know what's an eyesore to an honest man?" he asked, at length.

Mr. Cox smiled scornfully.

"Where is your warrant or order, or whatever you call it?" he demanded.

"I've shown it to Mrs. Cox," said Mr. Piper.

"Show it to me," said the other.

"I've complied with the law by showing it once," said Mr. Piper, bluffing, "and I'm not going to show it again."

Mr. Cox stared at him disdainfully, beginning at his little sleek grey head and travelling slowly downwards to his untidy boots and then back again. He repeated this several times, until Mr. Piper, unable to bear it patiently, began to eye him in the same fashion.

"What are you looking at, vulture?" demanded the incensed Mr. Cox.

"Three spots o' grease on a dirty weskit," replied Mr. Piper, readily, "a pair o' bow legs in a pair o' somebody else's trousers, and a shabby coat wore under the right arm, with carrying off"—he paused a moment as though to make sure—"with carrying off of a drawing-room clock."

He regretted this retort almost before he had finished it, and rose to his feet with a faint cry of alarm as the heated Mr. Cox first locked the door and put the key in his pocket and then threw up the window.

"Vulture!" he cried, in a terrible voice.

"Yes, sir," said the trembling Mr. Piper.

Mr. Cox waved his hand towards the window.

"Fly," he said, briefly.

Mr. Piper tried to form his white lips into a smile, and his knees trembled beneath him.

"Did you hear what I said?" demanded Mr. Cox. "What are you waiting for? If you don't fly out of the window I'll throw you out."

"Don't touch me," screamed Mr. Piper, retreating behind a table, "it's all a mistake. All a joke. I'm not a broker's man. Ha! ha!"

"Eh?" said the other; "not a broker's man? What are you, then?"

In eager, trembling tones Mr. Piper told him, and, gathering confidence as he proceeded, related the conversation which had led up to his imposture. Mr. Cox listened in a dazed fashion, and as he concluded threw himself into a chair, and gave way to a terrible outburst of grief.

"The way I've worked for that woman," he said, brokenly, "to think it should come to this! The deceit of the thing; the wickedness of it. My heart is broken; I shall never be the same man again—never!"

Mr. Piper made a sympathetic noise.

"It's been very unpleasant for me," he said, "but my niece is so masterful."

"I don't blame you," said Mr. Cox, kindly; "shake hands."

They shook hands solemnly, and Mr. Piper, muttering something about a draught, closed the window.

"You might have been killed in trying to jump out of that window," said Mr. Cox; "fancy the feelings of those two deceitful women then."

"Fancy *my* feelings!" said Mr. Piper, with a shudder. "Playing with fire, that's what I call it. My niece is coming this afternoon; it would serve her right if you gave her a fright by telling her you *had* killed me. Perhaps it would be a lesson to her not to be so officious."

"It would serve 'em both right," agreed Mr. Cox; "only Mrs. Berry might send for the police."

"I never thought of that," said Mr. Piper fondling his chin.

"I might frighten my wife," mused the amiable Mr. Cox; "it

would be a lesson to her not to be deceitful again. And, by Jove, I'll get some money from her to escape with; I know she's got some, and if she hasn't she will have in a day or two. There's a little pub at Newstead, eight miles from here, where we could be as happy as fighting-cocks with a fiver or two. And while we're there enjoying ourselves my wife'll be half out of her mind trying to account for your disappearance to Mrs. Berry."

"It sounds all right," said Mr. Piper, cautiously, "but she won't believe you. You don't look wild enough to have killed anybody."

"I'll look wild enough when the time comes," said the other, nodding. "You get on to the 'White Horse' at Newstead and wait for me. I'll let you out at the back way. Come along."

"But you said it was eight miles," said Mr. Piper.

"Eight miles easy walking," rejoined Mr. Cox. "Or there's a train at three o'clock. There's a sign-post at the corner there, and if you don't hurry I shall be able to catch you up. Goody-bye."

He patted the hesitating Mr. Piper on the back, and letting him out through the garden, indicated the road. Then he returned to the drawing-room, and carefully rumpling his hair, tore his collar from the stud, overturned a couple of chairs and a small table, and sat down to wait as patiently as he could for the return of his wife.

He waited about twenty minutes, and then he heard a key turn in the door below and his wife's footsteps slowly mounting the stairs. By the time she reached the drawing-room his tableau was complete, and she fell back with a faint shriek at the frenzied figure which met her eyes.

"Hush," said the tragedian, putting his finger to his lips.

"Henry, what is it?" cried Mrs. Cox. "What *is* the matter?"

"The broker's man," said her husband, in a thrilling whisper. "We had words—he struck me. In a fit of fury I—I—choked him."

"Much?" inquired the bewildered woman.

"*Much?*" repeated Mr. Cox, frantically. "I've killed him and hidden the body. Now I must escape and fly the country."

The bewilderment on Mrs. Cox's face increased; she was trying to reconcile her husband's statement with a vision of a trim little figure which she had seen ten minutes before with its head tilted backwards studying the sign-post, and which she was now quite certain was Mr. Piper.

"Are you sure he's dead?" she inquired.

"Dead as a door-nail," replied Mr. Cox, promptly. "I'd no idea he was such a delicate little man. What am I to do? Every moment adds to my danger. I must fly. How much money have you got?"

The question explained everything. Mrs. Cox closed her lips with a snap and shook her head.

"Don't play the fool," said her husband, wildly; "my neck's in danger."

"I haven't got anything," asseverated Mrs. Cox. "It's no good looking like that, Henry, I can't make money."

Mr. Cox's reply was interrupted by a loud knock at the hall-door, which he was pleased to associate with the police. It gave him a fine opportunity for melodrama, in the midst of which his wife, rightly guessing that Mrs. Berry had returned according to arrangement, went to the door to admit her. The visitor was only busy two minutes on the door-mat, but in that time Mrs. Cox was able in low whispers to apprise her of the state of affairs.

"That's my uncle all over," said Mrs. Berry, fiercely; "that's just the mean trick I should have expected of him. You leave 'em to me, my dear."

She followed her friend into the drawing-room, and having shaken hands with Mr. Cox, drew her handkerchief from her pocket and applied it to her eyes.

"She's told me all about it," she said, nodding at Mrs. Cox, "and it's worse than you think, much worse. It isn't a broker's man—it's my poor uncle, Joseph Piper."

"Your *uncle!*" repeated Mr. Cox, reeling back; "the broker's man your *uncle?*"

Mrs Berry sniffed. "It was a little joke on our part," she admitted, sinking into a chair and holding her handkerchief to her face. "Poor uncle; I dare say he's happier where he is."

Mr. Cox wiped his brow, and then, leaning his elbow on the mantelpiece, stared at her in well-simulated amazement.

"See what your joking has led to," he said, at last. "I have got to be a wanderer over the face of the earth, all on account of your jokes."

"It was an accident," murmured Mrs. Berry, "and nobody knows he was here, and I'm sure, poor dear, he hadn't got much to live for."

"It's very kind of you to look at it in that way, Susan, I'm sure," said Mrs. Cox.

"I was never one to make mischief," said Mrs. Berry. "It's no good crying over spilt milk. If uncle's killed he's killed, and there's an end of it. But I don't think it's quite safe for Mr. Cox to stay here."

"Just what I say," said that gentleman, eagerly; "but I've got no money."

"You get away," said Mrs. Berry, with a warning glance at her friend, and nodding to emphasise her words; "leave us some address to write to, and we must try and scrape twenty or thirty pounds to send you."

"Thirty," said Mr. Cox, hardly able to believe his ears.

Mrs. Berry nodded. "You'll have to make that do to go on with," she said, pondering. "And as soon as you get it you had better get as far away as possible before poor uncle is discovered. Where are we to send the money?"

Mr. Cox affected to consider.

"The 'White Horse,' Newstead," he said at length, in a whisper; "better write it down."

Mrs. Berry obeyed; and this business being completed, Mr. Cox, after trying in vain to obtain a shilling or two cash in hand, bade them a pathetic farewell and went off down the path, for some reason best known to himself, on tiptoe.

For the first two days Messrs. Cox and Piper waited with exemplary patience for the remittance, the demands of the landlord, a man of coarse fibre, being met in the meantime by the latter gentleman from his own slender resources. They were both reasonable men, and knew from experience the difficulty of raising money at short notice; but on the fourth day, their funds being nearly exhausted, an urgent telegram was dispatched to Mrs. Cox.

Mr. Cox was alone when the reply came, and Mr. Piper, returning to the inn-parlour, was amazed and distressed at his friend's appearance. Twice he had to address him before he seemed to be aware of his presence, and then Mr. Cox, breathing hard and staring at him strangely, handed him the message.

"Eh?" said Mr. Piper, in amaze, as he read slowly: "'*No—need—send—money—Uncle—Joseph—has—come—back.*—BERRY.' What does it mean? Is she mad?"

Mr. Cox shook his head, and taking the paper from him, held it at arm's length and regarded it at an angle.

"How can you be there when you're supposed to be dead?" he said, at length.

"How can I be there when I'm here?" rejoined Mr. Piper, no less reasonably.

Both gentlemen lapsed into a wondering silence, devoted to the attempted solution of their own riddles. Finally Mr. Cox, seized with a bright idea that the telegram had got altered in transmission, went off to the post-office and dispatched another, which went straight to the heart of things:—

"*Don't—understand—is—Uncle—Joseph—alive?*"

A reply was brought to the inn-parlour an hour later on. Mr. Cox opened it, gave one glance at it, and then with a suffocating cry handed it to the other. Mr. Piper took it gingerly, and his eyebrows almost disappeared as he read:—

"*Yes—smoking—in—drawing-room.*"

His first strong impression was that it was a case for the Psychical Research Society, but this romantic view faded in favour of a simple solution, propounded by Mr. Cox with much crispness, that Mrs. Berry was leaving the realms of fact for those of romance. His actual words were shorter, but the meaning was the same.

"I'll go home and ask to see you," he said, fiercely; "that'll bring things to a head, I should think."

"And she'll say I've gone back to London, perhaps," said Mr. Piper, gifted with sudden clearness of vision. "You can't show her up unless you take me with you, and that'll show *us* up. That's her artfulness; that's Susan all over."

"I never did like Susan," said Mr. Piper, with acerbity, "never."

Mr. Cox said he could easily understand it, and then, as a forlorn hope, sat down and wrote a long letter to his wife, in which, after dwelling at great length on the lamentable circumstances surrounding the sudden demise of Mr. Piper, he bade her thank Mrs. Berry for her well-meant efforts to ease his mind, and asked for the immediate dispatch of the money promised.

A reply came the following evening from Mrs. Berry herself. It was a long letter, and not only long, but badly written and crossed. It began with the weather, asked after Mr. Cox's health, and referred to the writer's; described with much minuteness a strange headache which had attacked Mrs. Cox, together with a long list of the remedies prescribed and the effects of each, and wound up in an out-of-the-way corner, in a vein of cheery optimism which reduced both readers to the verge of madness.

"Dear Uncle Joseph has quite recovered, and, in spite of a little nervousness—he was always rather timid—at meeting you again, has consented to go to the 'White Horse' to satisfy you that he is alive. I dare say he will be with you as soon as this letter—perhaps help you to read it."

Mr. Cox laid the letter down with extreme care, and, coughing gently, glanced in a sheepish fashion at the goggle-eyed Mr. Piper.

For some time neither of them spoke. Mr. Cox was the first to break the silence and—when he had finished—Mr. Piper said "Hush."

"Besides, it does no good," he added.

"It does *me* good," said Mr. Cox, recommencing.

Mr. Piper held up his hand with a startled gesture for silence. The words died away on his friend's lips as a familiar voice was heard in the passage, and the next moment Mrs. Berry entered the room and stood regarding them.

"I ran down by the same train to make sure you came, uncle," she remarked. "How long have you been here?"

Mr. Piper moistened his lips and gazed wildly at Mr. Cox for guidance.

"'Bout—'bout five minutes," he stammered.

"We were so glad dear uncle wasn't hurt much," continued Mrs. Berry, smiling, and shaking her head at Mr. Cox; "but the idea of your burying him in the geranium-bed; we haven't got him clean yet."

Mr. Piper, giving utterance to uncouth noises, quitted the room hastily, but Mr. Cox sat still and stared at her dumbly.

"Weren't you surprised to see him?" inquired his tormentor.

"Not after your letter," said Mr. Cox, finding his voice at last, and speaking with an attempt at chilly dignity. "Nothing could surprise me much after that."

Mrs. Berry smiled again.

"Ah, I've got another little surprise for you," she said, briskly. "Mrs. Cox was so upset at the idea of being alone while you were a wanderer over the face of the earth, that she and I have gone into partnership. We have had a proper deed drawn up, so that now there are two of us to look after things. Eh? What did you say?"

"I was just thinking," said Mr. Cox.

SAM'S BOY

IT was getting late in the afternoon as Master Jones, in a somewhat famished condition, strolled up Aldgate, with a keen eye on the gutter, in search of anything that would serve him for his tea. Too late, he wished that he had saved some of the stale bread and damaged fruit which had constituted his dinner.

Aldgate proving barren, he turned up into the quieter Minories, skilfully dodging the mechanical cuff of the constable at the corner as he passed, and watching with some interest the efforts of a stray mongrel to get itself adopted. Its victim had sworn at it, cut at it with his stick, and even made little runs at it—all to no purpose. Finally, being a soft-hearted man, he was weak enough to pat the cowering schemer on the head, and, being frantically licked by the homeless one, took it up in his arms and walked off with it.

Billy Jones watched the proceedings with interest, not un-tempered by envy. If he had only been a dog! The dog passed in the man's arms, and, with a whine of ecstasy, insisted upon licking his ear. They went on their way, the dog wondering between licks what sort of table the man kept, and the man speculating idly as to a descent which appeared to have included, among other things, an ant-eater.

"'E's all right," said the orphan, wistfully; "no coppers to chivvy 'im about, and as much grub as he wants. Wish I'd been a dog."

He tied up his breeches with a piece of string which was lying on the pavement, and, his hands being now free, placed them in a couple of rents which served as pockets, and began to whistle. He was not a proud boy, and was quite willing to take a lesson even from the humblest. Surely he was as useful as a dog!

The thought struck him just as a stout, kindly-looking seaman passed with a couple of shipmates. It was a good-natured face, and the figure was that of a man who lived well. A moment's

114

hesitation, and Master Jones, with a courage born of despair, ran after him and tugged him by the sleeve.

"Halloa!" said Mr. Samuel Brown, looking round. "What do you want?"

"Want you, father," said Master Jones.

The jolly seaman's face broke into a smile. So also did the faces of the jolly seaman's friends.

"I'm not your father, matey," he said, good-naturedly.

"Yes, you are," said the desperate Billy; "you know you are."

"You've made a mistake, my lad," said Mr. Brown, still smiling. "Here, run away."

He felt in his trouser-pocket and produced a penny. It was a gift, not a bribe, but it had by no means the effect its donor intended. Master Jones, now quite certain that he had made a wise choice of a father, trotted along a yard or two in the rear.

"Look here, my lad," exclaimed Mr. Brown, goaded into action by intercepting a smile with which Mr Charles Legge had favoured Mr. Harry Green, "you run off home."

"Where do you live now?" inquired Billy, anxiously.

Mr. Green, disdaining concealment, slapped Mr. Legge on the back, and, laughing uproariously, regarded Master Jones with much kindness.

"You mustn't follow me," said Sam, severely; "d'ye hear?"

"All right, father," said the boy, dutifully.

"And don't call me father," vociferated Mr. Brown.

"Why not?" inquired the youth, artlessly.

Mr. Legge stopped suddenly, and, putting his hand on Mr. Green's shoulder, gaspingly expressed his inability to go any farther. Mr. Green, patting his back, said he knew how he felt, because he felt the same, and, turning to Sam, told him he'd be the death of him if he wasn't more careful.

"If you don't run away," said Mr. Brown, harshly, as he turned to the boy, "I shall give you a hiding."

"Where am I to run to?" whimpered Master Jones, dodging off and on.

"Run 'ome," said Sam.

"That's where I'm going," said Master Jones following.

"Better try and give 'im the slip, Sam" said Mr. Legge, in a confidential whisper; "though it seems a unnatural thing to do."

"Unnatural? What d'ye mean?" demanded his unfortunate friend. "Wot d'ye mean by unnatural?"

"Oh, if you're going to talk like that, Sam," said Mr. Legge, shortly, "it's no good giving you advice. As you've made your bed, you must lay on it."

"How long is it since you saw 'im last, matey?" inquired Mr. Green.

"I dunno; not very long," replied the boy, cautiously.

"Has he altered at all since you see 'im last?" inquired the counsel for the defence, motioning the fermenting Mr. Brown to keep still.

"No," said Billy, firmly; "not a bit."

"Wot's your name?"

"Billy," was the reply.

"Billy wot?"

"Billy Jones."

Mr. Green's face cleared, and he turned to his friends with a smile of joyous triumph. Sam's face reflected his own, but Charlie Legge's was still overcast.

"It ain't likely," he said, impressively; "it ain't likely as Sam would go and get married twice in the same name, is it? Put it to yourself, 'Arry—would you?"

"Look 'ere," exclaimed the infuriated Mr. Brown, "don't you interfere in my business. You're a crocodile, that's wot you are. As for you, you little varmint, you run off, d'ye hear?"

He moved on swiftly, accompanied by the other two, and set an example of looking straight ahead of him, which was, however, lost upon his friends.

"'E's still following of you, Sam," said the crocodile, in by no means disappointed tones.

"Sticking like a leech," confirmed Mr. Green. "'E's a pretty little chap, rather."

"Takes arter 'is mother," said the vengeful Mr. Legge.

The unfortunate Sam said nothing, but strode a haunted man down Nightingale Lane into Wapping High Street, and so to the ketch *Nancy Bell*, which was lying at Shrimpett's Wharf. He stepped on board without a word, and only when he turned to descend the forecastle-ladder did his gaze rest for a moment on the small, forlorn piece of humanity standing on the wharf.

"Halloa boy, what do you want?" cried the skipper, catching sight of him.

"Want my father, sir—Sam," replied the youth, who had kept his ears open.

The skipper got up from his seat and eyed him curiously; Messrs. Legge and Green, drawing near, explained the situation. Now the skipper was a worldly man; and Samuel Brown, A.B., when at home, played a brass instrument in the Salvation Army band. He regarded the boy kindly and spoke him fair.

"Don't run away," he said, anxiously.

"I'm not going to, sir," said Master Jones, charmed with his manner, and he watched breathlessly as the skipper stepped forward, and, peering down the forecastle, called loudly for Sam.

"Yes, sir," said a worried voice.

"Your boy's asking after you," said the skipper, grinning madly.

"He's not my boy, sir," replied Mr. Brown, through his clenched teeth.

"Well, you'd better come up and see him," said the other. "Are you sure he isn't, Sam?"

Mr. Brown made no reply, but coming on deck met Master Jones's smile of greeting with an icy stare, and started convulsively as the skipper beckoned the boy aboard.

"He's been rather neglected, Sam," said the skipper, shaking his head.

"Wot's it got to do with me?" said Sam, violently. "I tell you I've never seen 'im afore this arternoon."

"You hear what your father says," said the skipper—— ("Hold your tongue, Sam.) Where's your mother, boy?"

"Dead, sir," whined Master Jones. "I've on'y got 'im now."

The skipper was a kind-hearted man, and he looked pityingly at the forlorn little figure by his side. And Sam was the good man of the ship and a leading light at Dimport.

"How would you like to come to sea with your father?" he inquired.

The grin of delight with which Master Jones received this proposal was sufficient reply.

"I wouldn't do it for everybody," pursued the skipper, glancing severely at the mate, who was behaving foolishly, "but I don't mind obliging you, Sam. He can come."

"*Obliging*?" repeated Mr. Brown, hardly able to get the words out. "Obliging *me*? I don't want to be obliged."

"There, there," interrupted the skipper. "I don't want any thanks. Take him forrard and give him something to eat—he looks half starved, poor little chap."

He turned away and went down to the cabin, while the cook, whom Mr. Brown had publicly rebuked for his sins the day before, led the boy to the galley and gave him a good meal. After that was done Charlie washed him, and Harry going ashore, begged a much-worn suit of boy's clothes from a foreman of his acquaintance. He also brought back a message from the foreman to Mr. Brown to the effect that he was surprised at him.

The conversation that evening after Master Jones was asleep turned upon bigamy, but Mr. Brown snored through it all, though Mr. Legge's remark that the revelations of that afternoon had thrown a light upon many little things in his behaviour which had hitherto baffled him, came perilously near to awaking him.

At six in the morning they got under way, the boy going nearly frantic with delight as sail after sail was set, and the ketch, with a stiff breeze, rapidly left London behind her. Mr. Brown studiously ignored him, but the other men pampered him to his heart's content, and even the cabin was good enough to manifest a little concern in his welfare, the skipper calling Mr. Brown up no fewer than five times that day to complain about his son's behaviour.

"I can't have somersaults on this 'ere ship, Sam," he remarked, shaking his head; "it ain't the place for 'em."

"I wonder at you teaching 'im such things," said the mate, in grave disapprobation.

"Me?" said the hapless Sam, trembling with passion.

"He must 'ave seen you do it," said the mate, letting his eye rove casually over Sam's ample proportions. "You must ha' been leading a double life altogether, Sam."

"That's nothing to do with us," interrupted the skipper, impatiently. "I don't mind Sam turning cart-wheels all day if it amuses him, but they mustn't do it here, that's all. It's no good standing there sulking, Sam; I can't have it."

He turned away, and Mr. Brown, unable to decide whether he was mad or drunk, or both, walked back, and, squeezing himself up in the bows, looked miserably over the sea. Behind him the men disported themselves with Master Jones, and once, looking over his shoulder, he actually saw the skipper giving him a lesson in steering.

By the following afternoon he was in such a state of collapse that, when they put in at the small port of Withersea to discharge a portion of the cargo, he obtained permission to stay below in his bunk. Work proceeded without him, and at nine o'clock in the evening they sailed again, and it was not until they were a couple of miles on their way to Dimport that Mr. Legge rushed aft with the announcement that he was missing.

"Don't talk nonsense," said the skipper, as he came up from below in response to a hail from the mate.

"It's a fact, sir," said Mr. Legge, shaking his head.

"What's to be done with the boy?" demanded the mate, blankly.

"Sam's a unsteady, unreliable, tricky old man," exclaimed the skipper, hotly; "the idea of going and leaving a boy on our hands like that. I'm surprised at him. I'm disappointed in Sam—deserting!"

"I expect 'e's larfing like anything, sir," remarked Mr. Legge.

"Get forrard," said the skipper, sharply; "get forrard at once, d'ye hear?"

"But what's to be done with the boy?—that's what I want to know," said the mate.

"What d'ye think's to be done with him?" bawled the skipper. "We can't chuck him overboard, can we?"

"I mean when we get to Dimport?" growled the mate.

"Well, the men'll talk," said the skipper, calming down a little, "and perhaps Sam's wife'll come and take him. If not, I suppose he'll have to go to the workhouse. Anyway, it's got nothing to do with me. I wash my hands of it altogether."

He went below again, leaving the mate at the wheel. A murmur of voices came from the forecastle, where the crew were discussing the behaviour of their late colleague. The bereaved Master Jones, whose face was streaky with the tears of disappointment, looked on from his bunk.

"What are you going to do, Billy?" inquired the cook.

"I dunno," said the boy, miserably.

He sat up in his bunk in a brown study, ever and anon turning his sharp little eyes from one to another of the men. Then, with a final sniff to the memory of his departed parent, he composed himself to sleep.

With the buoyancy of childhood he had forgotten his trouble by the morning, and ran idly about the ship as before, until in the afternoon they came in sight of Dimport. Mr. Legge, who had a considerable respect for the brain hidden in that small head, pointed it out to him, and with some curiosity waited for his remarks.

"I can see it," said Master Jones, briefly.

"That's where Sam lives," said his friend, pointedly.

"Yes," said the boy, nodding, "all of you live there, don't you?"

It was an innocent enough remark in all conscience, but there was that in Master Jones's eye which caused Mr. Legge to move away hastily and glance at him in some disquietude from the other side of the deck. The boy, unconscious of the interest excited by his movements, walked restlessly up and down.

"Boy's worried," said the skipper, aside, to the mate; "cheer up, sonny."

Billy looked up and smiled, and the cloud which had sat on his brow when he thought of the cold-blooded desertion of Mr. Brown gave way to an expression of serene content.

"Well, what's he going to do?" inquired the mate, in a low voice.

"That needn't worry us," said the skipper. "Let things take their course; that's my motto."

He took the wheel from Harry; the little town came closer; the houses separated and disclosed roads, and the boy discovered to his disappointment that the church stood on ground of its own, and not on the roof of a large red house as he had supposed. He ran forward as they got closer, and, perching up in the bows until they were fast to the quay, looked round searchingly for any signs of Sam.

The skipper locked up the cabin, and then calling on one of the shore-hands to keep an eye on the forecastle, left it open for the convenience of the small passenger. Harry, Charlie, and the cook stepped ashore. The skipper and mate followed, and the latter, looking back from some distance, called his attention to the desolate little figure sitting on the hatch.

"I s'pose he'll be all right," said the skipper, uneasily; "there's food and a bed down the fo'c's'le. You might just look round to-night and see he's safe. I expect we'll have to take him back to London with us."

They turned up a small road in the direction of home and walked on in silence, until the mate, glancing behind at an acquaintance who had just passed, uttered a sharp exclamation. The skipper turned, and a small figure which had just shot round the corner stopped in mid-career and eyed them warily. The men exchanged uneasy glances.

"Father," cried a small voice.

"He—he's adopted you now," said the skipper, huskily.

"Or you," said the mate. "I never took much notice of him."

He looked round again. Master Jones was following briskly, about ten yards in the rear, and twenty yards behind him came the crew, who, having seen him quit the ship, had followed with the evident intention of being in at the death.

"Father," cried the boy again, "wait for me."

One or two passers-by stared in astonishment, and the mate began to be uneasy as to the company he was keeping.

"Let's separate," he growled, "and see who he's calling after."

The skipper caught him by the arm. "Shout out to him to go back," he cried.

"It's you he's after, I tell you," said the mate. "Who do you want, Billy?"

"I want my father," cried the youth, and, to prevent any mistake, indicated the raging skipper with his finger.

"*Who* do you want?" bellowed the latter, in a frightful voice.

"Want you, father," chirruped Master Jones.

Wrath and dismay struggled for supremacy in the skipper's face, and he paused to decide whether it would be better to wipe Master Jones off the face of the earth or to pursue his way in all the strength of conscious innocence. He chose the latter course, and, a shade more erect than usual, walked on until he came in sight of his house and his wife, who was standing at the door.

"You come along o' me, Jem, and explain," he whispered to the mate. Then he turned about and hailed the crew. The crew, flattered at being offered front seats in the affair, came forward eagerly.

"What's the matter?" inquired Mrs. Hunt, eyeing the crowd in amazement as it grouped itself in anticipation.

"Nothing," said her husband, off-handedly.

"Who's that boy?" cried the innocent woman.

"It's a poor little mad boy," began the skipper; "he came aboard——"

"I'm not mad, father," interrupted Master Jones.

"A poor little mad boy," continued the skipper, hastily, "who came aboard in London and said poor old Sam Brown was his father."

"No—you, father," cried the boy, shrilly.

"He calls everybody his father," said the skipper, with a smile of anguish; "that's the form his madness takes. He called Jem here his father."

"No, he didn't," said the mate, bluntly.

"And then he thought Charlie was his father."

"No, sir," said Mr. Legge, with respectful firmness.

"Well, he said Sam Brown was," said the skipper.

"Yes, that's right, sir," said the crew.

"Where is Sam?" inquired Mrs. Hunt, looking round expectantly.

"He deserted the ship at Withersea," said her husband.

"I see," said Mrs. Hunt, with a bitter smile, "and these men have all come up prepared to swear that the boy said Sam was his father. Haven't you?"

"Yes, mum," chorused the crew, delighted at being understood so easily.

Mrs. Hunt looked across the road to the fields stretching beyond. Then she suddenly brought her gaze back, and, looking full at her husband, uttered just two words—

"Oh, Joe!"

"Ask the mate," cried the frantic skipper.

"Yes, I know what the mate'll say," said Mrs. Hunt. "I've no need to ask him."

"Charlie and Harry were with Sam when the boy came up to them," protested the skipper.

"I've no doubt," said his wife. "Oh, Joe! Joe! Joe!"

There was an uncomfortable silence, during which the crew, standing for the most part on one leg in sympathy with their chief's embarrassment, nudged each other to say something to clear the character of a man whom all esteemed.

"You ungrateful little devil," burst out Mr. Legge, at length; "arter the kind way the skipper treated you, too."

"Did he treat him kindly?" inquired the captain's wife, in conversational tones.

"Like a fa—like a uncle, mum," said the thoughtless Mr. Legge. "Gave 'im a passage on the ship and fairly spoilt 'im. We was all surprised at the fuss 'e made of 'im; wasn't we, Harry?"

He turned to his friend, but on Mr. Green's face there was an expression of such utter scorn and contempt that his own fell. He glanced at the skipper, and was almost frightened at his appearance.

The situation was ended by Mrs. Hunt entering the house and closing the door with an ominous bang. The men slunk off, headed by Mr. Legge; and the mate, after a few murmured words of encouragement to the skipper, also departed. Captain Hunt looked first at the small cause of his trouble, who had drawn off to some distance, and then at the house. Then, with a determined gesture, he turned the handle of the door and walked in. His wife, who was sitting in an armchair, with her eyes on the floor, remained motionless.

"Look here, Polly——," he began.

"Don't talk to me," was the reply. "I wonder you can look me in the face."

The skipper ground his teeth, and strove to maintain an air of judicial calm.

"If you'll only be reasonable——," he remarked, severely.

"I thought there was something secret going on," said Mrs. Hunt. "I've often looked at you when you've been sitting in that chair, with a worried look on your face, and wondered what it was. But I never thought it was so bad as this. I'll do you the credit to say that I never thought of such a thing as this. . . . What did you say? . . . What?"

"I said 'damn!'" said the skipper, explosively.

"Yes, I've no doubt," said his wife, fiercely. "You think you're going to carry it off with a high hand and bluster; but you won't bluster me, my man. I'm not one of your meek and mild women who'll put up with anything. I'm not one of your——"

"I tell you," said the skipper, "that the boy calls everybody his father. I dare say he's claimed another by this time."

Even as he spoke the handle turned, and the door opening a few inches disclosed the anxious face of Master Jones. Mrs. Hunt, catching the skipper's eye, pointed to it in an ecstasy of silent wrath. There was a breathless pause, broken at last by the boy.

"Mother!" he said, softly.

Mrs. Hunt stiffened in her chair and her arms fell by her side as she gazed in speechless amazement. Master Jones, opening the door a little wider, gently insinuated his small figure into the room. The skipper gave one glance at his wife, and then, turning hastily away, put his hand over his mouth, and, with protruding eyes, gazed out of the window.

"Mother, can I come in?" said the boy.

"Oh, Polly!" sighed the skipper. Mrs. Hunt strove to regain the utterance of which astonishment had deprived her.

"I . . . what . . . Joe . . . don't be a fool!"

"Yes, I've no doubt," said the skipper, theatrically. "Oh, Polly! Polly! Polly!"

He put his hand over his mouth again and laughed silently, until his wife, coming behind him, took him by the shoulders and shook him violently.

"This," said the skipper, choking; "this is what . . . you've been worried about. . . . This is the secret what's——"

He broke off suddenly as his wife thrust him by main force into a chair, and standing over him with a fiery face dared him to say another word. Then she turned to the boy.

"What do you mean by calling me 'mother'?" she demanded. "I'm not your mother."

"Yes, you are," said Master Jones.

Mrs. Hunt eyed him in bewilderment, and then, roused to a sense of her position by a renewed gurgling from the skipper's chair, set to work to try and thump that misguided man into a more serious frame of mind. Failing in this, she sat down, and, after a futile struggle, began to laugh herself, and that so heartily that Master Jones, smiling sympathetically, closed the door, and came boldly into the room.

The statement, generally believed, that Captain Hunt and his wife adopted him, is incorrect, the skipper accounting for his continued presence in the house by the simple explanation that he had adopted them,—an explanation which Mr. Samuel Brown, for one, finds quite easy of acceptance.

A WILL AND A WAY

THE old man sat over the tap-room fire at the "Cauliflower," his gnarled, swollen hands fondled the warm bowl of his long pipe, and an ancient eye watched with almost youthful impatience the slow warming of a mug of beer on the hob.

He had just given unasked-for statistics to the visitor at the inn who was sitting the other side of the hearth. His head was stored with the births, marriages, and deaths of Claybury, and with a view of being entertaining he had already followed, from the cradle to the altar and the altar to the grave, the careers of some of the most uninteresting people that ever breathed.

"No, there ain't been a great sight o' single men hereabouts," he said, in answer to a question. "Claybury 'as always been a marrying sort o' place—not because the women are more good-looking than others, but because they are sharper."

He reached forward, and, taking up his beer, drank with relish. The generous liquor warmed his blood, and his eye brightened.

"I've buried two wives, but I 'ave to be careful myself, old as I am," he said, thoughtfully. "There's more than one woman about 'ere as would like to change 'er name for mine. Claybury's got the name for being a marrying place, and they don't like to see even a widow-man.

"Now and agin we've 'ad a young feller as said as 'e wouldn't get married. There was Jem Burn, for one, and it ain't a month ago since four of 'is grandchildren carried him to the churchyard; and there was Walter Bree: 'e used to prove as 'ow any man that got married wasn't in 'is right mind, and 'e got three years in prison for wot they call bigamy.

"But there used to be one man in these parts as the Claybury women couldn't marry, try as they might. He was a ugly little man with red 'air and a foxy face. They used to call 'im Foxy Green, and 'e kept 'appy and single for years and years.

"He wasn't a man as disliked being in the company o' women

though, and that's wot used to aggeravate 'em. He'd take 'em out for walks, or give 'em a lift in 'is cart, but none of 'em could get 'old of 'im, not even the widders. He used to say 'e loved 'em all too much to tie hisself up to any one of 'em, and 'e would sit up 'ere of a night at the "Cauliflower" and send men with large families a'most crazy by calkerlating 'ow many pints o' beer their children wore out every year in the shape o' boots.

"Sometimes 'is uncle, old Ebenezer Green, used to sit up 'ere with 'im. He was a strong, 'earty old man, and 'e'd sit and laugh at Foxy till 'is chair shook under 'im. He was a lively sporting sort o' man, and when Foxy talked like that 'e seemed to be keeping some joke to hisself which nearly choked 'im.

"'You'll marry when I'm gone, Foxy,' he'd say.

"'Not me,' ses Foxy.

"Then the old man 'ud laugh agin and talk mysterious about fox-hunts and say 'e wondered who'd get Foxy's brush. He said 'e'd only got to shut 'is eyes and 'e could see the pack in full cry through Claybury village, and Foxy going 'is 'ardest with 'is tongue 'anging out.

"Foxy couldn't say anything to 'im, because it was understood that when the old man died 'e was to 'ave 'is farm and 'is money; so 'e used to sit there and smile as if 'e liked it.

"When Foxy was about forty-three 'is uncle died. The old man's mind seemed to wander at the last, and 'e said what a good man 'e'd always been, and wot a comfort it was to 'im now that 'e was goin. And 'e mentioned a lot o' little sums o' money owed 'im in the village which nobody could remember.

"'I've made my will, Foxy,' he ses, 'and schoolmaster's takin' care of it; I've left it all to you.'

"'All right,' ses Foxy. 'Thankee.'

"'He's goin' to read it arter the funeral,' ses 'is uncle, 'which is the proper way to do it. I'd give anything to be there, Foxy, and see your face.'

"Those were 'is last words, but 'e laughed once or twice, and for a long time arter 'e'd gone Foxy Green sat there and wondered at 'is last words and wot there was to laugh about.

"The old man was buried a few days after, and Foxy stood by the grave 'olding a 'andkerchief to 'is eyes, and behaving as though 'e 'ad lost money instead of coming in for it. Then they went back to the farm, and the first thing the schoolmaster did was to send all the women off before reading the will.

"'Wot's that for?' ses Foxy, staring.

"'You'll see,' ses the schoolmaster; 'them was my instructions.

It's for your sake, Mr. Green; to give you a chance—at least, that's wot your uncle said.'

"He sat down and took out the will and put on 'is spectacles. Then 'e spread it out on the table and took a glass o' gin and water and began to read.

"It was all straightforward enough. The farm and stock, and two cottages, and money in the bank, was all left to Josiah Green, commonly called Foxy Green, on condition——

"There was such a noise o' clapping, and patting Foxy on the back, that the schoolmaster 'ad to leave off and wait for quiet.

"'On condition,' he ses, in a loud voice, 'that he marries the first Claybury woman, single or widow, that asks 'im to marry her in the presence of three witnesses. If he refuses, the property is to go to 'er instead.'

"Foxy turned round like mad then, and asked Henery Walker wot 'e was patting 'im on the back for. Then, in a choking voice, he asked to 'ave it read agin.

"'Well, there's one thing about it, Mr. Green,' ses Henery Walker; 'with all your property you'll be able to 'ave the pick o' the prettiest gals in Claybury.'

"'Ow's that?' ses Joe Chambers, very sharp; 'he's got to take the first woman that asks 'im, don't matter wot 'er age is.'

"He got up suddenly, and, without even saying good-bye to Foxy, rushed out of the 'ouse and off over the fields as 'ard as 'e could go.

"'Wot's the matter with 'im?' ses Foxy.

"Nobody could give any answer, and they sat there staring at each other, till all of a sudden Henery Walker jumps up and goes off if anything 'arder than wot Joe Chambers had done.

"'Anything wrong with the drink?' ses Foxy, puzzled like.

"They shook their 'eads agin, and then Peter Gubbins, who'd been staring 'ard with 'is mouth open, got up and gave the table a bang with 'is fist.

"'Joe Chambers 'as gone arter 'is sister,' he ses, 'and Henery Walker arter 'is wife's sister, as 'e's been keeping for this last six months. That's wot they've gone for.'

"Everybody saw it then, and in two minutes Foxy and the schoolmaster was left alone looking at each other and the empty table.

"'Well, I'm in for a nice thing,' ses Foxy. 'Fancy being proposed to by Henery Walker's sister-in-law! Ugh!'

"'It'll be the oldest ones that'll be the most determined,' said the schoolmaster, shaking 'is 'ead. 'Wot are you going to do?'

"'I don't know,' ses Foxy, 'it's so sudden. But they've got to 'ave three witnesses, that's one comfort. I'd like to tell Joe Chambers wot I think of 'im and 'is precious sister.'

"It was very curious the way the women took it. One an' all of 'em pretended as it was an insult to the sex, and they said if Foxy Green waited till 'e was asked to marry he'd wait long enough. Little chits o' gals o' fourteen and fifteen was walking about tossing their 'eads up and as good as saying they might 'ave Green's farm for the asking, but they wouldn't ask. Old women of seventy and over said that if Foxy wanted to marry them he'd 'ave to ask, and ask a good many times too.

"Of course, this was all very well in its way, but at the same time three Claybury gals that was away in service was took ill and 'ad to come 'ome, and several other women that was away took their holidays before their relations knew anything about it. Almost every 'ouse in Claybury 'ad got some female relation staying in it, and they was always explaining to everybody why it was they 'ad come 'ome. None of 'em so much as mentioned Foxy Green.

"Women are artful creatures and think a lot of appearances. There wasn't one of 'em as would ha' minded wot other folks said if they'd caught Foxy, but they'd ha' gone half crazy with shame if they'd tried and not managed it. And they couldn't do things on the quiet because of the three witnesses. That was the 'ardship of it.

"It was the only thing talked about in Claybury, and Foxy Green soon showed as he was very wide-awake. First thing 'e did was to send the gal that used to do the dairy-work and the 'ouse-work off. Then 'e bought a couple o' large, fierce dogs and chained 'em up, one near the front door and one near the back. They was very good dogs, and they bit Foxy hisself two or three times so as to let 'im see that they knew wot they was there for.

"He took George Smith, a young feller that used to work on the farm, into the 'ouse, and for the fust week or two 'e rather enjoyed the excitement. But when 'e found that 'e couldn't go into the village, or even walk about 'is own farm in safety, he turned into a reg'lar woman-hater.

"The artful tricks those women 'ad wouldn't be believed. One day when Foxy was eating 'is dinner William Hall drove up to the gate in a cart, and when George came out to know wot 'e wanted, 'e said that he 'ad just bought some pigs at Rensham and would Foxy like to make fust offer for 'em.

"George went in, and when 'e came out agin he said William

Hall was to go inside. He 'eld the dog while William went by, and as soon as Foxy 'eard wot 'e wanted 'e asked 'im to wait till 'e'd finished 'is dinner, and then he'd go out and 'ave a look at 'em.

"'I was wantin' some pigs bad,' he ses, 'and the worst of it is I can't get out to buy any as things are.'

"'That's wot I thought,' ses William Hall; 'that's why I brought 'em to you.'

"'You deserve to get on, William,' ses Foxy. 'George,' he ses, turning to 'im.

"'Yes,' ses George.

"'Do you know much about pigs?'

"'I know a pig when I see one,' ses George.

"'That's all I want,' ses Foxy; 'go and 'ave a look at 'em.'

"William Hall gave a start as George walked out, and a minute afterwards both of 'em 'eard an awful noise, and George came back rubbing 'is 'ead and saying that when 'e lifted up the cloth one o' the pigs was William Hall's sister and the others was 'er nephews. William said it was a joke, but Foxy said he didn't like jokes, and if William thought that 'e or George was going to walk with 'im past the dog 'e was mistook.

"Two days arter that, Foxy, 'appening to look out of 'is bedroom window, saw one o' the Claybury boys racing 'is cows all up and down the meadow. He came down quietly and took up a stick, and then 'e set out to race that boy up and down. He'd always been a good runner, and the boy was 'alf-blown like. 'E gave a yell as 'e saw Foxy coming arter 'im, and left the cow 'e was chasin' and ran straight for the 'edge, with Foxy close behind 'im.

"Foxy was within two yards of 'im when 'e suddenly caught sight of a blue bonnet waiting behind the 'edge, and 'e turned round and went back to the 'ouse as fast as 'e could go and locked 'imself in. And 'e 'ad to sit there, half-busting, all the morning, and watch that boy chase 'is best cows up and down the meadow without daring to go out and stop 'im.

"He sent George down to tell the boy's father that night, and the father sent back word that if Foxy 'ad got anything to say agin 'is boy why didn't 'e come down like a man and say it hisself?

"Arter about three weeks o' this sort o' thing Foxy Green began to see that 'e would 'ave to get married whether he liked it or not, and 'e told George so. George's idea was for 'im to get the oldest woman in Claybury to ask 'im in marriage, because then he'd soon be single agin. It was a good idea, on'y Foxy didn't seem to fancy it.

"'Who do you think is the prettiest gal in Claybury, George?' he ses.

"'Flora Pottle,' ses George, at once.

"'That's exactly my idea,' ses Foxy; 'if I've got to marry, I'll marry 'er. However, I'll sleep on it a night and see 'ow I feel in the morning.'

"'I'll marry Flora Pottle,' he ses, when 'e got up. 'You can go round this arternoon, George, and break the good news to 'er.'

"George tidied hisself up arter dinner and went. Flora Pottle was a very fine-looking gal, and she was very much surprised when George walked in, but she was more surprised when 'e told 'er that if she was to go over and ask Foxy to be 'er 'usband he wouldn't say 'No.'

"Mrs. Pottle jumped out of 'er skin for joy a'most. She'd 'ad a 'ard time of it with Flora and five young children since 'er 'usband died, and she could 'ardly believe 'er ears when Flora said she wouldn't.'

"''E's old enough to be my father,' she ses.

"'Old men make the best 'usbands,' ses George, coaxing 'er; 'and, besides, think o' the farm.'

"'That's wot you've got to think of,' ses her mother. 'Don't think o' Foxy Green at all; think o' the farm.'

"Flora stood and leaned herself up agin a chest o' drawers and twisted 'er hands, and at last she sent back word to say that she wanted time to think it over.

"Foxy Green was very much astonished when George took back that answer. He'd thought that any gal would ha' jumped at 'im without the farm, and arter going upstairs and looking at hisself in the glass 'e was more astonished than ever.

"When George Smith went up to the Pottles agin the next day Flora made a face at 'im, and 'e felt as orkard as if 'e'd been courting 'er hisself a'most. At first she wouldn't 'ave anything to say to 'im at all, but went on sweeping out the room, and nearly choking 'im. Then George Smith, wot was a likely young feller, put 'is arm round 'er waist, and, taking the broom away from 'er, made 'er sit down beside 'im while 'e gave 'er Foxy's message.

"He did Foxy's courting for 'im for an hour, although it on'y seemed about five minutes to both of 'em. Then Mrs. Pottle came in, and arter a lot of talk Flora was got to say that George Smith might come agin for five minutes next day.

"Foxy went on dreadful when 'e 'eard that Flora 'adn't given an answer, but George Smith, who liked the job much better than farming or making beds, told 'im she was coming round, and that it was on'y natural a young gal should like to be courted a bit afore givin' in.

"'Yes,' ses Foxy, biting 'is lip, 'but 'ow 's it to be done?'

"'You leave it to me,' ses George Smith, 'and it'll be all right. I sit there and talk about the farm as well as wot you could.'

"'And about me too, I s'pose?' ses Foxy, catching 'im up.

"'Yes,' ses George; 'I tell 'er all sorts o' lies about you.'

"Foxy looked at 'im a moment, and then 'e went off grumbling. He was like a good many more men, and because Flora Pottle didn't seem to want 'im 'e on'y fancied 'er the more. Next day 'e sent George Smith up with an old brooch as a present, and when George came back 'e said 'e thought that if it 'ad been a new one it would 'ave done wot was wanted.

"You can't keep secrets in Claybury, and it soon got round wot Foxy Green was arter. That made the other women more determined than ever, and at last Foxy sent up word that if Flora wo'ldn't ask 'im to let 'im know, as 'e was tired o' being a prisoner, and old Mrs. Ball 'ad nearly 'ad 'im the day afore.

"It took George Smith two hours' 'ard courtin' afore he could get Flora Pottle to say 'Yes,' but at last she did, and then Mrs. Pottle came in, and she shook 'ands with George, and gave 'im a glass o' beer. Mrs. Pottle wanted to take 'er up to Green's farm there and then, but Flora said no. She said they'd go up at eight o'clock in the evening', and the sacrifice should be made then.

"Foxy didn't like the word 'sacrifice' at all, but if 'e'd got to be married 'e'd sooner marry Flora than anybody, and 'e 'ad to put up with it.

"'There'll be you for one witness,' he ses to George, 'and Mrs. Pottle is two; wot about the third?'

"'I should 'ave 'alf a dozen, so as to make sure,' ses George.

"Foxy thought it was a good idea, and without letting 'em know wot it was for, 'e asked Henery Walker and Joe Chambers, and three or four more 'e 'ad a grudge against for trying to marry 'im to their relations, to come up and see that 'e'd been able to pick and choose.

"They came at ha'-past seven, and at eight o'clock there was a knock at the door, and George, arter carefully looking round, let in Mrs. Pottle and Flora. She was a fine-looking gal, and as she stood there looking at all them astonished men, 'er face all blushes and 'er eyes large and shining, Foxy thought getting married wasn't such a bad thing arter all. He gave 'er a chair to sit on, and then 'e coughed and waited.

"'It's a fine night,' he ses, at last.

"'Beautiful,' ses Mrs. Pottle.

"Flora didn't say anything. She sat there shuffling 'er feet on the carpet, and Foxy Green kept on looking at 'er and waiting for 'er to speak, and 'oping that she wouldn't grow up like 'er mother.

"'Go on, Flora,' ses Mrs. Pottle, nudging 'er.

"'Go on, Flora,' ses Henery Walker, mimicking 'er. 'I s'pose you've come to ask Foxy a question by the look of it?'

"'Yes,' ses Flora, looking up. 'Are you quite well, Mr. Green?'

"'Yes, yes,' ses Foxy; 'but you didn't come up 'ere to ask me that.'

"'It's all I could do to get 'er 'ere at all, Mr. Green,' says Mrs. Pottle; 'she's that shy you can't think. She'd rather ha' 'ad you ask 'er yourself.'

"'That can't be done,' ses Foxy, shaking 'is 'ead. 'Leastways, I'm not going to risk it.'

"'Now, Flora,' ses 'er mother, nudging 'er agin.

"'Come on, Flora Pottle,' ses Bob Hunt; 'we're all a-waitin'.'

"'Shut your eyes and open your mouth, as if Foxy was a powder,' ses Henery Walker.

"'I can't,' ses Flora, turning to her mother. 'I can't and I won't.'

"'Flora Pottle,' ses 'er mother, firing up.

"'I won't,' ses Flora, firing up too; 'you've been bothering me all day long for ever so long, and I won't. I 'ate the sight of 'im. He's the ugliest man in Claybury.'

"Mrs. Pottle began to cry and say that she'd disgraced 'er; but Foxy Green looked at 'er and 'e ses, 'Very well, Flora Pottle, then we'll say no more about it. Good evening.'

"'Good evening,' ses Mrs. Pottle, getting up and giving Flora a shake. 'Come along, you tantalising mawther, do. You'll die an old maid, that's what you'll do.'

"'That's all you know,' ses Flora, smiling over at George Smith; 'but if you're so fond o' Mr. Green why don't you ask 'im yourself? He can't say "No."'

"For half a minute the room was as quiet as a grave, and the on'y thing that moved was Foxy Green's eyes as he looked fust at the door at the other end of the room and then at the window.

"'Lor' bless my soul!' ses Mrs. Pottle, in a surprised voice. 'I never thought of it.'

"She sat down agin and smiled at Foxy as if she could eat 'im.

"'I can't think why I didn't think of it,' she ses, looking round. 'I was going out like a lamb. Mr. Green——'

"'One moment,' ses Foxy, 'olding up 'is 'and. 'I should be a terrible, bad, cruel, unkind husband to anybody I didn't like.

Don't say words you'll be sorry for arterwards, Mrs. Pottle.'

"'I'm not going to,' ses Mrs. Pottle; 'the words I'm going to say will be good for both of us; I'm far more suitable for you than a young gal—Mr. Green, will you marry me?'

"Foxy Green looked at 'er for a moment, and then 'e looked round at all them grinning men wot he'd brought there by mistake to see 'im made a fool of. Then in a low, 'usky voice he ses, 'I will.'"

JERRY BUNDLER

IT wanted a few nights to Christmas, a festival for which the small market-town of Torchester was making extensive preparations. The narrow streets which had been thronged with people were now almost deserted; the cheap-jack from London, with the remnant of breath left him after his evening's exertions, was making feeble attempts to blow out his naphtha lamp, and the last shops open were rapidly closing for the night.

In the comfortable coffe-room of the old "Boar's Head," half a dozen guests, principally commercial travellers, sat talking by the light of the fire. The talk had drifted from trade to politics, from politics to religion, and so by easy stages to the supernatural. Three ghost stories, never known to fail before, had fallen flat; there was too much noise outside, too much light within. The fourth story was told by an old hand with more success; the streets were quiet, and he had turned the gas out. In the flickering light of the fire, as it shone on the glasses and danced with shadows on the walls, the story proved so enthralling that George, the waiter, whose presence had been forgotten, created a very disagreeable sensation by suddenly starting up from a dark corner and gliding silently from the room.

"That's what I call a good story," said one of the men, sipping his hot whisky. "Of course it's an old idea that spirits like to get into the company of human beings. A man told me once that he travelled down the Great Western with a ghost, and hadn't the slightest suspicion of it until the inspector came for tickets. My friend said the way that ghost tried to keep up appearances by feeling for it in all its pockets and looking on the floor was quite touching. Ultimately it gave it up and with a faint groan vanished through the ventilator."

"That'll do, Hirst," said another man.

"It's not a subject for jesting," said a little old gentleman who

134

had been an attentive listener. "I've never seen an apparition myself, but I know people who have, and I consider that they form a very interesting link between us and the after-life. There's a ghost story connected with this house, you know."

"Never heard of it," said another speaker, "and I've been here some years now."

"It dates back a long time now," said the old gentleman. "You've heard about Jerry Bundler, George?"

"Well, I've just 'eard odds and ends, sir," said the old waiter, "but I never put much count to 'em. There was one chap 'ere what said 'e saw it, and the gov'ner sacked 'im prompt."

"My father was a native of this town," said the old gentleman, "and knew the story well. He was a truthful man and a steady churchgoer, but I've heard him declare that once in his life he saw the appearance of Jerry Bundler in this house."

"And who was this Bundler?" inquired a voice.

"A London thief, pickpocket, highwayman—anything he could turn his dishonest hand to," replied the old gentleman; "and he was run to earth in this house one Christmas week some eighty years ago. He took his last supper in this very room, and after he had gone up to bed a couple of Bow Street runners, who had followed him from London but lost the scent a bit, went upstairs with the landlord and tried the door. It was stout oak, and fast, so one went into the yard, and by means of a short ladder got on to the window-sill, while the other stayed outside the door. Those below in the yard saw the man crouching on the sill, and then there was a sudden smash of glass, and with a cry he fell in a heap on the stones at their feet. Then in the moonlight they saw the white face of the pick-pocket peeping over the sill, and while some stayed in the yard, others ran into the house and helped the other man to break the door in. It was difficult to obtain an entrance even then, for it was barred with heavy furniture, but they got in at last, and the first thing that met their eyes was the body of Jerry dangling from the top of the bed by his own handkerchief."

"Which bedroom was it?" asked two or three voices together.

The narrator shook his head. "That I can't tell you; but the story goes that Jerry still haunts this house, and my father used to declare positively that the last time he slept here the ghost of Jerry Bundler lowered itself from the top of his bed and tried to strangle him."

"That'll do," said an uneasy voice. "I wish you'd thought to ask your father which bedroom it was."

"What for?" inquired the old gentleman.

"Well, I should take care not to sleep in it, that's all," said the voice, shortly.

"There's nothing to fear," said the other. "I don't believe for a moment that ghosts could really hurt one. In fact my father used to confess that it was only the unpleasantness of the thing that upset him, and that for all practical purposes Jerry's fingers might have been made of cotton-wool for all the harm they could do."

"That's all very fine," said the last speaker again; "a ghost story is a ghost story, sir; but when a gentleman tells a tale of a ghost in the house in which one is going to sleep, I call it most ungentlemanly!"

"Pooh! nonsense!" said the old gentleman, rising; "ghosts can't hurt you. For my own part, I should rather like to see one. Good night, gentlemen."

"Good night," said the others. "And I only hope Jerry'll pay you a visit," added the nervous man as the door closed.

"Bring some more whisky, George," said a stout commercial; "I want keeping up when the talk turns this way."

"Shall I light the gas, Mr. Malcolm?" said George.

"No; the fire's very comfortable," said the traveller. "Now, gentlemen, any of you know any more?"

"I think we've had enough," said another man; "we shall be thinking we see spirits next, and we're not all like the old gentleman who's just gone."

"Old humbug!" said Hirst. "I should like to put him to the test. Suppose I dress up as Jerry Bundler and go and give him a chance of displaying his courage?"

"Bravo!" said Malcolm, huskily, drowning one or two faint "Noes." "Just for the joke, gentlemen."

"No, no! Drop it, Hirst," said another man.

"Only for the joke," said Hirst, somewhat eagerly. "I've got some things upstairs in which I am going to play in the *Rivals*— knee-breeches, buckles, and all that sort of thing. It's a rare chance. If you'll wait a bit I'll give you a full-dress rehearsal, entitled, 'Jerry Bundler; or, The Nocturnal Strangler.'"

"You won't frighten us," said the commercial, with a husky laugh.

"I don't know that," said Hirst, sharply; "it's a question of acting, that's all. I'm pretty good, ain't I, Somers?"

"Oh, you're all right—for an amateur," said his friend, with a laugh.

"I'll bet you a level sov. you don't frighten me," said the stout traveller.

"Done!" said Hirst. "I'll take the bet to frighten you first and the old gentleman afterwards. These gentlemen shall be the judges."

"You won't frighten us, sir," said another man, "because we're prepared for you; but you'd better leave the old man alone. It's dangerous play."

"Well, I'll try you first," said Hirst, springing up. "No gas, mind."

He ran lightly upstairs to his room, leaving the others, most of whom had been drinking somewhat freely, to wrangle about his proceedings. It ended in two of them going to bed.

"He's crazy on acting," said Somers, lighting his pipe. "Thinks he's the equal of anybody almost. It doesn't matter with us, but I won't let him go to the old man. And he won't mind so long as he gets an opportunity of acting to us."

"Well, I hope he'll hurry up," said Malcolm, yawning; "it's after twelve now."

Nearly half an hour passed. Malcolm drew his watch from his pocket and was busy winding it, when George, the waiter, who had been sent on an errand to the bar, burst suddenly into the room and rushed towards them.

"'E's comin', gentlemen," he said, breathlessly.

"Why, you're frightened, George," said the stout commercial, with a chuckle.

"It was the suddenness of it," said George, sheepishly; "and besides, I didn't look for seein' 'im in the bar. There's only a glimmer of light there, and 'e was sitting on the floor behind the bar. I nearly trod on 'im."

"Oh, you'll never make a man, George," said Malcolm.

"Well, it took me unawares," said the waiter. "Not that I'd have gone to the bar by myself if I'd known 'e was there, and I don't believe you would either, sir."

"Nonsense!" said Malcolm. "I'll go and fetch him in."

"You don't know what it's like, sir," said George, catching him by the sleeve. "It ain't fit to look at by yourself, it ain't, indeed. It's got the—— *What's that?*"

They all started at the sound of a smothered cry from the staircase and the sound of somebody running hurriedly along the passage. Before anybody could speak, the door flew open and a figure bursting into the room flung itself gasping and shivering upon them.

"What is it? What's the matter?" demanded Malcolm. "Why, it's Mr. Hirst." He shook him roughly and then held some spirit to his lips. Hirst drank it greedily and with a sharp intake of his breath gripped him by the arm.

"Light the gas, George," said Malcolm.

The waiter obeyed hastily. Hirst, a ludicrous but pitiable figure in knee-breeches and coat, a large wig all awry, and his face a mess of grease paint, clung to him, trembling.

"Now, what's the matter?" asked Malcolm.

"I've seen it," said Hirst, with a hysterical sob. "O Lord, I'll never play the fool again, never!"

"Seen what?" said the others.

"Him—it—the ghost—anything!" said Hirst, wildly.

"Rot!" said Malcolm, uneasily.

"I was coming down the stairs," said Hirst. "Just capering down—as I thought—it ought to do. I felt a tap——"

He broke off suddenly and peered nervously through the open door into the passage.

"I thought I saw it again," he whispered. "Look—at the foot of the stairs. Can you see anything?"

"No, there's nothing there," said Malcolm, whose own voice shook a little. "Go on. You felt a tap on your shoulder——"

"I turned round and saw it—a little wicked head and a white dead face. Pah!"

"That's what I saw in the bar," said George. "'Orrid it was—devilish!"

Hirst shuddered, and, still retaining his nervous grip of Malcolm's sleeve, dropped into a chair.

"Well, it's a most unaccountable thing," said the dumbfounded Malcolm, turning round to the others. "It's the last time I come to this house."

"I leave to-morrow," said George. "I wouldn't go down to that bar again by myself, no, not for fifty pounds!"

"It's talking about the thing that's caused it, I expect," said one of the men; "we've all been talking about this and having it in our minds. Practically we've been forming a spiritualistic circle without knowing it."

"Hang the old gentleman!" said Malcolm, heartily. "Upon my soul, I'm half afraid to go to bed. It's odd they should both think they saw something."

"I saw it as plain as I see you, sir," said George, solemnly. "P'raps if you keep your eyes turned up the passage you'll see it for yourself."

They followed the direction of his finger, but saw nothing, although one of them fancied that a head peeped round the corner of the wall.

"Who'll come down to the bar?" said Malcolm, looking round.

"You can go, if you like," said one of the others, with a faint laugh; "we'll wait here for you."

The stout traveller walked towards the door and took a few steps up the passage. Then he stopped. All was quite silent, and he walked slowly to the end and looked down fearfully towards the glass partition which shut off the bar. Three times he made as though to go to it; then he turned back, and, glancing over his shoulder, came hurriedly back to the room.

"Did you see it, sir?" whispered George.

"Don't know," said Malcolm, shortly. "I fancied I saw something, but it might have been fancy. I'm in the mood to see anything just now. How are you feeling now, sir?"

"Oh, I feel a bit better now," said Hirst, somewhat brusquely, as all eyes were turned upon him. "I dare say you think I'm easily scared, but you didn't see it."

"Not at all," said Malcolm, smiling faintly despite himself.

"I'm going to bed," said Hirst, noticing the smile and resenting it. "Will you share my room with me, Somers?"

"I will with pleasure," said his friend, "provided you don't mind sleeping with the gas on full all night."

He rose from his seat, and bidding the company a friendly good-night, left the room with his crestfallen friend. The others saw them to the foot of the stairs, and having heard their door close, returned to the coffee-room.

"Well, I suppose the bet's off?" said the stout commercial, poking the fire and then standing with his legs apart on the hearthrug; "though, as far as I can see, I won it. I never saw a man so scared in all my life. Sort of poetic justice about it, isn't there?"

"Never mind about poetry or justice," said one of his listeners; "who's going to sleep with me?"

"I will," said Malcolm, affably.

"And I suppose we share a room together, Mr. Leek?" said the third man, turning to the fourth.

"No, thank you," said the other, briskly; "I don't believe in ghosts. If anything comes into my room I shall shoot it."

"That won't hurt a spirit, Leek," said Malcolm, decisively.

"Well the noise'll be like company to me," said Leek, "and it'll wake the house too. But if you're nervous, sir," he added, with a grin, to the man who had suggested sharing his room, "George'll be only too pleased to sleep on the door-mat inside your room, I know."

"That I will, sir," said George, fervently; "and if you gentlemen would only come down with me to the bar to put the gas out, I could never be sufficiently grateful."

They went out in a body, with the exception of Leek, peering carefully before them as they went. George turned the light out in the bar and they returned unmolested to the coffee-room, and, avoiding the sardonic smile of Leek, prepared to separate for the night.

"Give me the candle while you put the gas out, George," said the traveller.

The waiter handed it to him and extinguished the gas, and at the same moment all distinctly heard a step in the passage outside. It stopped at the door, and as they watched with bated breath, the door creaked and slowly opened. Malcolm fell back open-mouthed, as a white, leering face, with sunken eyeballs and close-cropped bullet head, appeared at the opening.

For a few seconds the creature stood regarding them, blinking in a strange fashion at the candle. Then, with a sidling movement, it came a little way into the room and stood there as if bewildered.

Not a man spoke or moved, but all watched with a horrible fascination as the creature removed its dirty neckcloth and its head rolled on its shoulder. For a minute it paused, and then, holding the rag before it, moved towards Malcolm.

The candle went out suddenly with a flash and a bang. There was a smell of powder, and something writhing in the darkness on the floor. A faint, choking cough, and then silence. Malcolm was the first to speak. "Matches," he said, in a strange voice. George struck one. Then he leapt at the gas and a burner flamed from the match. Malcolm touched the thing on the floor with his foot and found it soft. He looked at his companions. They mouthed inquiries at him, but he shook his head. He lit the candle, and, kneeling down, examined the silent thing on the floor. Then he rose swiftly, and dipping his handkerchief in the water-jug, bent down again and grimly wiped the white face. Then he sprang back with a cry of incredulous horror, pointing at it. Leek's pistol fell to the floor and he shut out the sight with his hands, but the others, crowding forward, gazed spell-bound at the dead face of Hirst.

Before a word was spoken the door opened and Somers hastily entered the room. His eyes fell on the floor. "Good God!" he cried. "You didn't——"

Nobody spoke.

"I told him not to," he said, in a suffocating voice. "I told him not to. I told him——"

He leaned against the wall, deathly sick, put his arms out feebly, and fell fainting into the traveller's arms.

THE PEACEMAKER

THE harbour was crowded with fishing boats, and fresh arrivals were coming in every few minutes. Until the entrance was reached they came scudding along with every appearance of haste, but then their mainsails came tumbling down to the deck, and the boats with sufficient way left on them moved easily over the still water, and felt their way to a berth. Small boats conveyed the fish to the quay, where embryo fishermen were appraising the catch with a wisdom beyond their years.

There was a glut of whiting. So many whiting, and going so cheaply that it was enough to make them bite their tails from sheer vexation. Small flat fish which slid away from their pile were carefully looked after and coaxed back with the toe of a sea-boot, but whiting slid away unnoticed until they vanished from mortal ken in the pockets of predatory urchins.

In the small market, a short, red-faced man with a scrubby beard walked in a disparaging fashion from heap to heap, using a favourite briar in lieu of a hammer to knock down such fish as found bidders. The latter were few and wary, and turning a deaf ear to eloquence expressed opinions distasteful to an auctioneer's ear in crude English.

The sense of the meeting being against him, the auctioneer truckled to it, and coming to another heap consisting of a selection of the most undesirable fish that swim Britannia's realm, gazed at it indignantly. There was a titter behind him, and he voiced his wrath impetuously.

"That's Joe Gubbs's catch," he bawled. "S'elp me, I'd know that man's luck anywhere,"

He turned the fish over scornfully with his foot, and, with a severe glance at the hapless Gubbs, moved away to something more saleable.

"Where d' ye get 'em from, Gubbs?" inquired an aggravating

voice. "We never get such things in our nets. I've never seen some o' them things afore."

"There's a lot you ain't seen, Bob Tarbut," said Gubbs, turning upon him, "and what you do see don't do you much good."

"I'd be ashamed to bring home such a queer-looking lot," jeered the other.

"They mayn't be up to much, but there's none on 'em would care to change faces with you, I expect," related Gubbs.

"You leave my face alone," said Tarbut, whose physiognomy was much used in the village for purposes of comparison.

"A skate's handsome to you," said Gubbs, following up his advantage.

He jumped back suddenly as the fist of the sensitive Tarbut shot suddenly out, and treading on a small fish, whirled round wildly with his hands in the air in the effort to retain his balance, and sat down heavily. The bystanders instantly separated into two groups, and two or three anxious sympathisers helped the fallen man to his feet, and indicated those parts of Tarbut's frame which in their opinion were least adapted to offer resistance to his fist.

"Stand up," said Gubbs, sternly, as he shook himself free from these friends.

"I am a-standin' up!" said Tarbut, breathing hard.

The two combatants approached each other stealthily, and manoeuvring round the heaps of fish, struck safely at each other over these convenient barriers.

"Get 'em in the road," cried an excited voice, "they can't 'urt each other here."

A dozen kindly hands helped them there, and finding too much strategy for sport in a large ring, at the bidding of the resourceful individual who had last spoken, gradually made it smaller and smaller. Two or three small blows warmed the combatants, and they set to work in earnest. Then Gubbs, under a heavy blow from Tarbut, went to the ground and stayed there.

It was three minutes before he came thoroughly round, and then he sat up in a dazed fashion and looked round for his opponent.

"Did I kill 'im?" he inquired, in a whisper.

"No, not quite," said one of his friends, gently.

Gubbs rubbed his eyes. "What are they patting him on the back for?" he inquired, eyeing the group who were making a fuss over Tarbut.

"'Cos he's won," said his friend.

Gubbs staggered to his feet.

"It's no good," said the landlord of the "Three Fishers," who had run over to the scene of the fray; "you wasn't properly trained, you know. Now, look 'ere. If you put yourself in my hands, in three weeks you can beat him holler."

"You do as Mr. Larkins ses, Joe," said his friend, impressively.

"I lived among prizefighters afore I come down 'ere," said Mr. Larkins, expanding his small frame. "In three weeks' time, Gubbs, you'll be able to knock him silly."

"Well, what about Tarbut? He ought to be trained too," said one of the men. "Fair play's fair play any day."

"I'll train 'im," said an old ex-coastguardsman.

"I don't want no training," said Tarbut, surlily. "I've beat 'im, beat 'im easy."

"Well, beat 'im again, Tarbut," said one of his friends. "I'll put my five bob on you. Who'll take me?"

For the next five minutes, heedless of the assertions of both men that they wouldn't fight any more, bets were freely taken, Tarbut, in view of his recent success, being a hot favourite.

A jarring element was introduced into the proceedings by a small, elderly man wearing a piece of blue ribbon, who, pushing his way in eagerly, inquired what it was all about. Nobody troubling to give him a correct answer, he tried to solve it for himself, and was then caught, just in the nick of time, trying to make the enemies shake hands.

"You go off to your Mother's Meeting, Peter Morgan," said an incensed voice.

"It's a fight," said the little man, raising his voice. "Oh, my friends——"

"It's nothing o' the kind," said Larkins, hotly. "I'm training 'em for a race, that's all. They're just going to see who's the best runner."

Morgan, disregarding the publican, looked to others for information.

"It's quite right," said a bystander. "You can believe me, can't you?"

"When 's it going to be?" asked Morgan.

"I don't know," said the other, turning away.

"You ought to be ashamed of yourselves," said Morgan, warmly. "It's bad enough to make a couple of men fight what don't want to without telling a lot of lies about it."

"It's none o' your business," said Larkins, surlily. "Ask no questions and you'll hear no lies. You'll get some idea into that 'ead of yours and then go and split, and have it stopped."

"I never told of anything in my life," said Morgan, sharply. "My mates here know that. That ain't my way. My way's persuasion and example, not forcing people to do what I want."

"There's a purse o' fifteen and six made up for the winner," said Larkins, turning away and whispering the news to Gubbs. "The spot for the picnic'll be made known later on. Them what's in the know is respectfully asked to keep their mouths shut to save trouble all round."

He went back to his bar, and the other men, after standing about a bit, strolled off one by one to their teas. Mr. Morgan was one of the last to leave, and went as far as Tarbut's door with him to tell him an anecdote of a man who was struck behind the ear in a fight and killed on the spot.

A comfortable meal and a good night's rest restored Mr. Gubbs to his wonted serenity of mind, and he awoke at six o'clock feeling determined to shake hands with Tarbut and let the matter drop. A persistent hammering at the door, which gradually got louder and louder, interfering with his meditations, he roused Mrs. Gubbs, who was sleeping peacefully, and with some asperity bade her get up and stop it.

"It's Mr. Larkins, Joe," said the lady, hastily withdrawing her head from the window.

Mr. Gubbs sat up in bed, and then with a mighty yawn rose, and, pushing open the casement again, gazed indignantly at the small publican, who was standing below keeping up an incessant rapping on the door with a small cane.

"Morning, Mr. Larkins, sir," said Gubbs, sniffing at the cool morning air.

"Halloa!" said Larkins, looking up. "This won't do, you know. You're wasting time. You ought to be up and out by now."

"I've changed my mind," said Gubbs, leaning out and speaking in a low voice to defeat the intentions of Mrs. Gubbs, who was listening. "I dreamt I killed Tarbut, an' it's give me such a fright that I've resolved not to fight."

"That's all right," said Larkins, briskly; "dreams always go by contraries."

"Well there ain't much comfort in that," said Gubbs, who was anxious to get back to his warm bed, sharply.

"You dress and come down," said the imperious Larkins. "You ought to be ashamed of yourself after all the trouble I'm taking on your behalf."

Mr. Gubbs rubbed his eyes and pondered. "What's the towel for?" he demanded, suspiciously.

"Rub you down with after you've bathed," said the other.

"*Bathed*?" said Mr. Gubbs, with emphasis. "Bathed? What for?"

"Training," replied Mr. Larkins. "Hurry up."

"I don't believe old Bullock's going to make Tarbut bathe," said Gubbs, shivering; "it's weakening."

"You do as you're told," said the autocratic Larkins. "Bullock don't know nothing about it."

Mr. Gubbs sighed and withdrew his head, and explaining to his astonished wife that he was going for a little stroll, gloomily dressed himself and joined his trainer below.

"Shoulders back," said the small publican. "Head up."

He led the way down to the beach, and, ignoring the looks of aversion which Mr. Gubbs bestowed upon the silver sea, stood by while he disrobed and picked his way painfully over the shingle to the edge of the water. It was a bright morning, but somewhat chill, and Mr. Gubbs's breathless gaspings furnished an excellent clue to the temperature of the water.

"How do you feel?" inquired Mr. Larkins, anxiously, as he rubbed him down.

"I feel ill," said the other, shivering.

"You'll feel better when you've had your run," said Larkins, cheerily.

"'Ad my w—w—*wot*?" inquired Mr. Gubbs, staring at him offensively, and rubbing himself furiously with the towel.

"Your run," repeated Larkins, sternly. "You don't want your coat. I'll hold that. And mind, I don't want you to go running like a steam-engine, or a runaway horse."

"I wasn't goin' to," said Gubbs.

"Just trot easy," continued the other, "for about half a mile. Go as far as that gate over there, then rest two minutes and trot back again."

His manner was so dictatorial that Mr. Gubbs, remembering in time his score at the "Three Fishers," swallowed something he was going to say—and it was nearly strong enough to choke him—and set off at a strange, weird gait towards the indicated goal. He reached it at last, and after a long two minutes started back again in response to the semaphore-like appeals of the enthusiastic Larkins.

"I've got my work cut out for me, I can see," said the latter, as his victim, puffing and blowing, sat down on the ground. "But I'll soon get you in trim, and mind you keep quiet about it. I don't want Bullock to know."

"Why not?" demanded Mr. Gubbs.

"Because he'd train Tarbut the same way," said Larkins, with a cunning grin.

"Well, why shouldn't Tarbut 'ave a doing same as me?" said Mr. Gubbs, vindictively. "Why should 'e be a-laying in comfort in 'is bed while I'm catching cold bathing and killing myself running?"

"Don't you be a fool," said Larkins, affectionately patting him on the shoulder. "Come into my place when you have time, and I'll put the gloves on with you a bit; and be careful what you eat, mind, else you'll undo all the good I've done you."

If it is possible for a man to expectorate sarcastically, Mr. Gubbs achieved that feat.

"Only two cups of tea with your breakfast," continued Larkins, solemnly, "and no greens for dinner, and I'll send you in one pint of old ale every day free gratis."

The tensity of Mr. Gubbs's features relaxed, and he smiled faintly as he rose and accompanied his friend back. Larkins saw him to his door, and after explaining fluently to Mrs. Gubbs that her husband was training for a race, gave her explicit instructions as to his diet, and departed.

It was a source of much joy to Mr. Larkins, though he was unable to persuade Gubbs to share in his feelings, that Tarbut's trainer was satisfied with a less vigorous system for his man. He let Tarbut off with a cold sponging on rising, and as Tarbut had his own ideas as to what constituted a cold sponging, both parties were well pleased with each other.

The business-like nature of these proceedings was keenly appreciated by the inhabitants of the fishing quarter. Fights had happened before and doubtless would again, but they were mere rough-and-tumble affairs, and over before any proper excitement could be worked up. The purse had steadily mounted up to thirty-five shillings, and the betting varied from day to day.

Each man had his knot of supporters, and enthusiasm had reached such a pitch that Gubbs, who was naturally of a retiring disposition, had to take his matutinal tub before quite a circle of admirers. Opposition on the part of the ladies was balked by continuing to allude to the affair as a race, though Mrs. Gubbs, who got up one morning to see her man run, went home in a state of mind bordering upon stupefaction.

An uneasy feeling was caused by the anxiety of the excellent Mr. Morgan to discover the time and place of meeting. No information was afforded him, and as he had indignantly denied any intention of giving the alarm, the gentlemen interested were much exercised as to the reasons for his curiosity.

The battle was fixed for a Saturday evening, the two trainers, after much wordy warfare, having selected a site which Mr. Larkins insisted had been made purposely by Nature with a view to affairs of the kind. Lofty cliffs hid it from view, and the ground itself consisted of turf so soft and spongy that Larkins predicted that Tarbut would bounce up from it like an indiarubber ball. The principals expressed themselves as satisfied, though their niggardliness in the matter of thanks for the trouble which had been taken over the arrangements formed food for conversation for the trainers all the way home.

The boats got in early on Friday afternoon with their fish. The catch was small and soon disposed of, and then the attentive trainers, rescuing their men from admirers, who were feeling their arms and putting leading questions as to their wind and state of mind, sent them indoors with concise instructions as to how they were to spend the last evening. Larkins officiously sent his man off for a short, sharp walk after his tea, and later on, going to the quay, found that Bullock had given his man the same instructions.

"Don't you go worrying of 'em, mind," said Larkins sternly to the group, "an' let 'em have an easy time of it to-morrow in the boats. Both of 'em," he added, generously.

"Spoke like a Briton, Mr. Larkins," said an old fisherman.

"What I want is fair play and no favour," said Mr. Larkins; "it's to be a genuine sporting affair. No bad blood or anything of that kind. After the little affair, all what go to see it are welcome to one drink at my expense."

"It's time my man was back," said Bullock, looking up the road which led over the cliffs. "I told him to go just as far as the ground and back."

"Old Peter Morgan's gone down to the place too, I think," piped a small lad in huge boots. "I saw 'im following of Tarbut."

The landlord of the "Three Fishers" started uneasily. "It's on my mind," he said, in a melancholy voice, "that that blessed old teetotaller'll have the thing stopped. He'll tell the police or something."

"No he won't," said the old fisherman who had spoken before. "Me an' Peter was boys together, an' he's never done anything o' that sort in his life. Before old Peter got religious there was nothing he liked better than to see a fight, or to take part in one either, an' it's my opinion he'd like to see this one, only he don't like to say so."

"Well, he won't," said Larkins, grimly; "it may be as you say, but we're not going to take any risks."

Conversation became general, and in view of the nearness of the event, animated, but still the two gladiators failed to put in an appearance.

"He's overdoing it, that's what he is," said Mr. Larkins, referring to the ardent Gubbs. "You can 'ave a man too willing. He'll go and knock hisself up."

The small boy came up, his big boots clattering over the stones, and, shading his eyes with his hands, looked up the road. The other men, following his gaze, saw three men advancing lovingly arm-in-arm towards them.

"It—it can't be old Morgan with 'em?" said Mr. Larkins.

"It is, though," said the old fisherman, peering through screwed-up eyes. "They've made it up through old Peter, that's wot they've done. He's been talking at 'em and getting at 'em, and now there won't be no fight."

His disappointed auditors groaned in chorus. "Won't there," said Larkins, savagely. "Ho—won't there—— You don't think me and my friend Bullock here are going to slave three weeks for nothing, do you?"

"There won't be no fight," repeated the old man. "Look how loving they are! All three of 'em as close together as sweethearts."

The advancing trio certainly bore out the old man's words to the latter. Mr. Peter Morgan was in the centre, and appeared to be half-embracing his companions.

"Why, they can hardly walk," said Bullock; "they've been too far."

"Yes, that's what it is," said Larkins, in a hollow voice.

"Seems to me," said the boy, slowly, "that they've 'ad a bit of a scrap already."

The crowd, with bated breath, stepped out to meet them, Larkins and Bullock leading. It was evident that the two heroes were clinging to Mr. Morgan more for support than from any motives of affection, and it was no less evident that the lad's remark as to a bit of a scrap was capable of wide interpretation. In a few minutes both parties were face to face, and the two trainers gazing at their charges speechless with indignation.

"Which is Gubbs?" demanded Larkins at last, in an unnatural voice.

The figure on Morgan's right arm managed to open an eye and to twist its swollen lips into something intended for a smile.

"What 'ave you been doing?" vociferated the incensed landlord.

"Fightin'," said Gubbs, speaking with some difficulty; "it's all over now. It was a draw, and we're going to halve the money between us."

"Oh, are you," said Larkins, bitterly. "Well, you won't have a damned ha'penny of it. What do you mean by it? Eh?"

"I'll tell you all about it," said Morgan, who was looking radiantly happy. "I saw Tarbut going up the road and I followed him and talked to him, and by and by up comes Gubbs, and I talked to him. Then I found out what, of course, I knew before, that all you men were trying to induce these poor souls to knock each other about for money."

Mr. Larkins, choking helplessly, looked sternly at Mr. Morgan, and pointed an incriminating finger at Tarbut's visage.

"I urged 'em not to make such a brutal show of themselves for money," continued Mr. Morgan, "but they said as 'ow they would. Gubbs said it would be the easiest thirty-five shillings he'd ever earned, and Tarbut said it was him as was going to earn it. After a little talk o' this kind, Gubbs here 'it Tarbut smack in the eye."

Tarbut gave a faint groan in confirmation.

"Then they both started to peel," continued Mr. Morgan.

"Why didn't you stop 'em?" inquired the ex-coastguard; "it was your duty as a Christian to stop 'em."

"I thought it was better for 'em to fight like that than to make a brutal exhibition of themselves," said Mr. Morgan, with dignity. "It was a revolting spectacle, shocking, and I'm glad and thankful there was nobody there but me to see 'em make such brute beasts of themselves."

A threatening murmur broke from the crowd.

"There in that sweet secluded spot," said Mr. Morgan, shaking his head, "these two men, stripped to the waist, knocked one another about for fifteen rounds. First blood fell to Tarbut, he got in with his left on Gubbs's nose, then Gubbs up with a fearful blow and knocked him flat. It was as clean a blow as ever I see. I took Tarbut on my knee—poor fellow, he was doing wrong, but still he was suffering, and Peter Morgan's always got a knee for the sufferer. Second round he was more cautious, and watching 'is opportunity, he clenched and fell with Gubbs underneath. It was a disgusting spectacle."

Mr. Larkins bent savagely over to Mr. Bullock and whispered in his ear.

"When time was called"—said Mr. Morgan.

"Who called it?" inquired a voice, with the air of one making a point.

"I did," said Mr. Morgan; "there was nobody else;—both of 'em walked round each other a bit, sparring and looking for opportunities. I think the third round was the longest of all. Both of 'em kept getting in a lot of little knocks and then dodging away again. Then Tarbut caught Gubbs one in the bread-ba—in the wind— and then followed up on his jaw and knocked him down again. It was a disgusting spectacle."

"Must ha' been," said a dejected voice.

"After that there was twelve more rounds," continued the narrator; "sometimes Tarbut had the best of it, and sometimes Gubbs. Both men was very determined and fought very fair. It was good, solid hard hitting, and they were marked all over before they'd finished. Once Gubbs gave Tarbut a blow over the heart, and I thought he wouldn't get up to time."

"I wouldn't if you hadn't blowed water into my face out of that puddle," said Tarbut.

"It was a most disgusting spectacle," said Mr. Peter Morgan, hurriedly.

"Seems to me——" began Larkins, ferociously.

"Two fine strong men, stripped to the waist, hard as nails, knocking each other about for money," said Mr. Morgan. "They're never going to fight any more. I made 'em promise they wouldn't. They're good friends now; ain't you, lads?"

With an utter disregard of the feelings of the bystanders the two men shook hands.

"And though I regard fighting with horror," concluded Mr. Morgan, beaming on them, "I think that, as it was a bargain, you should divide the purse between 'em."

"They won't get a farthing of it," said Mr. Larkins, explosively, "unless you like to give it to 'em out of your own pocket."

"*Me!*" said Mr. Morgan, opening his eyes. "Why?"

"Ask yourself," said Mr. Larkins, pointedly. "I should say if any man ever 'ad thirty-five shillingsworth of sport all to hisself, you have; and, what's more, you know it, Mr. Peter Morgan."

The peacemaker sighed, and, turning, led his charges gently away. The crowd watched them as far as the "Three Fishers," and observing that they detached themselves by force from their guide and friend, crossed the road and followed them in.

FALSE COLOURS

"OF course, there is a deal of bullying done at sea at times," said the night-watchman, thoughtfully. "The men call it bullying an' the officers call it discipline, but it's the same thing under another name. Still, it's fair in a way. It gets passed on from one to another. Everybody aboard a'most has got somebody to bully, except, perhaps the boy; he 'as the worst of it, unless he can manage to get the ship's cat by itself occasionally.

"I don't think sailor-men mind being bullied. I never 'eard of its putting one off 'is feed yet, and that's the main thing, arter all's said and done.

"Fust officers are often worse than skippers. In the fust place, they know they ain't skippers, an' that alone is enough to put 'em in a bad temper, especially if they've 'ad their certifikit a good many years and can't get a vacancy.

"I remember, a good many years ago now, I was lying at Calcutta one time in the *Peewit*, as fine a barque as you'd wish to see, an' we 'ad a fust mate there as was a disgrace to 'is sects. A masty, bullying, violent man, who used to call the hands names as they didn't know the meanings of and what was no use looking in the dictionary for.

"There was one chap aboard, Bill Cousins, as he used to make a partickler mark of. Bill 'ad the misfortin to 'ave red 'air, and the way the mate used to throw that in 'is face was disgraceful. Fortunatey for us all, the skipper was a very decent sort of man, so that the mate was only at 'is worst when he wasn't by.

"We was sitting in the fo'c's'le at tea one arternoon, when Bill Cousins came down, an' we see at once 'e'd 'ad a turn with the mate. He sat all by hisself for some time simmering, an' then he broke out. 'One o' these days I'll swing for 'im; mark my words.'

"'Don't be a fool, Bill,' ses Joe Smith.

"'If I could on'y mark 'im,' ses Bill, catching his breath. 'Just mark 'im fair an' square. If I could on'y 'ave 'im alone for ten

152

minutes, with nobody standing by to see fair play. But, o' course, if I 'it 'im it's mutiny.'

"'You couldn't do it if it wasn't, Bill,' ses Joe Smith again.

"'He walks about the town as though the place belongs to 'im,' said Ted Hill. 'Most of us is satisfied to shove the niggers out o' the way, but he ups fist and 'its 'em if they comes within a yard of 'im.'

"'Why don't they 'it 'im back?' ses Bill. 'I would if I was them.'

"Joe Smith grunted. 'Well, why don't you?' he asked.

"''Cos I ain't a nigger,' ses Bill.

"'Well, but you might be,' ses Joe, very earnest. 'Black your face an' 'ands an' legs, and dress up in them cotton things, and go ashore and get in 'is way.'

"'If you will, I will, Bill,' ses a chap called Bob Pullin.

"Well, they talked it over and over, and at last Joe, who seemed to take a great interest in it, went ashore and got the duds for 'em. They was a tight fit for Bill, Hindoos not being as wide as they might be, but Joe said if 'e didn't bend about he'd be all right, and Pullin, who was a smaller man, said his was fust class.

"After they were dressed, the next question was wot to use to colour them with; coal was too scratchy, an' ink Bill didn't like. Then Ted Hill burnt a cork and started on Bill's nose with it afore it was cool, an' Bill didn't like that.

"'Look 'ere,' ses the carpenter, 'nothin' seems to please you, Bill—it's my opinion you're backing out of it.'

"'You're a liar,' ses Bill.

"'Well, I've got some stuff in a can as might be boiled-down Hindoo for all you could tell to the difference,' ses the carpenter; 'and if you'll keep that ugly mouth of yours shut, I'll paint you myself.'

"Well, Bill was a bit flattered, the carpenter being a very superior sort of a man, and quite an artist in 'is way, an' Bill sat down an' let 'im do 'im with some stuff out of a can that made 'im look like a Hindoo what 'ad been polished. Then Bob Pullin was done too, an' when they'd got their turbins on, the change in their appearance was wonderful.

"'Feels a bit stiff,' ses Bill, working 'is mouth.

"'That'll wear off,' ses the carpenter; 'it wouldn't be you if you didn't 'ave a grumble, Bill.'

"'And mind and don't spare 'im, Bill,' ses Joe. 'There's two of you, an' if you only do wot's expected of you, the mate ought to 'ave a easy time abed this v'y'ge.'

"'Let the mate start fust,' ses Ted Hill. 'He's sure to start on you if you only get in 'is way. Lord, I'd like to see his face when you start on '*im*!'

"Well, the two of 'em went ashore arter dark with the best wishes o' all on board, an' the rest of us sat down in the fo'c's'le spekerlating as to what sort o' time the mate was going' to 'ave. He went ashore all right, because Ted Hill see 'im go, an' he noticed with partickler pleasure as 'ow he was dressed very careful.

"It must ha' been near eleven o'clock. I was sitting with Smith on the port side o' the galley, when we heard a 'ubbub approaching the ship. It was the mate just coming aboard. He was without 'is 'at; 'is necktie was twisted round 'is ear, and 'is shirt and 'is collar was all torn to shreds. The second and third officers ran up to him to see what was the matter, and while he was telling them, up comes the skipper.

"'You don't mean to tell me, Mr. Fingall,' ses the skipper, in surprise, 'that you've been knocked about like that by them mild and meek Hindoos?'

"'Hindoos, sir?' roared the mate. 'Cert'nly not, sir. I've been assaulted like this by five German sailor-men. And I licked 'em all.'

"'I'm glad to hear that,' ses the skipper; and the second and third pats the mate on the back—just like you pat a dog you don't know.

"'Big fellows they was,' ses he, 'an' they give me some trouble. Look at my eye!'

"The second officer struck a match and looked at it, and it cert'n'y was a beauty.

"'I hope you reported this at the police-station?' ses the skipper.

"'No, sir,' ses the mate, holding up 'is 'ead. 'I don't want no p'lice to protect me. Five's a large number, but I drove 'em off, and I don't think they'll meddle with any British fust-officers again.'

"'You'd better turn in,' ses the second, leading him off by the arm.

"The mate limped off with him, and as soon as the coast was clear we put our 'eads together and tried to make out how it was that Bill Cousins and Bob 'ad changed themselves into five German sailor-men.

"'It's the mate's pride,' ses the carpenter. 'He didn't like being knocked about by Hindoos.'

"We thought it was that, but we had to wait nearly another hour afore the two came aboard, to make sure. There was a difference in the way they came aboard, too, from that of the mate. *They* didn't make no noise, and the fust thing we knew of their coming aboard was seeing a bare, black foot waving feebly at the top of the fo'c's'le ladder feelin' for the step below.

"That was Bob. He came down without a word, and then we see 'e was holding another black foot and guiding it to where it should go. That was Bill, an' of all the 'orrid, limp-looking blacks that you ever see, Bill was the worst when he got below. He just sat on a locker all of a heap and held 'is 'ead, which was swollen up, in 'is hands. Bob went and sat beside 'im, and there they sat, for all the world like two wax figgers instead o' human beings.

"'Well, you done it, Bill,' ses Joe, after waiting a long time for them to speak. 'Tell us all about it.'

"'Nothin' to tell,' ses Bill, very surly. 'We knocked 'im about.'

"'And he knocked us about,' ses Bob, with a groan. 'I'm sore all over, and as for my feet——'

"'Wot's the matter with them?' ses Joe.

"'Trod on,' ses Bob, very short. 'If my bare feet was trod on once they was a dozen times. I've never 'ad such a doing in all my life. He fought like a devil. I thought he'd ha' murdered Bill.'

"'I wish 'e 'ad,' ses Bill, with a groan; 'my face is bruised and cut about cruel. I can't bear to touch it.'

"'Do you mean to say the two of you couldn't settle 'im?' ses Joe, staring.

"'I mean to say we got a hiding,' ses Bill. 'We got close to him fust start off and got our feet trod on. Arter that it was like fighting a windmill, with sledge-hammers for sails.'

"He gave a groan and turned over in his bunk, and when we asked him some more about it, he swore at us. They both seemed quite done up, and at last they dropped off to sleep just as they was, without even stopping to wash the black off or to undress themselves.

"I was awoke rather early in the morning by the sounds of somebody talking to themselves, and a little splashing of water. It seemed to go on a long while, and at last I leaned out of my bunk and see Bill bending over a bucket and washing himself and using bad langwidge.

"'Wot's the matter, Bill?' ses Joe, yawning and sitting up in bed.

"'My skin's that tender, I can hardly touch it,' ses Bill, bending down and rinsing 'is face. 'Is it all orf?'

"'Orf?' ses Joe; 'no, o' course it ain't. Why don't you use some soap?'

"'Soap,' answers Bill, mad-like; 'why, I've used more soap

155

than I've used for six months in the ordinary way.'

"'That's no good,' ses Joe; 'give yourself a good wash.'

"Bill put down the soap then very careful, and went over to 'im and told him all the dreadful things he'd do to him when he got strong agin, and then Bob Pulling got out of his bunk an' a'd a try on *his* face. Him an' Bill kept washing, and then taking each other to the light and trying to believe it was coming off until they got sick of it, and then Bill, 'e up with his foot and capsized the bucket, and walked up and down the fo'c's'le raving.

"'Well, the carpenter put it on,' ses a voice, 'make 'im take it orf.'

"You wouldn't believe the job we 'ad to wake that man up. He wasn't fairly woke till he was hauled out of 'is bunk an' set down opposite them two pore black fellers an' told to make 'em white again.

"'I don't believe as there's anything will touch it,' he says, at last. 'I forgot all about that.'

"'Do you mean to say,' bawls Bill, 'that we've got to be black all the rest of our life?'

"'Cert'nly not,' ses the carpenter, indignantly, 'it'll wear off in time; shaving every morning'll 'elp it, I should say.'

"'I'll get my razor now,' ses Bill, in a awful voice; 'don't let 'im go, Bob. I'll 'ack 'is head orf.'

"He actually went off an' got his razor, but, o' course, we jumped out of our bunks and got between 'em and told him plainly that it was not to be, and then we set 'em down and tried everything we could think of, from butter and linseed oil to cold tea-leaves used as a poultice, and all it did was to make 'em shinier an' shinier.

"'It's no good, I tell you,' ses the carpenter, 'it's the most lasting black I know. If I told you how much that stuff is a can, you wouldn't believe me.'

"'Well, you're in it,' ses Bill, his voice all of a tremble; 'you done it so as we could knock the mate about. Whatever's done to us'll be done to you too.'

"'I don't think turps'll touch it,' ses the carpenter, getting up, 'but we'll 'ave a try.'

"He went and fetched the can and poured some out on a bit o' rag and told Bill to dab his face with it. Bill give a dab, and the next moment he rushed over with a scream and buried his head in a shirt wot Simmons was wearing at the time and began to wipe his face with it. Then he left the flustered Simmons an' shoved another chap away from the bucket and buried his face in it and kicked and carried on like a madman. Then 'e jumped into his bunk again and buried 'is face in the clothes and rocked hisself and moaned as if he was dying.

"'Don't you use it, Bob,' he ses, at last.

"''Tain't likely,' ses Bob. 'It's a good thing you tried it fust, Bill.'

"''Ave they tried holy-stone?' ses a voice from a bunk.

"'No, they ain't,' ses Bob, snappishly, 'and, what's more, they ain't goin' to.'

"Both o' their tempers was so bad that we let the subject drop while we was at breakfast. The orkard persition of affairs could no longer be disregarded. Fust one chap threw out a 'int and then another, gradually getting a little stronger and stronger, until Bill turned round in a uncomfortable way and requested of us to leave off talking with our mouths full and speak up like Englishmen wot we meant.

"'You see, it's this way, Bill,' ses Joe, soft-like. 'As soon as the mate sees you there'll be trouble for all of us.'

"'For all of us,' repeats Bill, nodding.

"'Whereas,' ses Joe, looking round for support, 'if we gets up a little collection for you and you should find it convenient to desart——'

"''Ear, 'ear,' ses a lot o' voices. 'Bravo, Joe.'

"'Oh, desart is it?' ses Bill; 'an' where are we goin' to desart to?'

"'Well, that we leave to you,' ses Joe; 'there's many a ship short-'anded as would be glad to pick up sich a couple of prime sailor-men as you an' Bob.'

"'Ah, an' wot about our black faces?' ses Bill, still in the same sneering, ungrateful sort o' voice.

"'That can be got over,' ses Joe.

"''Ow?' ses Bill and Bob together.

"'Ship as nigger-cooks,' ses Joe, slapping his knee and looking round triumphant.

"It's no good trying to do some people a kindness. Joe was perfectly sincere, and nobody could say but wot it wasn't a good idea, but o' course Mr. Bill Cousins must consider hisself insulted, and I can only suppose that the trouble he'd gone through 'ad affected his brain. Likewise Bob Pullin's. Anyway, that's the only excuse I can make for 'em. To cut a long story short, nobody 'ad any more breakfast, and no time to do anything until them two men was scrouged up in a corner an' eld there unable to move.

"'I'd never 'ave done 'em,' ses the carpenter, arter it was all over, 'if I'd known they was goin' to carry on like this. They wanted to be done.'

"'The mate'll half murder 'em,' ses Ted Hill.

"'He'll 'ave 'em sent to gaol, that's wot he'll do,' ses Smith. 'It's a serious matter to go ashore and commit assault and battery on the mate.'

"'You're all in it,' ses the voice o' Bill from the floor. 'I'm going to make a clean breast of it. Joe Smith put us up to it, the carpenter blacked us, and the others encouraged us.'

"'Joe got the clothes for us,' ses Bob. 'I know the place he got 'em from, too.'

"The ingratitude o' these two men was sich that at first we decided to have no more to do with them, but better feelings prevailed, and we held a sort o' meeting to consider what was best to be done. An' everything that was suggested one o' them two voices from the floor found fault with and wouldn't 'ave, and at last we 'ad to go up on deck with nothing decided upon, except to swear 'ard and fast as we knew nothing about it.

"'The only advice we can give you,' ses Joe, looking back at 'em, 'is to stay down 'ere as long as you can.'

"A'most the fust person we see on deck was the mate, an' a pretty sight he was. He'd got a bandage round 'is left eye, and a black ring round the other. His nose was swelled and his lip cut, but the other officers were making sich a fuss over 'im, that I think he rather gloried in it than otherwise.

"'Where's them other two 'ands?' he ses by and by, glaring out of 'is black eye.

"'Down below, sir, I b'lieve,' ses the carpenter, all of a tremble.

"'Go an' send 'em up,' ses the mate to Smith.

"'Yessir,' ses Joe, without moving.

"'Well, go on then,' roars the mate.

"'They ain't over and above well, sir, this morning,' ses Joe.

"'Send 'em up, confound you,' ses the mate, limping towards 'im.

"Well, Joe give 'is shoulders a 'elpless sort o' shrug and walked forward and bawled down the fo'c's'le.

"'They're coming, sir,' he ses, walking back to the mate just as the skipper came out of 'is cabin.

"We all went on with our work as 'ard as we knew 'ow. The skipper was talking to the mate about 'is injuries, and saying unkind things about Germans, when he give a sort of a shout and staggered back staring. We just looked round, and there was them two blackamoors coming slowly towards us.

"'Good heavens, Mr. Fingall,' ses the old man. 'What's this?'

"I never see sich a look on any man's face as I saw on the mate's then. Three times 'e opened 'is mouth to speak, and shut it agin without saying anything. The veins on 'is forehead swelled up tremendous and 'is cheeks was all blown out purple.

"'That's Bill Cousins' hair,' ses the skipper to himself. "It's Bill Cousins' hair. It's Bill Cous——'

"Bob walked up to him, with Bill lagging a little way behind, and then he stops just in front of 'im and fetches up a sort o' little smile.

"'Don't you make those faces at me, sir,' roars the skipper. 'What do you mean by it? What have you been doing to yourselves?'

"'Nothin', sir,' ses Bill, 'umbly; 'it was done to us.'

"The carpenter, who was just going to cooper up a cask which 'ad started a bit, shook like a leaf, and gave Bill a look that would ha' melted a stone.

"'Who did it?' ses the skipper.

"'We've been the wictims of a cruel outrage, sir,' ses Bill, doing all 'e could to avoid the mate's eye, which wouldn't be avoided.

"'So I should think,' ses the skipper. 'You've been knocked about, too.'

"'Yessir,' ses Bill, very respectful; 'me and Bob was ashore last night, sir, just for a quiet look round, when we was set on to by five furriners.

"'*What?*' ses the skipper; and I won't repeat what the mate said.

"'We fought 'em as long as we could, sir,' ses Bill, 'then we was both knocked senseless, and when we came to ourselves we was messed up like this 'ere.'

"What sort o' men were they?' asked the skipper, getting excited.

"'Sailor-men, sir,' ses Bob, putting in his spoke. 'Dutchies or Germans, or something o' that sort.'

"'Was there one tall man, with a fair beard,' ses the skipper, getting more and more excited.

"'Yessir,' ses Bill, in a surprised sort o' voice.

"'Same gang,' ses the skipper. "Same gang as knocked Mr. Fingall about, you may depend upon it. Mr. Fingall, it's a mercy for you you didn't get your face blacked too.'

"I thought the mate would ha' burst. I can't understand how any man could swell as he swelled without bursting.

"'I don't believe a word of it,' he ses, at last.

"'Why not?' ses the skipper, sharply.

"'Well, I don't,' ses the mate, his voice trembling with passion. 'I 'ave my reasons.'

"'I s'pose you don't think these two poor fellows went and blacked themselves for fun, do you?' ses the skipper.

"The mate couldn't answer.

"'And then went and knocked themselves about for more fun?' ses the skipper, very sarcastic.

"The mate didn't answer. He looked round helpless like, and see the third officer swopping glances with the second, and all the men looking sly and amused, and I think if ever a man saw 'e was done 'e did at that moment.

"He turned away and went below, and the skipper arter reading us all a little lecture on getting into fights without reason, sent the two chaps below agin and told 'em to turn in and rest. He was so good to 'em all the way 'ome, and took sich a interest in seeing 'em change from black to brown and from light brown to spotted lemon, that the mate daren't do nothing to them, but gave us their share of what he owed them as well as an extra dose of our own."